ALPENA COUNTY LIBRARY
W9-CLC-478

ALPENA COUNTY LIBRARY
211 N St.
Alpena, Mich. 49707

BLACK LEGACY

A HISTORY OF NEW YORK'S AFRICAN AMERICANS

Dedication

Beginning in the 1930s, Ben Katz (1903-1970) transformed an interest in jazz and blues into Black history research, a role in the Committee for the Negro in the Arts and in the councilmanic campaigns of Adam Clayton Powell Jr. and Benjamin J. Davis. A young boy accompanied him and was introduced to Ernest Crichlow, Sidney Bechet, and James P. Johnson, and many other of my heroes. Bunk Johnson sat at our table at the Stuyvesant Casino, and Dad brought me to Ernest Kaiser and Jean Blackwell Hutson at Harlem's Schomburg Center, a place he considered sacred ground.

W. E. B. Du Bois, Langston Hughes, and James Weldon Johnson were on our bookshelves, and King Oliver, Bessie Smith, and Louis Armstrong came from our record collection. In 1949 Dad and his great collaborator, Walter Christmas, created a historical play that was read in the Schomburg's basement by William Marshall, Alice Childress, Sidney Poitier, Frank Silvera, and Harry Belafonte.

Black Legacy synthesizes the love my father and I shared for this hidden New York heritage, and it is dedicated to the daring people who stride its pages, and to my majestic pioneers, Walter Christmas, Ernest Critchlow, Ernest Kaiser, and Ben Katz.

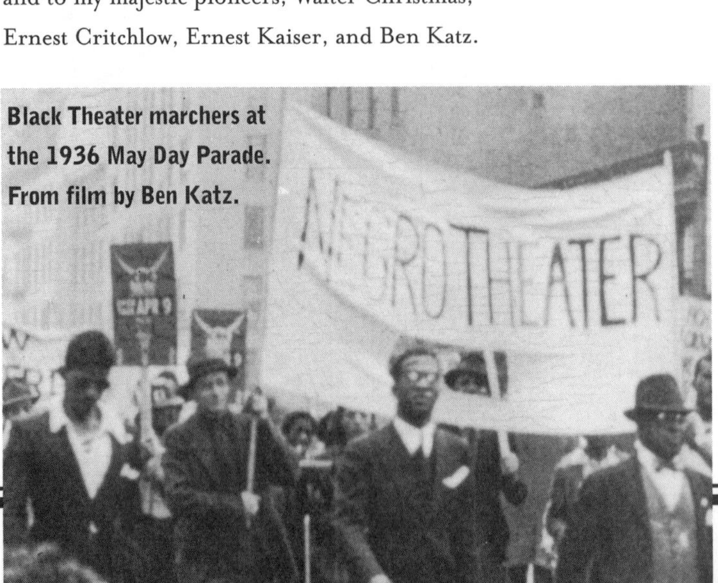

Black Theater marchers at the 1936 May Day Parade. From film by Ben Katz.

BLACK LEGACY

A HISTORY OF NEW YORK'S AFRICAN AMERICANS

WILLIAM LOREN KATZ

Illustrated with archival photographs and prints

ATHENEUM BOOKS FOR YOUNG READERS

Photo credits

The maps, frontis, and pages 13 and 19 are courtesy of the Prints Collection, Miriam and Ira D. Wallach Division of Art, Prints, and Photography, the New York Public Library, Astor, Lenox and Tilden Foundation. All other photos, except as noted, appear courtesy of the author.

Atheneum Books for Young Readers
An imprint of Simon & Schuster Children's Publishing Division
1230 Avenue of the Americas
New York, New York 10020

Book design by Patti Ratchford.
The text of this book is set in Mrs. Eaves.
First Edition
Printed in the United States of America
10 9 8 7 6 5 4 3 2 1
Library of Congress Cataloging-in-Publication Data:
Katz, William Loren.
Black legacy : A history of New York's African Americans / William Loren Katz ; illustrated with archival photographs and prints.—1st ed.
p. cm.
Includes bibliographical references and index.
Summary : Describes famous black leaders and cultural movements in New York City from its days as a Dutch colony to the 1990s.
ISBN 0-689-31913-4
1. Afro-Americans—New York (State)—New York—History—Juvenile literature. 2. New York (N.Y.)—History—Juvenile literature.
[1. Afro-Americans—New York (State)—New York—History. 2. New York (N.Y.)—History.] I. Title.
F128.9.N4K38 1997
974.7'100496073—dc20
96-18999 CIP AC

CONTENTS

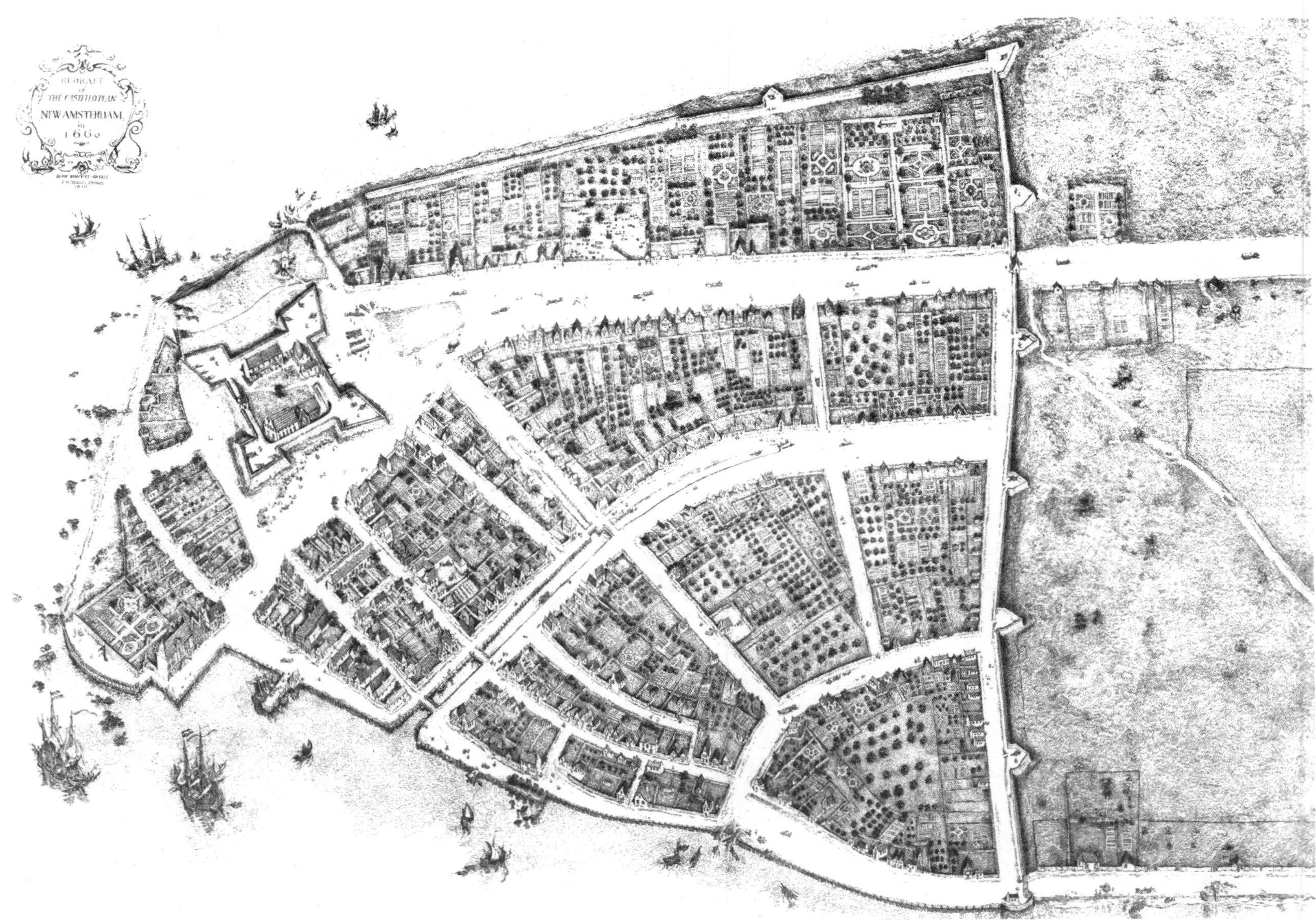
REDRAFT
of
THE CASTELLO PLAN
NEW AMSTERDAM
in
1660

CHAPTER ONE

THE AFRICANS OF NEW AMSTERDAM

Opposite: New Amsterdam in 1660.

In 1609 Africans were probably among the eighteen or so nameless seamen who helped navigate Captain Henry Hudson's sixty-three-foot *Half Moon* into New York Bay. The Algonquians, who called the island Manhattes, sang to these first foreigners and then began to trade their tobacco leaves for knives and beads.

The first Africans whose names appear in New York records, however, were translators for European explorers. During their early forays into Africa, Europeans discovered some Africans had unusual language skills. These Africans were eagerly sought out and hired for European explorations of the New World.

Dutch traders in the New Netherlands.

African interpreters, usually bearing European names, appear in early reports and diaries from the Americas. Matthieu da Costa translated for French traders in Canada. When he was hired by Holland, he may have visited New York with their expeditions in 1607 or 1609. French officials demanded his return to their service, but Costa assisted the Dutch for two more years.[1]

In 1612, when merchants from Holland arrived in Manhattes and built a first trading post of crude wooden huts near today's 45 Broadway, their interpreter was Jan Rodriguez. A free African, Rodriguez was recruited by Dutch captain Thijs Mossel in the West Indies.

In May 1613, when Mossel returned to Holland, Rodriguez remained behind to trade his hatchets and other goods with the Indians. The next year, when Hendrick Christaensen hired him as his agent, a furious Mossel claimed Rodriguez had been lured or spirited away. By 1614, when the Dutch built a fort, the Battery, on the island's southern tip, Africans such as Rodriguez had put their unique stamp on the island of Manhattan.[2]

The Dutch West India Company held a royal monopoly on trade with Manhattes, but its colony foundered. In 1624 New Netherland's first governor, Captain Cornelius Jacobsen May, arrived accompanied by thirty Walloon, or French-speaking Belgian, families. They were supposed to solve the colony's labor shortage, and May was sent to provide a sound government.

But May was a poor manager, and there were never enough laborers. Merchants had little interest in colonizing or farming when they could invest in the lucrative fur trade. Settlers abandoned farms for the woods, married Algonquian women, and became fur trappers. In Holland men and women who agreed to work as farmers for seven years were recruited as indentured servants. Soon many of these servants also fled farmwork for the fur trade. Crops rotted in the fields, and Manhattes seemed doomed by its lack of workers.[3]

To rescue their withering enterprise, in 1626 Holland dispatched a new governor, Peter Minuit, and more settlers. There was another dramatic change for the colony that year. A Dutch West India ship landed in Manhattes with eleven male Africans who were owned by the Dutch West India Company. Their last names may indicate their origin: Angola, Congo, Portuguese, and Santomee (São Tomé, Africa). Two years later three enslaved Angola women arrived and African American family life had begun in New York.[4]

The Africans of 1626 arrived to find Manhattes a muddy village of thirty wooden houses and less than two hundred citizens. The Dutch called it New Amsterdam but had not yet brought in their first crop and had no teacher or ordained minister.[5] A

The slave residence at the Knickerbocker mansion in the New Netherlands.

narrow Indian path wound through the village until African laborers widened it into De Herre Straet and later into Broadway. There was no Wall Street, no Fort Amsterdam, and only Algonquians living in Greenwich Village, Harlem, Brooklyn, the Bronx, and Queens. It would be another twenty-seven years before New Amsterdam would become the first self-governing municipality chartered in the Americas.

The Dutch West India Company's enslaved Africans made up 5 percent of New Amsterdam's people and were kept in a "Negroes house" at today's 86 Broad Street. Their initial work assignments were to clear land, build homes, and cut firewood.[6] Next they were told to tend cattle, plant and harvest crops, and build roads, fortifications, and bridges. In 1639 at the tip of Manhattan they rebuilt Fort Amsterdam.[7] African families also grew crops near their homes, an independence they probably cherished.

In November 1626 Dutch officials at Bowling Green handed trinkets worth sixty Dutch guilders or twenty-four dollars to the Canarsie Indians. The Canarsies thought they merely had received a tribute. But Dutch officials saw the transaction as a formal purchase of Manhattan island from its owners.

Some Africans became skilled craft workers, others were part of the fur trade, and still others served as household cooks and servants. One group of Africans was armed with axes and sent off to capture a white murder suspect. Enslaved laborers, writes historian Edgar McManus, turned the Dutch possession into a more stable settlement.

The skills of Africans almost immediately stirred concern among European laborers, who feared their competition. In 1628 Dutch West India officials had to assure worried white laborers that Africans would not be assigned as bricklayers or carpenters.

Enslaved Africans tried to free themselves or expand their opportunities. In 1634 five Africans petitioned the colony's directors in Holland for unpaid wages but received no answer. Some Africans converted to Dutch Calvinism, asked for church marriages, or had their children baptized—hoping these steps would lead to liberty. In 1641 New Amsterdam recorded the first marriage between Africans when Anthony van Angola and Lucie d'Angola exchanged vows in a Dutch Reformed Church ceremony. Other Africans soon were married by ordained ministers.

By 1640, when recently arrived enslaved Africans had tried to flee the colony, Dutch colonial law imposed a fifty-guilder fine on anyone who harbored a runaway. Additional laws against aiding fugitives were passed in 1648 and 1658, indicating an unflagging determination of Africans to gain freedom and a willingness of some white citizens to aid them.

The new colony did not prosper because few Europeans were willing to labor on farms. Day laborers and wealthy merchants hoped to make fortunes without hard work. Governors were incompetent and corrupt, men who invested in get-rich-quick schemes and made no long-range plans. Of the first four governors, three served less than a year, and Peter Minuit was recalled in disgrace. New Amsterdam's survival often rested on Africans.

In 1638, when Willem Kieft began his nine-year rule of the colony's five hundred residents, they represented many cultures. The settlement's first poet and its first bricklayer were Danes. Half a dozen others, including the first teacher, were Lithuanians married to Dutch women. Walloons formed 20 percent of the white population. In the 1630s 40 percent of arriving immigrants were from Norway, England, or Germany. Dozens of other residents were Africans. In 1643 visitor Jesuit Father Isaac Jogues was told that on "Manhate [*sic*] . . . four or five hundred men of different sects and nations [spoke] eighteen different languages."[8]

An unusual murder in January 1641 spotlighted the importance of the colony's African laborers. One of the enslaved, Jan de Primero, was found slain, and nine fellow workers were suspects. None would point out the murderer, but convinced they would be tortured until they did, the nine said they were all guilty. The New Amsterdam Council sitting as a court had no intention of executing nine of its best laborers, so the men were ordered to draw lots. Manuel de Gerritt, or the Giant, picked the unlucky straw and was marched to the Black hangman at City Hall.

However, the rope broke and Gerritt fell to the ground alive. The crowd "called out for mercy with great earnestness," and Governor Kieft pardoned Gerritt and the others. Primero's murder remained a mystery, one that deepened years later when his widow married Jan of Fort Orange, one of the nine who had confessed to the crime.[9]

The nine were soon to play a crucial role in Manhattan's defense after Dutch leaders instigated attacks on peaceful Algonquians. To Governor Kieft, Indians were a primitive and inferior people he planned to tax, or failing that, destroy. In 1640 the Algonquians refused to pay his taxes and angrily called him and the Dutch "Materiotty, or men of bad blood," tolerable at sea but "good for nothing" on land.

On a cold February night Kieft ordered two unprovoked and simultaneous Indian attacks. Maryn Adriaensen commanded Dutch forces, who killed forty sleeping Indians near today's Manhattan bridge. A larger column massacred eighty sleeping

Native Americans are massacred near Hoboken, New Jersey, by Dutch troops.

Indians on the banks of the Hudson near Pavonia, New Jersey. David de Vries "heard the shrieks" and saw Indians "butchered in their sleep." Infants were "cut to pieces," and after driving their children into the cold river, soldiers fired on parents who tried to save them.

To Governor Kieft his troops had performed a "deed of Roman valor." His cold-blooded massacres had the countryside in flames and white colonists fleeing to Fort Amsterdam to avoid retaliations. Dutch colonization of Staten Island came to a halt.[10]

Kieft's support among colonists deteriorated. Adriaensen was arrested for attempting to assassinate the governor, and two hours later Adriaensen's servant fired two shots at Kieft and was slain by a sentry. By spring Dutch troops had dwindled to fifty, facing an estimated fifteen hundred armed Algonquians. In July nine soldiers refused to obey orders and were arrested.[11]

White colonists abandoned their farms north of Wall Street, refugees crowded into Fort Amsterdam, and normal life ground to a halt. That September, to rouse popular support, Kieft asked "Eight Men" to serve as his advisers. But these prominent citizens saw themselves as the colony's first self-governing body. They also issued Manhattan's first white protest. "We are not safe even for an hour whilst the Indians daily threaten to overwhelm us," they wrote to the Dutch West India Company in Holland. The Eight Men spoke of the plight of their families, who feared to leave the fort and did not dare to "fetch a stick of firewood without an escort." With armed foes outside and frightened, disloyal Dutch settlers within, Kieft was a besieged man.[12]

That July warfare reached a crescendo. When a dozen enslaved African men petitioned for liberty, the Dutch rulers devised a new strategy. Within a month Kieft and the Council of New Amsterdam awarded them "conditional freedom with their wives on the same footing as other free people." Gerritt and others who confessed to the Primero murder became free, but their children remained enslaved by the Dutch West India Company.[13]

Kieft and the council, calling it a reward for "long and faithful service," next began to grant those freed Blacks farms and plantations north of New Amsterdam. Kieft's policies had united the Indians and driven his best citizens to the edge of treason. Perhaps he had hit upon a way to secure his power, win loyalty at home, and create a buffer zone against the Indians. The Dutch land grants of two hundred acres to formerly enslaved men and women—stretching from today's Canal Street to 34th Street—placed grateful Black landowners between the white settlers and Algonquian troops poised for combat.

As land was handed to the Africans, Kieft and his council also discussed building a physical buffer zone, a fence that would stretch from New Amsterdam north to a plantation owned by a Black man named Emmanuel. The Dutch wrote this justification: "Because the Indians daily commit much damage, both to men and cattle, and there is danger that the lives of many Christians, who go looking for straying cattle, may be lost. . . ."[14]

Free African families, then, were placed in the path of any Algonquian march on New Amsterdam's "Christians." The governor hoped to count on the Africans, as owners of new homes, farms, and plantations, to defend them. He also might have reasoned the Africans would be willing to aid their Dutch sponsors. And, finally, he knew that the Africans, unlike others in New Amsterdam, had no part in anti-Indian violence nor any role in his calculated massacres that provoked the war. Land grants north of the village to Africans continued throughout the war.[15]

In the summer of 1645 the war ebbed, and calm had returned to New Amsterdam. Black frontier farmers in today's Midtown had built peaceful relations with their Algonquian neighbors.

The land grants marked a proud moment for New York's first free African American community. Black farmers owned a broad, two-mile slice of Manhattan from Canal Street to 34th

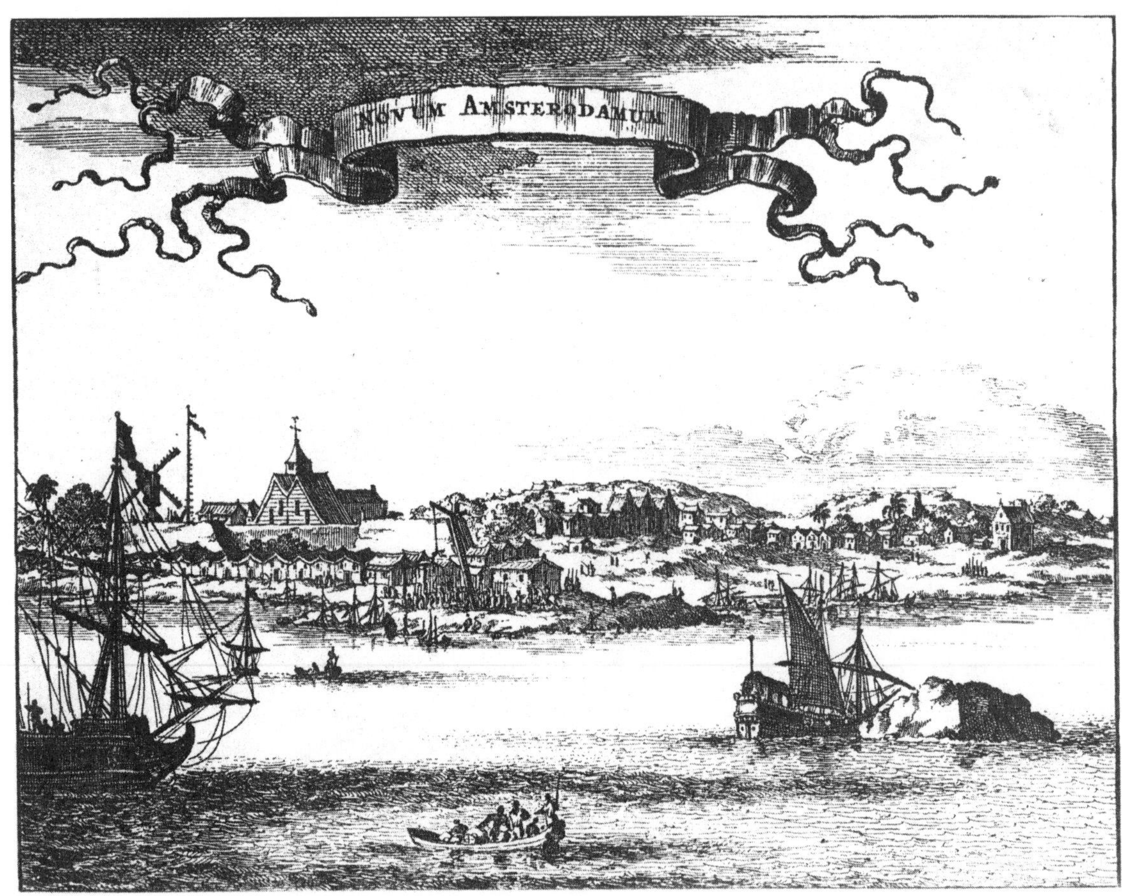

New Amsterdam in 1650, according to a sketch drawn by a European artist in 1671. From Iconography of Manhattan Island.

Street. Dozens of farms owned by formerly enslaved people, later to become a hundred city blocks, meant a dream come true for the Africans. Gerritt's land grant included part of today's Washington Square Park. Anthony Portuguese owned another huge piece of it. Simon Congo's forty-five-acre farm contained what is now Union Square from Broadway to Sixth Avenue.

Paul D'Angola's farm stretched along today's Bleecker Street to West Third Street and from Minetta Lane (then Minetta Creek) to Thompson Street. Each of these families had to agree to pay taxes to the Dutch West India Company in corn, wheat, and one fat hog each year. But for these landowners, such payments were a small price for precious liberty and a deed to one's home and farm.

Some scholars have said the land grants were on a useless swamp. Domingo Antony's and Paul D'Angola's parcels did include the "Kolck," or pond of fresh water, and a Collect Pond, which a century later became putrid and had to be filled in. Others have noted that Governor Wouter Von Twiller earlier had run a profitable tobacco plantation at the northeast corner of Washington Square. Either way, Greenwich Village remained the African American neighborhood. A path along Minetta Lane was named the Negro Causeway.[16]

One of the emancipated was Jan Francisco, a former slave for the Dutch West India Company. In 1661 he became one of twenty-three founders of Boswyck (today's Bushwick) in Brooklyn.

In *Black Manhattan* James Weldon Johnson refers to the early form of bondage in the New Netherlands as a "half-slavery," since it often was more lenient than that in other European colonies. Masters in New Amsterdam claimed the right to a slave's labor but not to control his or her private life. The Dutch West India Company leased out the enslaved under its control. Owners often worked alongside slaves and indentured servants. Unlike other white colonists, the Dutch claimed no legal right to whip either enslaved or free servants without official permission. But owning human beings has always invited cruelty and harsh treatment.[17]

Equal punishment for crimes marked Dutch rule in New Amsterdam.

Some Dutch owners treated their slaves well. Africans in the New Netherlands enjoyed rights to assemble, to walk around without a pass, and to own property. Enslaved couples had legal marriages, and husbands could protect wives and daughters from evil masters. People of African descent could appeal to the Dutch courts to redress grievances and could testify against white citizens. Anna Negrine, a widow, was able to hire Claes Manuell, a Dutch attorney, to represent her legal interests.[18]

Lucie or Dorothy d'Angola, in 1641, was a godparent and witness at the baptism of an infant, Anthony, whom she adopted after the boy's parents died, the first African adoption in the colony. In 1661, after she married Emmanuel Pieterson, she petitioned the Dutch to free their beloved Anthony. She told the court how she reared him "as her own . . . without aid of anyone in the world." The couple's fervent plea was granted.[19]

Unlike other colonies, New Amsterdam had no laws mandating discrimination. Free Africans could marry each other, have servants, and try to enjoy the rights of European colonists. At least one Dutch citizen was sentenced "to work three months with the Negroes in chains." In 1651 Captain Johan de Vries had a child with an African woman, who may have been his wife and "for whom," it was said, "he made ample provision."[20]

Another sea captain from England who visited the colony found an easy mixing of people:

> Their blacks . . . were very free and familiar; sometimes sauntering about among the whites at meal time, with hat on head, and freely joining occasionally in conversation, as if they were one and all of the same household.[21]

People of color took every opportunity to enlarge their horizons. Lucas Santomee, son of Peter, one of the freed Africans, became a noted physician in the colony. Manuel Sanders, an African, "was affluent enough to employ his medical advisor by the year." There were no restrictions on African women inheriting, owning, or trading in property. The earliest Black land grant in July 1643 was for former slave Catelina Anthony. Other women, including wives and widows, also became owners of farms, plantations, and other real estate.[22]

The subject of slavery was an often unsettling one for the Dutch. Some agreed with a resident who, in 1650, wrote a pamphlet to challenge slavery's legality, but another writer defended bondage. The colony's "half-slavery" policy may have benefited masters and the enslaved. A lack of brutal treatment and arbitrary rules may have reduced the number of runaways. Slave

An African is cheered on to victory in a New Netherlands horse race.

rebellions marked the colonial era, but no revolt disturbed New Amsterdam. "Half-slavery" may have reduced the rage that sparks flight and rebellion, and might have encouraged workers.

Africans continued to enrich their lives. They danced in the streets at Christmas, and some were described as "exquisite performers on three-stringed fiddles." Although African drums were banned in other North American colonies, they sounded along the Hudson River. Owners brought enslaved men and women from as far as fifty miles away for what amounted to Manhattan cultural festivals to enjoy African chants and dances.[23]

The enslaved carried on a long struggle for freedom. Slave Lysbet Antonis expressed her view publicly—she was accused of setting her master's home on fire, the colony's first resistance by an African woman. In 1654 slave Anthony Jansen sued his master for illegal use of his labor and was awarded compensation for his work. Few were that lucky.

Some Dutch residents offered Africans education and religious instruction. In 1638 white citizens petitioned for a "school master to teach and train the youth of both Dutch and Blacks in the knowledge of Jesus Christ." In 1644 the Dutch Reformed Church in Holland ordered the "instruction of Negroes in the Christian religion." Religious training grew under Governor Stuyvesant. When he established St. Mark's Church at Second Avenue and Tenth Street, scores of Africans enrolled. Others were able to join the town's six other main Dutch Reformed churches.

So many Africans sought to baptize their children that one white minister said it had more to do with liberty than godliness: "They wanted nothing else than to deliver their children from bodily slavery, without striving for piety or Christian virtues." Political, economic, and military changes began to alter New Amsterdam's "half-slavery." Between 1636 and 1646 slave prices tripled, from one hundred to three hundred guilders each. According to historian Edgar McManus, annual wages for laborers on the island averaged six hundred guilders, so owning slaves drastically cut labor costs.

In 1647 Peter Stuyvesant, who would rule for the next eighteen years, arrived to replace Governor Kieft. Since the colony's labor shortage was never solved, he also agreed to incentives for African workers. In 1652 Stuyvesant freed three of his own slaves but required that they help in his house when asked. His wife later freed another slave and sold him valuable land near today's Second Avenue and Tenth Street.

In 1660 the governor opened his militia ranks to Africans, but it is unclear if any accepted his offer. Dutch landowners issued Africans weapons so they could march off to arrest white tenants who failed to pay their rent. In 1660, when the island's first two hospitals opened, they were intended to serve "sick soldiers and Negroes."

But Stuyvesant also believed that enslaved Africans ought to be used "to promote and advance the population and agriculture of the province." As director of New Netherlands and the Dutch slave-trading center at Curaçao, he began to increase importations of enslaved Africans to his colony. As the master of forty men and women, he also was the largest slave owner in the New Netherlands.

A 1642 print shows Blacks and whites in New Amsterdam.

In 1653, when New Amsterdam received the first municipal charter for self-government in the Americas, slaves completed a fortified wall alongside a path to be called Wall Street.

In 1654, life changed for the enslaved of Manhattan. When Portugal drove Holland from its colony in Brazil, Holland's slave-trading center shifted to New Amsterdam. In 1655 and 1659 Dutch slave vessels that once traded with Brazil brought hundreds of African women, children, and men to Manhattan, and from there some were shipped to other European colonies.

The Dutch West India Company began to encourage the sale of the enslaved to individual colonists. It even announced an attractive new plan: "Trades as carpentering, bricklaying, black-

Surrender by the Dutch to the English.

smithing and others ought to be taught to the negroes . . . this race has sufficient fitness for it and it would be very advantageous." In 1660, after a shipment of enslaved Africans landed, Stuyvesant supervised what was probably Manhattan's first public auction of human beings.[24]

In 1658 Governor Peter Stuyvesant established a distant farming village called Nieuw Haerlem after a city in Holland. It stood in the bottomlands and meadows far to the north where today's 125th Street touches the Harlem River. Its first known foreign residents were twenty Dutch, French, Danes, Germans, Belgians, and Swedes, who huddled near crude stockades. That year African slave laborers widened an Indian footpath into the first crude road to connect New Amsterdam with Harlem.

Harlem probably also served as a home for slaves who fled New

Amsterdam. Enslaved Black men and women sought a life of freedom in its dense woods. Those who settled near the North (Hudson) River shared their liberty with deer, bears, and wolves.

To draw business and more laborers to their colony, the Dutch West India Company advertised New Amsterdam as "a maritime empire where milk and honey flowed." Instead they attracted another aggressive European power. In August 1664 Colonel Richard Nicolls, commanding four British ships and several hundred soldiers, sailed into New Amsterdam harbor.

A surprised Governor Stuyvesant surrendered without firing a shot. His fort's walls badly needed repairs and were unfit to withstand assault, most of his gunpowder was useless, and he had only 150 men with arms. During the panic caused by the arrival of the British fleet, some slaves fled.

Governor Stuyvesant blamed his surrender on others. Just before the enemy landed, he said, three hundred Africans had been brought to New Amsterdam. These enslaved men, women, and children had eaten the surplus food and left his troops too hungry to fight.[25]

Scholar Michael Kammen has estimated that in 1664 about eight thousand whites and seven hundred Africans lived in New Amsterdam. The British, in a minority, agreed to tolerate Dutch religious practices and culture and to respect property rights.

To the dismay of Africans, however, the English soon began to replace the Dutch lenient "half-slavery" with their own profit-driven, mean-spirited bondage. Africans in Manhattan faced new hardships and challenges as they pressed their search for liberty and justice.[26]

CHAPTER TWO

IN BRITISH NEW YORK

The Duke of York, New Amsterdam's new ruler, renamed the colony New York and appointed its first English governor, Richard Nicolls. The new governor dealt firmly with slavery for the good reason that his patron, the Duke of York, held a major interest in the Royal African Company, a slave-trading company. The Royal African Company soon established a slave market at Wall Street and the East River.

Among the governor's first acts was to sign a law that benefited those who traded in African slaves and to issue a warrant for the arrest of four Black runaways. Nicolls also extended the patent of Nieuw Haerlem from 74th Street northward to 129th Street and from the Hudson River to the East River. But when he tried to rename this northern outpost of his colony Lancaster, his non-English residents rebelled and forced a compromise: "New Harlem," the English version of the Dutch name.

This early sketch of Colonial New York emphasizes the importance of the fur trade.

Throughout the rest of the seventeenth century, Dutch customs continued to shape life in Manhattan. This was largely because so few English settlers arrived that after ten years they made up only 16 percent of New

The stockade punished both white and Black citizens of Colonial New York.

York's population. For decades courts followed Dutch laws that permitted slaves to testify against whites.

However, New York increasingly came under the rule of merchants committed to the commerce in slaves. The colony's Common Council of four aldermen were businessmen who expected enormous profits from slavery. British entrepreneurs imported more and more Africans, and British commercialism put an end to the humanity and charity of Dutch "half-slavery."

In 1677 a New York court stated that any person of color brought to trial was presumed to be a slave. In 1682 New York officials strengthened the laws of bondage and granted masters life-and-death power over their slaves. Slaves had to carry a pass and could not leave their owners' homes on Sundays. Two years later one city ordinance prohibited more than four Africans and Native Americans from meeting together and any African or Native American from possessing guns. In 1706 a court made it clear that if a slave converted to Christianity, this act did not entitle him or her to liberty.

Protected by law and custom, slave trading flourished in New York. In 1698, when the city had five thousand people, slaves numbered only seven hundred. But from 1730 to 1750 more slaves arrived in New York than Europeans. By 1746 one in five

Opposite: The Northeastern United States and, inset, a view of New York as seen in 1673.

New Yorkers was of African descent. So many had arrived that the price of a slave fell to 50 percent of what it had been earlier.

Reputable merchants imported most slaves, but large numbers (never officially counted) arrived illegally on pirate ships. New York Harbor was often filled with vessels owned or commanded by pirates. New York's wealthiest merchants were pleased to deal with Captain Kidd and other pirates because they sold enslaved Africans at such low prices. Since trade with pirates enriched the city, businessmen blurred the line that separated legal from illegal profits.[1]

Prominent city investors such as the Ludlows and Livingstons gathered up enormous profits by trading in Africans. This gave slave trading a virtuous face. Buying slaves carried no stigma, produced great wealth, and attracted financial speculators, reputable businessmen, and government officials. Those made rich by their commerce in human beings built the city's churches and contributed to its leading charities.

Some enslaved New Yorkers were house servants and skilled laborers.

Slave traders found that political power came with their increased profits, and they were able to persuade British officials not to tax them. Only once in colonial New York, in a 1703 military emergency, were slave traders taxed to pay for city defense.

Slave owners hired the services of lawyers, insurers, shipbuilders, and auctioneers and fattened their salaries. They paid for office clerks, warehouse laborers, and dockworkers. The commerce in slaves also increased the profits of restaurants, office suppliers, and messenger agencies. Newspaper owners earned revenues from advertisements of slave sales and auctions, and they rented out their offices so merchants could conduct business meetings.

Some of New York's docks were turned into slave markets. Auctions were held at five locations in downtown Manhattan. In 1709, at what is now 60 Wall Street, the city fathers established an official slave market. By 1711, reported a newspaper, the location was a "place where Negroes and Indians could be bought, sold or hired."

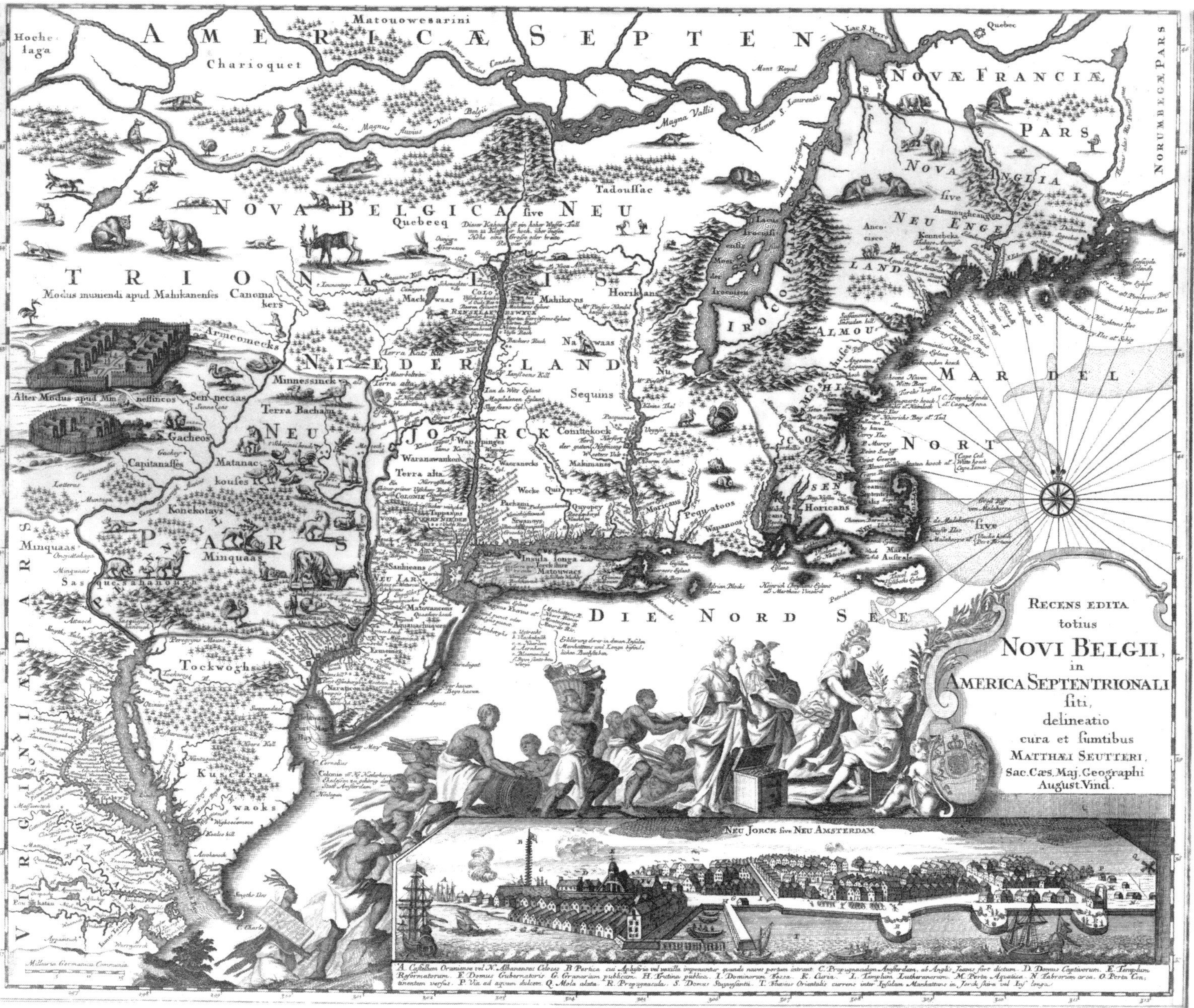
RECENS EDITA totius NOVI BELGII, in AMERICA SEPTENTRIONALI siti, delineatio cura et sumtibus MATTHÆI SEUTTERI, Sac. Cæs. Maj. Geographi August. Vind.
NEU JORCK sive NEU AMSTERDAM
AMERICÆ SEPTEN TRIONALIS
NOVA BELGICA sive NEU NIEDERLAND
NOVÆ FRANCIÆ PARS
NOVA ANGLIA sive NEU ENGELAND
NORUMBEGÆ PARS
VIRGINIÆ PARS
MAR DEL NORT
DIE NORD SEE
Insula longa
Chariocquet
Matouowesarini
Hochelaga
Quebec
Tadoussac
Modus muniendi apud Mahikanenses
Alter Modus apud Minquas
Tockwoghs
Minquaas
Sequins
Pequatoos

One could also purchase white indentured servants.

Newspaper reward notices described the varied backgrounds of the enslaved. In 1732 the New York *Gazette* offered for sale, "Englishmen, Negro men, a Negro girl, and a few Welshmen." Another paper printed an ad for the sale of a "Negro Indian Man Slave . . . a Fiddler."

Free and enslaved Africans served in every trade and neighborhood. Some were farmers, day laborers, bakers, tailors, tanners, goldsmiths, blacksmiths, shoemakers, tobacconists, carpenters, caulkers, shipyard workers, porters, and sailors. Others were cooks, gardeners, coachmen, or launderers. Artisans with valuable skills were rented out by owners for the day, week, or year.

Africans sought to relieve a life of hard work. In Manhattan's Catherine Market, slaves bringing produce from New Jersey and Long Island met. As they peddled eggs, fish, and berries for cash, African women, men, and children danced, sang, or recited poems. Some dancers, such as "Ned" and "Bobolink Bob," wrote one eyewitness, "scarcely knew they were in bondage."

African slaves were welcomed in the foremost English religious congregations. Trinity Episcopal Church at Broadway and Wall Street, which received its Royal Charter in 1697 as the colony's Church of England branch, had dozens of African American members. In 1766 the city's first Methodist congregation included slaves and free people. Some churches created segregated sections and pews, but a number of African couples, including slaves, had their marriages solemnized by the Church of England.

Colonial New York was a turbulent urban world with four hundred taverns, one for every twelve adult males, and no police force. At night its streets were noisy, dangerous, and unhealthy. Disease and death lived in every block, and occasional epidemics tore through neighborhoods. Death rates were high, but no higher for people of color than whites. In a 1730 epidemic only 71 of the 509 recorded dead were Africans, a 12 percent death rate for a Black population that was 15 percent of Manhattan's total. From 1690 through the American Revolution, New York was the most populous city in the New World, and during the

Slaves performed the hard work in New York and other English colonies.

eighteenth century only Charleston, South Carolina, counted more slaves. In the 1703 census 40 percent of New York City households owned slaves, though most owned two people or less. By the 1771 census African Americans made up 14.3 percent of the city population, including a third of Kings County (Brooklyn) and 20 percent of Richmond and Queens. By 1776 New York City had twenty-five thousand residents and 15 percent were slaves.

White city craftsmen worried more about economic competition from skilled slaves than they did about crime, disease, or death. Colonial legislatures passed new laws to bar slaves from skilled trades and professions, but masters who profited from their being hired often evaded the law. In 1737 Lieutenant Governor George Clarke of New York met with a delegation of white mechanics who complained that slave owners had trained their slaves in various crafts and then hired them out to replace white workers.

Some white masters feared slave education was a threat to the system of bondage. Training or learning might enhance an African's sense of worth, they reasoned, and also give them reasons to move around the city. African artisans had opportunities to meet both Europeans and other people of color. Some worked for money they did not turn over to their masters. Many artisans earned enough to pay for new clothes and strutted in their finery. Slaves tried to earn enough cash to liberate their families. These acts of independence frightened most white New Yorkers.

Criminal punishments were harsh in New York City and they fell equally on women and men of both races. Officials ordered two Black women whipped on their bare backs, and a few months later two white women received the same punishment. In 1703 Queen Anne decreed that for "the willful killing of Indians and Negroes," whites should suffer the death penalty. However, no white was ever tried for the murder of a person of color.

New York's strict laws created the illusion that the enslaved were carefully supervised, but this was not true. They *were* prohibited from illegal trading that might help them gain the cash to flee or to purchase their freedom. In 1738, however, a court held masters liable for fines when their slaves caused trouble.

Though slave life could be harsh, individuals were rarely brutalized. Runaway notices in Southern newspapers often listed the scars, brandings, and mutilations inflicted by cruel masters and overseers. Reward notices in New York papers did not mention such signs of mistreatment.

Unlike slaves in the South, some New York slaves enjoyed the legal right to marriage, which was solemnized by the church. But since laws did not prevent slave families from being sold apart, separation was always a fear. Some owners tried to keep African American families intact, but not all. Most masters allowed visitations of husbands and wives who lived near each other.

Though their property rights had no standing in English courts, slaves had owned land, particularly in Greenwich Village, from Dutch times. Some left their inheritance to loved ones in their wills. One white owner left his entire estate to his three children born to their slave mother.

Though both slaves and masters followed Christianity, they

brought different interpretations to the Scriptures. In the sufferings of Christ and the Hebrews, enslaved people saw their own misery and found ways to seek salvation and express feelings. African Americans hoped conversion to Christianity was one way to liberty. Owners hoped slaves would learn "Christian obedience" from worship services. In their own Christian rituals some people of African descent buried their dead in the old Indian burial ground near Washington Square Park.

In 1704, with the arrival of Elias Neau, a white Protestant missionary employed by the Society for the Propagation of the Gospel in Foreign Parts, African education became more organized. Moved by Black suffering, Neau began visiting the homes of people of color and invited them to his home. He started a Catechism school, the city's first for African Americans. Over the next four years, he brought systematic religious instruction to an estimated two hundred people of color.

Whites blamed Neau for planting unsafe thoughts in Africans, and his life was briefly in danger. But the governor and Trinity Church endorsed his efforts, and Neau was able to continue his teaching until his death in 1722. In 1737 the Society for the Propagation of the Gospel in Foreign Parts opened missionary schools for people of color north of the city, in New Rochelle and Newburgh. The society also welcomed Africans to its general meetings.

Whites repeatedly passed new laws to protect their system. In 1682 no more than four slaves were allowed to meet. Later this was reduced to three. By 1702 the number that could meet was lowered to two, and a sunset curfew was imposed on slave men and women over the age of fourteen. That year New York governor Lord Cornbury, a relative of Queen Anne, tried to prevent slaves from assembling in a "riotous" manner. He urged deadly force: "if any of them refuse to submit, then fire upon them, kill or destroy them, if they cannot otherwise be taken."

In 1720 any people of color out after dark were required to carry a lantern. Each New York town hired a man whose job it was to flog slaves. Whipping was also used to punish poor whites.

New York legislation prohibited slave testimony in court against free people. Despite all efforts, slave insubordination was common and found its way into newspaper reports. Rebelliousness took many forms. Some slaves slighted or sabotaged their work. Others tried to earn money at extra jobs to buy their freedom. Despite every precaution, men and women fled their chains. Recently arrived Africans fled before they learned to speak English, and others fled after they learned many languages. One runaway, according to his reward notice, spoke English, Dutch, Spanish, and Danish. Slaves, always seeking allies, tried to learn the language of nearby Native Americans.[2]

Fugitives headed for Long Island, where some were adopted by Indian nations such as the Shinnacocks on the southern shore and the Montauks. Others headed northward toward Albany, seeking liberty among the French, Mohawks, or the Algonquians.

Runaways found a welcome in many Native American villages. In 1712 two Indians were charged with aiding a city slave revolt. By 1717 white New Yorkers complained that runaways not only received aid from but had intermarried with Native Americans. In 1723 the governor of New York asked the Six Iroquois Nations to return fugitive slaves they harbored, but none were returned. In 1733 the governor renewed his request, but Indian negotiators replied with an untruth: "we know not one that there is among any of the Six Nations."

In 1749 a group of Africans from a Spanish ship no sooner arrived in the city than they tried to flee. A paper warned whites that slaves "always aim at their deliverance at any rate, as 'tis likely our freemen would were they in slavery among the Spaniards."

Since New York City slaves often tried to reach freedom in French Canada, in 1705 a law imposed the death penalty on those caught forty miles north of Albany or Saratoga. White fears of resistance and revolt led to other laws. In 1712 New York prohibited anyone from helping a fugitive and again forbade Africans and Native Americans to carry firearms. By 1730 the colony's General Assembly mandated fines for whites who invited slaves into their homes.

In 1745 the colony passed a new death penalty for runaways. But this had no impact on a new ally, the Mohawk nation's Chief Joseph Brant. Born in 1742 and educated in a British school, Brant became a British ally during the Revolution. He was also known for welcoming runaways in his villages in Ontario and for encouraging marriages with his Mohawks.

Chief Joseph Brant and his Mohawks welcomed slave runaways from New York.

Some of the enslaved fled New York aboard ships bound for the Caribbean. Still others headed east to Connecticut, or west into New Jersey or Pennsylvania. Generally fugitives were young men between eighteen and thirty. Most were sailors, carpenters, butchers, tailors, bakers, shoemakers, or goldsmiths, but some were unskilled day laborers or house servants. About a tenth of escapees were women, and some dared to bring babies and children with them.

Some ran away to reunite with relatives who had been sold to nearby or distant masters. They headed toward the next town or to far-off villages in New England, Virginia, or the Carolinas. Reward descriptions for runaways provided clues about how they avoided capture in a strange land. Light-skinned slaves passed for white. Others had white friends or free people of color who forged passes for them.

Many escapees demonstrated personal ingenuity. One runaway hired a horse and charged his master's account. A Brooklyn man fled with two sheep and a beehive full of honey. A Long Island fugitive carried his bed as he raced for liberty.

The flight of slaves meant a loss of money for masters, but the thought of an armed slave rebellion struck terror in all whites. New York governor Cornbury worried that the "great insolency" of city slaves could lead to revolts. Newspapers reported minor offenses by slaves, such as throwing snowballs or getting drunk. Nervous Europeans feared that slaves might turn violent at any moment. To prevent plots, the British passed a law limiting

African American burials to daytime hours and only twelve mourners.

Slaves continued to launch revolts. In 1708 slaves on Long Island rose and killed seven whites. Four slaves, including an Indian and a woman, were executed. In 1744 an owner found his most trusted slave had broken into his warehouse and stolen its contents. Was this slave improving his lot or was a rebellion in the making? Mere mention of revolts created white panic. Owners also feared that any expression of leniency toward slaves might lead to a revolt. When the French Acadians from Nova Scotia, who had settled on Long Island, befriended slaves, whites became alarmed. White New Yorkers blamed mysterious fires on slaves. If food, muskets, and knives disappeared, did this mean an uprising?

In 1755, during the French and Indian War, Lieutenant Governor De Lancey announced that a French attack on the city could trigger a slave revolt. His words stirred more panic than the advancing French armies.

Colonial New York experienced two major rebellion scares. On an April night in 1712, about twenty-four slaves, commanded by recent arrivals from Africa, armed themselves with guns, knives, and hatchets. They assembled in a Maiden Lane orchard and set fire to a building, and as whites rushed to put out the fires, they killed nine whites and wounded six others. White males armed, and Governor Robert Hunter ordered out the militia.

When the outnumbered rebels fled to the woods of northern Manhattan, a white said, "Had it not been for the Garrison there, the city would have been reduced to ashes, and the greatest part of the inhabitants murdered." A hunt began and in two weeks seventy Blacks were arrested. Others committed suicide rather than face capture.

A reign of terror followed: Twenty-seven men, including some Indians, were brought to trial; twenty-one were convicted; and thirteen hanged (including two Indians). One was left to die in chains, four were burned, and one was broken on the wheel. Finally denouncing this as a "blind fury" by whites, Governor Hunter halted the executions.[3]

New York authorities next passed stricter laws. One sought to discourage manumissions, the freeing of slaves, by requiring owners to provide cash if the liberated became a pauper. Another act warned that revolt stemmed from missionaries' stories of redemption from the Bible. One law denied African Americans the right to own or inherit property. At the same time, in Pennsylvania and Massachusetts, legislators temporarily halted the slave trade and began to openly discuss whether it should be phased out.

In 1741, when England was at war with Spain, New York's African American population stood at 18 percent of the total. Whites' fears of invasion soon started another, greater, slave-revolt panic. Would there be a Spanish naval bombardment and landing? Would the slaves remain loyal in the confusion? Winter ice and winds had frozen the harbor, so supply ships could not land. The bakers went on strike, and the price of wheat soared. How would the city survive its troubles at home and from abroad?

One January night in Hackensack, across the river in New Jersey, two African Americans burned several barns. Though they were captured and executed, terror rose. In late February the burglary of a New York merchant's home was followed by rumors of a planned slave revolt that had secret white support.

For several nights in New York City, fires mysteriously erupted at a fort, a chapel, a barracks, and the governor's house. When a slave was caught looting a burning building in March, Black suspects were jailed for a plot to leave the city "in ashes."

Centuries later, no one knows exactly what happened. Mary Burton, a white indentured servant, tavern worker, and perhaps a dealer in stolen goods, pointed her finger at a Black terrorist plot, and whites were ready to believe her tales.

Encouraged by officials, Burton's stories of a conspiracy became more elaborate and involved more plotters. Next a convicted thief corroborated some of her charges. Tales passing as evidence continued to mount, but the sources were white convicted felons or slaves who had been threatened with death. Authorities inflated minor or vague charges into high crimes and acts of violence. Slave testimony had long been illegal in

English colonial courts, but there was no one willing to point this out.

Fear gripped the city judicial system. Two slaves charged with "having things . . . unbecoming the condition of slaves" were executed. White attorneys, outraged by the unfolding slave plot, refused to defend the prisoners, so they lacked any legal advice.

Most of the accused denied guilt and the existence of a plot. Slave owners swore under oath that their slaves who had been accused, were at home during the arson attack. Then, two of the arrested, Quak and Cuffee, were sentenced to burn at the stake. The two swore they were innocent until piles of wood were placed at their feet. Quak and Cuffee began to name plotters.

New Yorkers who attended the Church of England feared Catholics. They had passed a law imposing the death penalty on any priest who entered the city. The tension of the winter made the time ripe for a "Catholic" plot. A teacher, James Ury, who had arrived a few months before the fire, was suspected of being a Catholic priest because he knew Latin and was a masterful debater. Mary Burton suddenly altered her original tale, which had held that a white tavern keeper had engineered the conspiracy. No, she insisted now, Ury was its leader.

Alarm soared at news of a popish (Catholic) plot. Black prisoners were persuaded to identify Ury as their leader. But when Burton began to name such prominent whites as the governor's wife, authorities finally realized the plot was a hoax.

By then official violence had taken a fearful toll. Fifty people still sat trembling in dank cells, but they were the lucky ones. Four whites and eighteen African Americans had been hanged, fourteen other slaves had been burned to death, and seventy others—called the Beasts of the People—had been shipped to Africa. Mary Burton was rewarded and quietly left the colony. Half a century after the Salem witch-hunts in Massachusetts took nineteen lives, white New Yorkers had fused their fanaticism with a deadly racial hysteria.[4]

Slave resistance did not end in 1741. That same year a major slave rebellion erupted in Stono, South Carolina. In 1761 slaves were arrested in a plan to burn Schenectady, and some fled to

Canada. Armed resistance and massive flights by the enslaved in New York and elsewhere characterized the years leading to the American Revolution.

A slave named Jupiter Hammon was born in 1711 on the Long Island estate of the Lloyd family. The young man was educated, perhaps with the Lloyd children, and his interest in writing was encouraged. His poetry and prose, imbued with a strong religious faith, were filled with Biblical allusions and read like church sermons.

Hammon's earliest poem, composed on December 25, 1760, was the first published by an African in the Americas. Addressing his Black sisters and brothers, Hammon spoke of the "salvation" of the human spirit. He insisted liberty was in God's hands and foretold a "divine assistance to enlighten the minds of my brethren."

In 1786, after the Revolutionary War was over, Hammon's "An Address to the Negroes in the State of New York" (republished in 1806 after his death) stated:

> That liberty is a great thing, we may know from our own feelings, and we may likewise judge from the conduct of the white people in the late war. How much money has been spent, and how many lives have been lost to defend their liberty. I must say that I hoped that God would open their eyes, when they were so much engaged for liberty, to think of the state of the poor blacks, and to pity us.[5]

NEW YORK COUNTY POPULATION FIGURES[6]

	Whites	Blacks
1698	4,237	700
1703	3,745	630
1723	5,886	1,362
1731	7,045	1,577
1737	8,945	1,719
1746	9,273	2,444
1749	10,926	2,368
1756	10,768	2,278

CHAPTER THREE

SLAVERY OR FREEDOM IN A REVOLUTIONARY ERA

Black patriots took part in burning the British stamps in Boston and elsewhere.

Even before courageous minutemen stood at Lexington and Concord, enslaved men and women saw reason to hope for their own liberty in the talk of natural rights by colonial leaders who opposed the tyranny of King George III.

In 1765, when patriot James Otis spoke for natural rights, he said, "The colonists, black and white, born here, are free born British subjects, and entitled to all the essential civil rights of such." In 1767 patriot Nathaniel Appleton said abolishing slavery would "show all the world, that we are true sons of liberty."

Leading supporters of American independence identified their cause with ending slavery. In 1772 Benjamin Franklin applauded Quaker Anthony Benezet's early labors against bondage and expressed his hope that colonial legislatures would abolish slavery. (In 1688 the Society of Friends, or Quakers, had denounced bondage and asked members to liberate their slaves.)

Thomas Jefferson's first published work called for an end to slavery, and Tom Paine's first pamphlet, "African Slavery in America," urged abolition. Abigail Adams wrote her husband, John, that it "was wrong to fight ourselves for what we are daily plundering from others." In 1774 New York City's distillers voted unanimously not to distill molasses intended for sale in the slave trade.

Early in the Revolution, antislavery sentiments soared. Slaves, insisted Abigail Adams, "have as good a right to freedom as we have." As minutemen fired on the British at Concord Bridge, slaves and masters signed agreements that granted liberty after a specified number of years. By April 1776 the Continental Congress voted to end the importation of slaves.

African Americans, inspired by the Declaration of Independence, began to petition for liberty. Some adopted the slogan "no taxation without representation." Others did not rely on mere words. During the Revolution more men, women, and children fled their chains than ever before. Many sought to hide in crowded cities such as New York.[1]

By 1771 the city's slave population had increased dramatically. An Englishman touring the city in 1774 was saddened to see "so many negro slaves upon the streets." He estimated the city population between twenty-six thousand and thirty thousand and said non-whites were a fifth of the total.

Cities such as New York offered slaves a chance to be near people of their color and to find marriage partners and the sheltering arm of Black communities. In ports such as New York, runaways also found ships leaving for other cities. Some drifted into tough street gangs such as the Long Bridge Boys, Freemasons, and Smith Fly Boys.

In 1776 New York fell into British hands. During the summer, British general William Howe captured Manhattan, drove Washington's Continentals north of the Harlem River, and remained in command of the city until the war ended in 1783. He used slaves to drive wagons, serve as teamsters, and build military installations. General George Washington was told that the British forces in the city included seven hundred runaways.

Howe armed African Americans, and his quartermaster corps hired runaways. In Jamaica, Queens, the eight workers of the British forage service were Black men. At Saratoga, hundreds of African Americans served as laborers for General John Burgoyne. At Fort Meadows, sixty-three were on the payroll of the 17th Regiment of Light Dragoons. From Albany and Schenectady southward to New York, British employment of slaves raised patriot anxiety. White men in the colony feared to leave their families to go to the front.

At first the Founding Fathers denied people of color a role in the Revolution. In 1775 New York exempted slaves and even indentured servants from militia service. George Washington, Benjamin Franklin, and other patriots opposed recruitment of free or enslaved African Americans. Then, on November 7, 1775, British Lord Dunmore changed the rules when he issued an order promising liberty and a musket to any slave who reached his lines. Black volunteers poured into Dunmore's Virginia camps, and a southern white wrote, "The flame runs like wildfire through the slaves." Fugitives also joined pro-British Tory guerrillas, such as Delancy's Rangers, organized in New York during the war.[2]

In January 1776 George Washington responded to Lord Dunmore's challenge by asking the Continental Congress to enlist free people of color, and the Revolution changed course. By March the commanding officer of each city and county of New York even recruited male slaves to build defenses.

Slaves were committed to the principle of freedom. They fought on whichever side offered it, and picked their own time and place to seize it. Thomas Jefferson estimated that thirty thousand slaves escaped in 1778 alone. By the British surrender at Yorktown in 1781 about a hundred thousand had fled.

Free African Americans served with Ethan Allen's Green Mountain Boys when they captured Fort Ticonderoga. At Bunker Hill, Peter Salem's musket brought down British commander Major Pitcairn. African Americans fought at Saratoga, Trenton, White Plains, Princeton, and Monmouth, and shiv-

New Yorkers rejoiced when the statue of King George III was toppled from its pedestal in lower Manhattan.

ered in the snow at Valley Forge. Phillip Field of Duchess County joined the 2nd New York Regiment and died in 1778 during Valley Forge's harsh winter. Captain Stephen Decatur's *Royal Lewis* had twenty Black sailors.

In 1781 the New York General Assembly authorized the enlistment of slaves in two regiments with these words: "And such slave . . . who shall serve for a term of three years, or until regularly discharged, shall immediately after such service or discharge be, and is hereby declared to be a free man of this state."

African Americans in New York played a key military role. When the British forces left Boston in 1776, it was anticipated they would head toward New York City. New York's Provincial Congress asked the commanding officers of each corps in the city and county to enlist all adult Black males, including slaves, in the building of defenses. Slaves worked every day, free men of color every second day. On Long Island the Provincial Congress told officials to recruit all men of color for work on fortifica-

Black men served in New York regiments.

tions. When Washington's forces left Long Island in 1776, his retreat was covered by 140 African American soldiers.

The many fugitive slaves who reached New York City created problems for both sides. British officials in the city established a Commission for Detecting and Defeating Conspiracies. In 1778 General Lafayette wrote about a slave plot to burn Albany. Two years later six slaves were jailed in Albany for attempting to flee to Canada. In 1780 New York's *Weekly Mercury* reported that the "desire of obtaining freedom . . . reigns" among slaves.

About eight thousand African Americans fought in the armies of George Washington and the navy of John Paul Jones. Some five thousand were regular soldiers and on average served longer terms than white men. A captured Hessian soldier wrote "no [Continental] regiment is to be seen in which there are not Negroes in abundance, and among them are able-bodied, strong and brave fellows."

Black volunteers flocked to the patriot ranks, but not all were volunteers. Owners who delivered their slaves to recruiters received a grant of five hundred acres of choice land. Sometimes a master refused to serve and instead sent a slave in his place. David Belknap, a patriot, instead of reporting to Fort Montgomery, sent a slave man who later was captured and died a prisoner of war.

No matter how they entered the ranks, African Americans became crucial to Washington's major campaigns. The drummer in Captain Benjamin Egbert's company in New York City in March 1776 was an African American named Tom. In 1781, at the battle of White Plains, New York, African American soldiers made up a fourth of the Continental army. That year Colonel Christopher Greene's Black regiment was wiped out in one of the Revolution's bloodiest battles near Points Bridge, New York. In February 1783, when the Continental army marched from Saratoga to Oswego, African Americans formed a majority.[3]

In July 1779 a slave name Pompey discovered the British password and helped General Anthony Wayne surprise and capture Stony Point and six hundred prisoners. Pompey was awarded his liberty. The next year two African American men helped capture British spy Major John André in New York.

Young Peter Williams, born a slave on Beekman Street, loyally supported the patriots. He was in New Jersey when he heard that British troops intended to arrest patriot leader Parson Chapman. Williams mounted his horse and rode off to warn the parson of the danger. Then he helped Chapman move his goods to safety. Captured by the British, who threatened to cut his head off if he withheld information, Williams remained silent.

On the day the British left New York City in 1783, Williams's fellow Methodists at the John Street church paid forty dollars to liberate their friend from bondage. To pay off this debt, Williams worked as a church sexton for two years. Later Williams became a prosperous tobacco merchant and undertaker, and by 1800 a founder and leading financial supporter of New York's first Black church.

On November 30, 1783, New York City became the last port evacuated by the British. Washington demanded the surrender

The British shipped some Africans to the West Indies at the end of the Revolution.

of all runaway slaves, but the British refused to return those who had fled expecting liberty. Washington strongly objected, but four thousand African Americans left on British vessels. The Royal Navy also evacuated four thousand people of color from Savannah and six thousand from Charleston and allowed most of them to settle in the West Indies.

For the enslaved of New York the Revolution changed little. Slaves and slave-owning classes grew. From 1790 to 1800 city slaves increased by 22 percent and slaveholders increased by 33 percent. Slaves now were only 10 percent of the city's population, but this was because of a vast increase in white immigration.

One in five white city households owned at least one slave. Every third resident of Kings County, on Long Island (now Brooklyn), was African American, and 60 percent of its white households held slaves. Slaveholding households in Kings, Queens, and Richmond Counties boasted a greater percentage of slaves than those who crowded the British colony of South

Carolina. For example, 58 percent of Kings' households had slaves, and people of color were 41 percent of the population.[4]

In 1787 a visitor found New York City filled with "miserable wooden hovels and strange looking brick houses, constructed in the Dutch fashion." Slaves lived no better, but no worse than others. In the first U.S. census in 1790, of New York City's 31,229 residents, 10 percent were African Americans and of these 7 percent were slaves and 3 percent were free.

Black labor helped accelerate business expansion after the war. The city's 248 merchants in 1790 rose to 1,102 by 1800, and many had amassed fortunes by trading in slaves. When the world's first stock exchange opened in New York City in 1792, half of its 177 stockholders were slave owners. Prominent Federalist governor George Clinton held eight slaves, and Aaron Burr and John Jay owned five each.

English visitor Alexander Conventry in the 1780s noted that "every respectable family had slaves . . . who did the drudgery." But slaveholding in the city cut across class. Artisans and professionals ranked as New York's largest slave-holding class. One in eight artisans and one in three professionals were owners. About 13 percent of owners were women. The white lower class was half of the city population and controlled only 6.6 percent of the wealth, but it owned 12 percent of the city's slaves, triple the percentage owned by poor whites in Boston and Philadelphia.

The demands of white owners and the nature of working conditions disrupted Black family life. With 75 percent of masters owning only one or two people, slave families were often divided among several owners and homes. Some 36 percent of free people also lived with those they served because it was required by the work or by their employers. The free people were often paid too little to afford a private apartment. Shane White, in his *Somewhat More Independent: The End of Slavery in New York City, 1770–1810* found this "brutal and little short of devastating in its impact on the black family."

Black households in New York averaged more members than those in Philadelphia or Boston, but compared to white New Yorkers most African American families had fewer children.

Black families tried as best they could to survive. John Moranda negotiated his liberty in 1795 and in a few months purchased his daughter, Susan, age four, for fifty dollars, and in three years paid $160 for his wife Susan, thirty-three, and his son, John. By 1800 Moranda was living on Warren Street with his family and supporting them.

Slaves continued to fly to freedom after the war. One in six escapees was under sixteen. Some fugitives left without anything but their clothes, but others took money and one carried his master's gold watch and half his linen. Masters to the north and east, in Long Island and Westchester, believed that one in three runaways headed toward New York City.

For every six male fugitives, one woman fled bondage. Most women escaped alone, but one in seven brought an infant or child. Those who fled to New York hoped to pass as free people and find good jobs. In 1795 one fugitive known as Calypso was seen racing along Pearl and Rutgers streets carrying a bundle of clothes and her shoes. Black residents took her in.

Sporadic slave rebelliousness also followed the war. In 1798 four slaves murdered a white Long Island family of seven. They were captured and executed.[5]

As part of the city's poor, people of color shared many perils and few opportunities. In 1786 eight hundred taverns served the city's population of thirty thousand including its large underclass. Tavern patrons filled the night with noise, quarrels, and occasional violence. African Americans turned their cellar homes into nightclubs, where they could drink and dance to fiddle music. Hazzard's Pete, a slave, was described as a "great dancer . . . in the negro dancing cellars in the city."

In New York Black religious and self-help organizations also sprouted after the Revolution. In 1786 at 42 Baxter Street, the New York African Society for Mutual Relief, the first Black mutual aid society, opened its doors. It offered members illness and death insurance and provided intellectual stimulation as well.

In 1808 the New York African Society for Mutual Relief had magazine editor William Hamilton as its president, and its board included a famous caterer, Thomas Downing, and inventor

Thomas Jennings. In 1818 the society was legally incorporated and soon built a headquarters on a Baxter Street lot, which also served as its station on the Underground Railroad. Society headquarters later moved to 27 Greenwich Avenue in Greenwich Village. It began the agitation over slavery that helped lead to the Civil War.

Despite city color barriers, African Americans made significant gains after American independence was achieved. They won new rights to own and inherit land, to marriages that were sanctified by churches and the state, and the right to live in any neighborhood. More than a few owned their own homes. In 1793 African American Catherine Ferguson, twenty-five, organized the first Sunday school in New York City. In 1796 William Platt, a Black artisan, willed the house he owned at 49 Cedar Street to his wife. By 1797 over two thousand African Americans lived and worked in the city as free people.

By 1800 some had made striking advances. Former slaves in New York had decided to reshape their identities by rejecting insulting names (such as Mistake) bestowed by owners. Many chose new names that were less likely to represent former masters and instead showed a pride in their free status. Tom became Thomas, Will became William, and Pete became Peter. Biblical names increased. Some 94 percent of free people were recorded as having surnames, not just given names. Another gain came in 1809 when New York law further sanctioned marriages between people of African descent, affirming the Black family.

Some African Americans scaled economic and social walls. James Derham had been the slave of an owner who fled with the British. Derham paid for his freedom, learned to speak several languages, and became a noted physician. Dr. Benjamin Rush, surgeon general of the American army, conceded that Derham knew more than he did about medicine.[6] Sally Gale, born in Huntington, Long Island, came to the city in 1797 and worked for nine months as a nurse at New York Hospital. At that time Manhattan also claimed two Black teachers. Timothy Weeks and William Johnson set up a thriving business partnership on Prince Street.

The most significant institution to arise from the ashes of the

Peter Williams founded New York's first independent African American church in 1800.

Revolution was an independent Black church. It all began in 1795 with Peter Williams, who worked as sexton for the John Street Methodist Church on what is now William near Nassau Street. Stung by insults from white parishioners, Williams and other Black members started their own gatherings the next year. In 1800 Williams used his own money and began to build on an empty lot he owned on Church and Leonard streets. Williams and the congregation built their Mother African Methodist Episcopal Zion Church. Others followed, and in 1806 James Varick, fifty-six, and two others in the African Methodist Episcopal Zion Church became the first of African descent to serve as ordained ministers in New York State. In 1808 an Abyssinian Baptist Church opened on Anthony Street with Reverend Thomas Paul as its minister. In 1809 Black members who withdrew from Trinity Episcopal Church because of discrimination formed the St. Philip's Protestant Episcopal Church. By 1820 it was welcomed into the Episcopal diocese and Peter Williams Jr. was its ordained rector.

In New York, as elsewhere, the Black church served as a house of hope and a sheltering arm for families as much as a home of God. For people of color it was spiritual healer, community meeting hall, and learning center. Churches helped build African American identity and served members as havens in every human storm. Under its roof the sick, hungry, poor, and homeless were cared for and republican principles were advanced. Basements and attics became sanctuaries for fugitive slaves and stations on the Underground Railroad. Movements to demand liberation were often born in rooms that echoed with songs in praise of God.[7]

NEW YORK COUNTY POPULATION FIGURES[8]

	WHITES	BLACKS
1771	18,726	3,137
1786	21,507	2,103
1790	29,661	3,470

CHAPTER FOUR

EDUCATION IN OLD NEW YORK

By 1800 New York's 15 percent African population gave it the largest Black percentage of any Northern city. A third of white households in the city either owned slaves or hired free Blacks. New York City in the early nineteenth century largely rested on an African American labor force that was both slave and free.

By 1810 free people of color had replaced slaves as servants in most white homes. The slave system was gradually fading away in the state. But even at this time 1,686 men, women, and children in the city were still enslaved. More than 30 percent of them had been trained as artisans—carpenters, coopers, cabinetmakers, upholsterers, sail makers, butchers, and bakers—and white artisans still tried to block their entrance to the skilled trades.

Free African Americans also began to redefine their personal identity through their choice of names. In New York City between 1776 and 1820, those who chose English names rose from 30 percent to 72 percent, and the number who selected Biblical names doubled.

African Americans in New York formed charitable and self-help societies. After African Americans organized the New York Society for Mutual Relief, an African Woolman Benevolent Society was begun in 1810. In 1817 African Americans established the New York African Bible Society. Five years later the city boasted a Phoenix Society to promote literary and educational interests among members. In 1827 a Brooklyn African Tompkins Society was started. The next year Reverend Peter Williams Jr. formed the Dorcas Society, an early self-help organization. In 1839 a Black women's group, Abyssinian

Benevolent Daughters of Esther Assocation of the City of New York was formed and printed its constitution.[1]

Free Black people, particularly women, migrated to New York eager to live among their own race, to meet marriage partners, and to enjoy the city's flourishing cultural and social life. Since job discrimination impacted more on men than women, in 1820 New York had three Black women for every two men.

That year New York's Black households averaged 6.3 people, more per household than households in Boston or Philadelphia. This represented not more children per family but more individuals living in single-housing units. Ninety-six percent of New York African American children lived with both their parents.

During the War of 1812, as they had in the Revolution, free African Americans in New York tried to prove their value to the country. They called a public meeting and offered to defend the city from the British. Speakers talked of a duty to volunteer. African Americans participated in the U.S. victories at Plattsburgh and Lake Champlain, New York. By 1814 the legislature authorized formation of a Black New York regiment and two thousand enlisted. One act mandated equal pay for all soldiers and declared that slaves whose masters let them enlist would be freed at the war's end.

Black New Yorkers continued to pursue their economic agenda. In 1810 New York City's lucrative oyster trade was dominated by twenty-seven African Americans—nine slaves and eighteen free people. Oystermen from Long Island and New Jersey sold their products in the city. The best oyster restaurants in the city were run by African Americans. Black women had also become prominent street vendors in city markets.

However, life for the average working African American was hard. One in three lived as domestics in a white household, and most had to share small attic or basement rooms. Others were cramped into dank cellars or rooms in the back of buildings.

Often people of color moved into neighborhoods that boasted a Black church. By 1818 discrimination at the Sands Street Methodist Church in Brooklyn drove its members to establish an African Wesleyan Methodist Episcopal Church. In 1821

The mixed Five Points area of New York City in 1859.

African Americans in Manhattan began Demeter Presbyterian church in a small building on Rose Street with Reverend Samuel Cornish as spiritual leader.

In 1825 Reverend Theodore Wright, the first Black graduate of Princeton's Theological Seminary, became pastor of the First Colored Presbyterian Church. Soon a dozen Black congregations rented or owned buildings in lower Manhattan.

African Americans also lived among poor Irish Americans in the notorious Five Points area on Center Street where Bayard and Worth streets met, east of the New York Courthouse and southwest of today's Chinatown. By the 1820s Five Points had a fearful reputation based on its criminal population, which included the jobless of all races. Visiting English writer Charles Dickens found Five Points "decayed," "loathsome," "reeking everywhere with filth," and filled with "hideous tenements which take their name from robbery and murder."

By 1825 more than a fifth of Manhattan's people of color lived in the unhealthy, dangerous Sixth Ward that stretched from Five Points to the Hudson River. When cholera struck the city in 1832, the death rate in this ward soared above the city average. Others still lived in Greenwich Village, near the Hudson River or on West Broadway, or eastward on Leonard, Sullivan, Greene, Mulberry, and Mercer streets.

When an epidemic swept through the Fourth Ward, the mixed community east of Broadway, one report noted: "Out of the 48 blacks, living in 10 cellars, 33 were sick, of whom 14 died; while, out of 120 whites, living immediately over their heads in the apartments of the same houses, not one even had the fever."

Even in these poor neighborhoods a few Black women and men became landlords and hotel keepers. Many others, including escaped slaves, joined local gangs—the Dead Rabbits, the Bowery Boys, and the Plug Uglies. These criminals were so well-armed and defiant that slave catchers—called "Blackbirders"—feared to enter their neighborhood.

Young David Broderick, a stonecutter, was born to poor Irish immigrants and lived alongside African Americans in Five Points. Later, drawn by the 1849 gold rush to California, Broderick entered politics successfully and in 1856 was elected to the U.S. Senate. He was a rarity, a Democrat opposed to slavery. Challenged to a duel by his proslavery opponent, the senator showed he was a gentleman when he fired into the early morning air. His foe took careful aim and shot him in the heart. In his last gasp Broderick said he died because he was against slavery.[2]

Before and after the Revolution, free people of color had the vote in New York and the New England states. They usually supported wealthy Federalists who, though they owned slaves, spoke for abolition. Middle- and lower-class whites, on the other hand, supported Thomas Jefferson's Democratic Republicans, which called itself the party of the common man.

In 1810 five of Brooklyn's thirteen Federalist candidates had freed their slaves, but their Democratic Republican opponents had not. When African Americans voted for the Federalist candidates, the Democratic Republicans were infuriated. Three years later three hundred Black voters provided the Federalists with the margin of victory they needed to win in the city. One Democratic leader warned about "the dangerous importance" of the Black vote. He claimed it "decided the political character of the [state] legislature." Democrats spoke of people of color as "degraded, dependent and unfit" voters or as Federalist "pawns."

In 1821 Democrats changed the suffrage laws at New York's Constitutional Convention. They were determined to limit voting to white men only and to strip the Federalists of their Black supporters. Led by Martin Van Buren, they made a major democratic advance when they struck down all property qualifications for white male voters. At the same time, they limited the suffrage for African American men to those who owned at least $250 in property. The democratic movement associated with Andrew Jackson served notice that it was for white males only.[3]

Their path to the ballot box almost entirely blocked, African Americans sought a new path that led to the schoolhouse. New York became the first city in the United States to offer systematic free education for African American children. This first experiment in public education began in 1787, two years before the United States Constitution was ratified. The New York Manumission Society called their project "the African Free Schools," and it sought to teach Christian beliefs and useful skills.[4]

The society's first school provided instruction for forty boys and girls in a single room at 245 William Street between Beekman and Ferry streets. Its white teacher, Cornelius Davis, left a white school for his new position. No Black teachers were hired.

In 1791 the school hired a woman to instruct Black girls in needlework. Classes focused on reading, writing, and navigation. Girls were instructed in domestic arts and boys in the manual arts.

The African Free Schools triggered heated debate. Some white citizens insisted education was wasted on people of color, while others enthusiastically supported the idea. Newspapers lauded the school's educational success, and the City Corporation gave small grants to the school until 1801 when the state legislature voted it more than fifteen hundred dollars.

In 1814 the first school was destroyed by fire, but a brick build-

The chapel in an early school for Black children. From <u>Frank Leslie's Illustrated Newspaper</u>, April 24, 1869.

ing was erected the next year on William Street near Duane, on land purchased by the city. Funds raised by philanthropists of both races insured the school's success.

In 1820 a second African Free School for five hundred students opened on Mulberry between Grand and Hester streets. A teacher taught girls sewing, reading, writing, arithmetic, English grammar, and geography. One pupil, Samuel R. Ward, said he felt his teachers showed commitment, understanding, and "great kindness."

In May 1824 city council representatives attended students' examinations and returned with glowing reports on their abilities in arithmetic, grammar, geography, spelling, writing, reading, and needlework. Talented pupils, they said, offered "prompt and satisfactory" answers. The popular *Commercial Advertiser* declared that the answers given by the now six hundred children were "highly interesting and gratifying." "We never beheld a white school," the reporter wrote, ". . . [with]

more order, and neatness of dress, and cleanliness of person." Journalists were particularly impressed with the girls' classes.

That year the famous Revolutionary hero Marquis de Lafayette was an honored guest at the school and was welcomed "as a friend of African emancipation" by student James McCune Smith for the staff and pupils. Lafayette praised the school's academic achievements and its students and teachers.

Then, on graduation day, Blacks suddenly had to enter a world that still judged them not by their intellect but by their color. In 1819 a pupil had addressed his graduating class:

> What are my prospects? To what shall I turn my hand? Shall I be a mechanic? No one will employ me; white boys won't work with me. Shall I be a merchant? No one will have me in his office. Can you be surprised at my discouragement?[5]

Samuel Ward found he had graduated into an angry city.

> Poverty compelled me to work, but inclination led me to study. . . . Added to poverty, however, in the case of a black lad in that city, is the ever-present, ever-crushing Negro-hate, which hedges up his path, blasts his hope, and embitters his spirits.

New York African Free School No. 2. Engraved from a drawing made by Patrick Reason, a pupil, age thirteen.

In 1832 one brilliant graduate, Charles Reason, fourteen, was hired as an instructor at the African Free School. However, even the African Free Schools never eliminated a glaring inequity. When Black teachers were hired, they were paid less than white teachers, even those with poorer performance ratings.

In 1835 three graduates, Henry Highland Garnet, Alexander Crummell, and Thomas Sidney, were invited to enroll in the Canaan, New Hampshire, Academy. Along the four-hundred-mile route few inns offered them food or lodging, but at the academy they were welcomed by the white students.

Henry Highland Garnet escaped from slavery and became a noted minister and abolitionist.

Canaan's local farmers, however, devised a different reception. Beginning on the Fourth of July and for two nights, they hitched ninety oxen to drag the main academy building into a swamp. Some then returned with guns to drive off the three Black students. Young Garnet, armed and ready, fired a double-barreled shotgun through a window. Lights flashed on all over the countryside and the startled farmers fled. But the days of the three at the academy were numbered, and they soon left.[6]

In New York City the African Free Schools merged with the New York City Public School Society in 1834 to better serve some fourteen hundred registered Black pupils. The average daily attendance stood at 50 percent and would have been higher except that white violence in the city persuaded many African American parents to keep their children at home.

New York's white bureaucracy began to make drastic changes in these African Free Schools. Elementary school courses were left intact, but Black teachers were fired and secondary school classes were closed. Pupil attendance and morale fell until a Black man was hired to recruit more pupils.

In 1836 a new school opened for Blacks on Laurens Street with 210 pupils and an African American principal, R. F. Wake. In 1847 another society promoting African American education opened a school on Thomas Street and another on Center Street, and soon it began an educational center for adult women and men. (By 1848 this society boasted 1,375 students and in 1852 had enrolled 319 others for after-work classes.)

Graduates of the earlier African Free Schools began to play a prominent role in New York's political and intellectual life. Henry Highland Garnet, Alexander Crummell, and Samuel R. Ward became important ministers and commanding abolitionist voices. James McCune Smith became a noted doctor and a statistical scholar with a worldwide reputation.[7]

Actor Ira Aldridge as he appeared in London, England.

But the school's shining star was actor Ira Aldridge, born in the city to a lay preacher and a mother from North Carolina who died when he was a child.

Aldridge began his theatrical career with a behind-the-stage job at the Chatham Theater. Then he joined the African Grove Theater, a Black Shakespearean acting troupe that opened a playhouse in 1821 on Bleecker and Mercer streets. For nine years the troupe ran an "entertainment agreeable to the ladies and gentlemen of color." Their performances were so popular they could charge high prices of twenty-five to seventy-five cents and still fill the playhouse.

The actors, however, found that white patrons caused a commotion during serious plays. To keep the peace, the troupe began to intersperse Shakespearean scenes with comedy routines. Then to further preserve the peace and since "whites do not know how to conduct themselves" with people of color, their handbill stated, whites were seated in rear seats.

In 1824 Aldridge left for England and a spectacular stage career. Though he spoke only English, by 1852 he was hailed as an acting genius from Dublin, Ireland, to St. Petersburg, Russia. Although he achieved fame as Shakespeare's Othello the Moor, he also triumphed in white roles such as Macbeth, Shylock, and King Lear. In 1867 he was in Poland and finishing plans to return to the United States for a new debut when he died.

Tom Molineaux, a Virginia slave, was born in 1784. His father, Zachary, has been credited with introducing boxing to the United States. Young Tom Molineaux earned his freedom and a hundred dollars when he outboxed another slave, and then left for New York City.[8]

Boxing champion Tom Molineaux in 1810.

Molineaux took a job at the Catherine Street produce market, a boxers' meeting place, and quickly demonstrated an ability to defeat men of all sizes and weights. Prodded by a sea captain to challenge the reigning boxing champion in London, Tom Molineaux sailed off to England. He was met by Bill Richmond, forty-seven, another former New York slave renowned for his boxing skills. Richmond, brought to England by his master when the British fled New York in 1783, agreed to serve as Molineaux's ring manager.

On December 18, 1810, Molineaux fought Tom Cribb for the world heavyweight crown. In the twenty-ninth round Cribb could not rise from his corner, but his second, Joe Ward, began a heated argument with Molineaux's second. This gave Cribb time to recover, and in round forty Cribb was awarded the decision, though many believed Molineaux was the victor.

In a scheduled rematch with Cribb the next year, Molineaux lost badly. Instead of continuing to box professionally, he toured Ireland to teach boxing as an art. Molineaux never recovered from his defeat, fell into poverty, and died a poor man in London. But he had become the first significant Black heavyweight contender, and some saw him as the world champion.

NEW YORK COUNTY POPULATION FIGURES[9]

	Total	Blacks	Slave	Free
1800	60,515	6,382	2,868	3,514
1810	96,373	9,823	1,686	8,137
1820	123,706	10,886	518	10,368

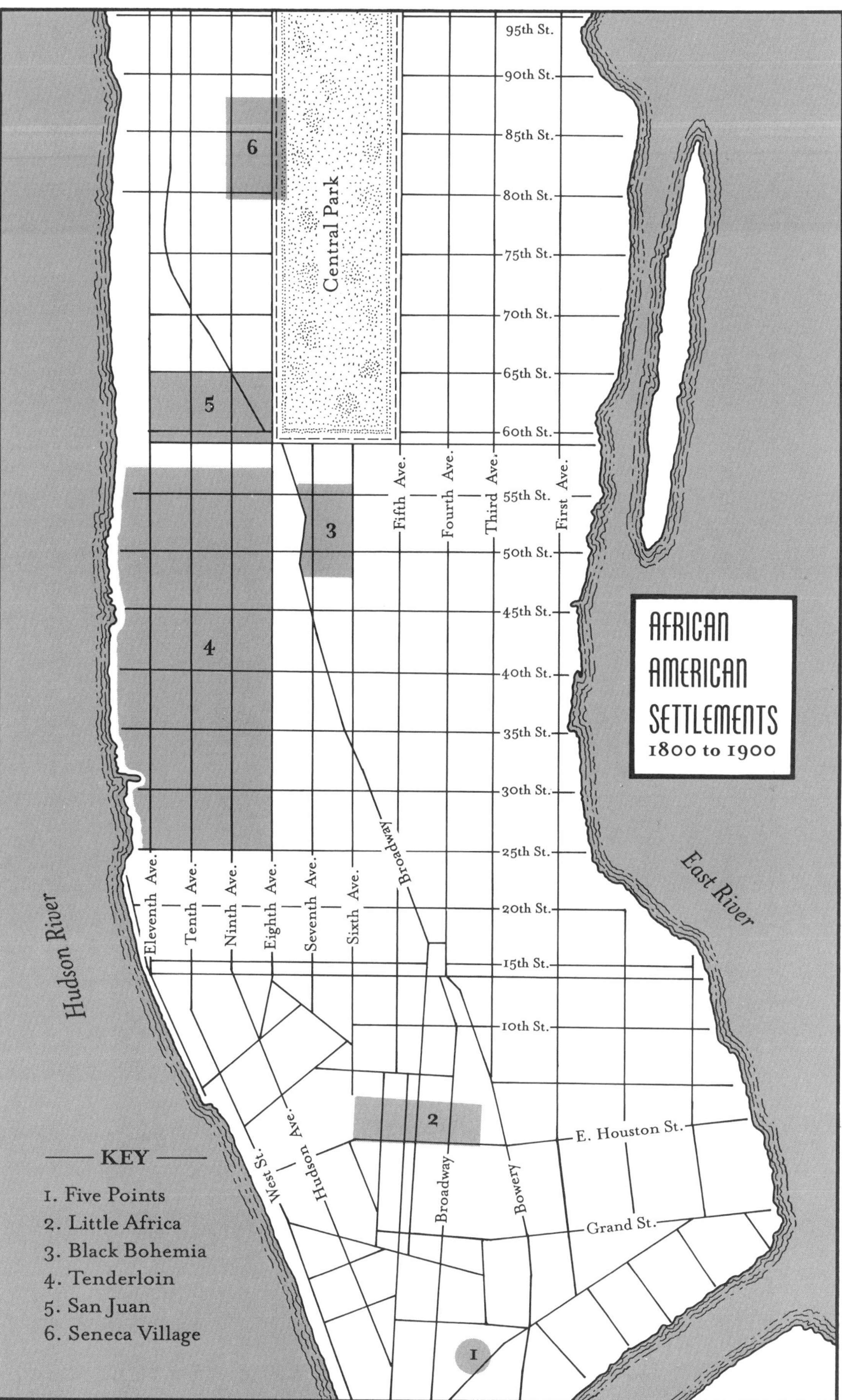

AFRICAN AMERICAN SETTLEMENTS
1800 to 1900
KEY
1. Five Points
2. Little Africa
3. Black Bohemia
4. Tenderloin
5. San Juan
6. Seneca Village
Central Park
Hudson River
East River
95th St.
90th St.
85th St.
80th St.
75th St.
70th St.
65th St.
60th St.
55th St.
50th St.
45th St.
40th St.
35th St.
30th St.
25th St.
20th St.
15th St.
10th St.
E. Houston St.
Grand St.
Fifth Ave.
Fourth Ave.
Third Ave.
First Ave.
Eleventh Ave.
Tenth Ave.
Ninth Ave.
Eighth Ave.
Seventh Ave.
Sixth Ave.
Broadway
West St.
Hudson Ave.
Bowery

CHAPTER FIVE

EMANCIPATION COMES TO NEW YORK

In the decades that followed the Revolution, Northern states moved to adopt emancipation. The talk about natural rights and the importance of the individual, and the defeat of British tyranny, brought a new antislavery spirit to the land.

In 1777, Vermont, by constitutional amendment, became the first state to prohibit slavery. Between 1777 and 1784 Pennsylvania, Massachusetts, Connecticut, and Rhode Island also voted for emancipation. Massachusetts outlawed slavery in 1783 after two slaves, Elizabeth Freeman and Quork Walker, in separate legal actions, sued in court and won their liberty.

Almost all patriot leaders had called for abolition during the war. In New York John Jay and Alexander Hamilton said American independence ought to be followed by emancipation. In 1779 Hamilton said, "I have not the least doubt that the Negroes will make very excellent soldiers," and added, "their natural faculties are as good as ours." To "give them freedom with their swords," he hoped, would open "a door to their emancipation." But state action was exceedingly slow, and emancipation was not completed in New York until 1827.

As early as 1777 John Jay, who headed the city's delegation to New York's Provincial Congress, urged an emancipation law, but it narrowly failed to pass. That same year at New York's first Constitutional Convention, a majority voted for a clause guaranteeing gradual emancipation. Gouverneur Morris wrote a document endorsed by thirty-one of the thirty-five delegates that read: "Every human being who breathes the air of the state shall enjoy the privileges of a freeman." The New York legislature, however, took no action until the war's end and then voted only to free slaves who had fought for independence.

A slave named Preston (without hat) is seized in New York City as his wife begs for his release (center).

Though favoring rule by white aristocrats, Alexander Hamilton in 1779 said: "The contempt we have been taught to entertain for the blacks, makes us fancy many things that are founded neither in reason nor experience." That same year John Jay's antislavery voice became louder when he became president of the Continental Congress.

In 1782 Jefferson's *Notes on Virginia* called slavery despotism, and Lafayette, French hero of the Revolution, announced, "I would never have drawn my sword in the cause of America if I could have conceived that thereby I was founding a land of slavery." Polish hero of the Revolution Thaddeus Kosciusko, Washington's chief of engineers, willed his money to the cause of abolition and Black education in the hope that Black men and women would become "defenders of their liberty and their country."[1] In 1801 a woman about to ship twenty slaves to the South faced an angry shouting crowd of 250 people of color outside her city home.

People of color and antislavery reformers in New York drew inspiration from the revolutions in France and in Haiti. Revolutionaries in France issued a Declaration of the Rights of Man and called for "Liberty, Equality and Fraternity." In 1791 a French society, *Amis de noirs* (Friends of Blacks), said, "All men are born free and with equal rights, regardless of their color" and insisted that "no society can legitimate such crime [as slavery]."

The first legal emancipation in New York had begun during the Revolution when some towns liberated slaves owned by loyalists. In 1784 the New York legislature declared slaves of former loyalists forever free.

In 1785 New York's legislature voted to outlaw the slave trade. The legislators also debated whether emancipation should be immediate or gradual. By more than three to one, they favored gradual abolition, and although they rejected Aaron Burr's bill for immediate emancipation, no further action was taken.

Many slave-owning legislators rejected any quick act of emancipation. They also had no intention of sharing political power with their former slaves. So although the legislature voted for gradual emancipation, it denied the vote to the African Americans who would be freed. The city's Council of Revision vetoed this action. Antislavery feeling remained strong, and in 1786 the *New York Journal* suggested those who owned human beings deserved to be "plundered, tormented and even massacred."

New York City became home to the first official antislavery society on U.S. soil, the Society for Promoting the Manumission of Slaves. Its first meeting in 1785 at Trinity Church on Broadway and Wall streets predated the U.S. Constitution, and its creators were Founding Fathers John Jay and Alexander Hamilton. Jay and Hamilton served as the society's first president and vice president. Nineteen other supporters included illustrious city Federalist families as the Schuylers, Duanes, and Livingstons. The society opened branches around the state and began to lobby state legislators to vote for a gradual approach to the abolition of slavery.[2]

In 1788 New York's legislature took its first concrete step toward liberty: It voted to free any slave sold in the state. When masters tried to avoid the law by claiming they had "leased" their slaves, the state supreme court called this a subterfuge. Legislators next voted to make manumission less costly for masters. They also granted a basic human right: In death penalty cases, slaves had a right to a trial by jury.

New Yorkers also began to challenge cruel slave masters. Abusers of slaves suffered public disapproval. The Albany town council banned flogging for slaves who violated the night curfew and instead fined their owners. Some owners, claiming they could not discipline disobedient slaves, began to free them.

U.S. chief justice John Jay

The slow pace toward emancipation gave some masters and slaves a chance to negotiate an earlier time release from bondage. But other owners began to sell their slaves to the South. In 1790 only 15 percent of African Americans in Manhattan and Brooklyn were free, but by 1820 the percentage reached 84 percent.

By 1790 the Society for Promoting the Manumission of Slaves gained branches in every local community and among every class of whites. John Jay advanced his cause from new positions of power, first in 1789 as chief justice of the United States Supreme Court and then in 1795 as governor of New York.

Besides lobbying legislators to pass an emancipation law, the society tried to persuade individual owners to release those held in bondage. Society members, shocked at how slave-hunting posses from the Southern states seized people on New York streets, offered slaves free attorneys and legal aid. The society also circulated the names of New Yorkers engaged in slave trading. Societal pressure virtually ended slave auctions in the city.

In 1795 Governor Jay sent a letter to the state legislature calling slavery unacceptable. At his urging in 1799 the Gradual Manumission Act finally passed on a voice vote when Aaron Burr and the Democratic Republicans united with the Federalists. Legislators decided to ignore the issue of equal rights that divided them fourteen years earlier.

However, the new law provided only gradualism. It freed no one and only stated that of children born to slave women after 1799, males would be freed at twenty-eight and females at twenty-five years old. The ruling Federalists were only able to whittle away at the corners of the slave power.

In 1805 New York City officials denied use of city jails to hold slaves. In 1808 antislavery forces were heartened by the passage of the federal law outlawing the slave trade. African Americans in

Though outlawed by 1808, slave trading continued. Finally, in 1862 a slave trader, Captain Nathaniel Gordon, was executed in New York City.

the city celebrated the day with three huge parades. Some marchers carried antislavery signs that asked: "Am I not a man and a brother?" Church sermons hailed the law.

But slave traders still breathed defiance. "New York," Captain James Smith said years later, was the slave traders' "chief port in the world." *"It is the greatest place in the universe for it,"* Smith said over and over. "New York is our headquarters." From an office at Beaver and Pearl streets slave traders carried on their illegal business, transporting Africans to Cuba for sale. In 1860 U.S. Naval officer Robert W. Schufeldt reported the *Wildfire* "was loaded in broad daylight with a regular slave cargo—at a pier in the East River . . .direct to Africa—everybody knew it, except the U.S. Marshal."[3]

State legislators, prodded by the Society for Promoting the Manumission of Slaves, continued to press antislavery laws. In 1809 the law prohibited the separate sale of spouses, giving slave marriages additional legal recognition and legitimizing children born to married slaves.

Finally, in 1817 the New York legislature voted a complete end to bondage—with all slaves to be freed by 1827. (The law did not affect citizens of other states, who could still bring slaves to New York for nine months at a time. When the state rescinded this nine-month rule in 1841, New York was free of slaves.)

After twenty-eight years of slow and painful progress, Emancipation Day dawned on July 4, 1827. Reverend William Hamilton welcomed the day with a special sermon at the African Zion Church. James McCune Smith, by then a leading civil rights activist, also spoke. Some ten thousand human beings in New York State had been freed.[4]

Emancipation dramatically altered the lives of African Americans in the city. Free people could move and live where they wished. The 7,470 free people of color in the city in 1810 became 14,083 in 1830 but comprised only 2.3 percent of the city population because of massive white migration. More than thirty thousand other African Americans resided outside the city.

Many African American men worked as sailors, particularly on whaling ships. At sea they could rise from a deckhand job to become a harpooner or first or second mate. By 1839 so many Black men worked on ships that they established their own seaman's boardinghouse in New York.

But freedom did not mean equality, and the change increased acts of hatred from whites in the city. A French visitor reported being rudely treated because he had a friendly conversation with a Black woman employee of a rooming house. A barber admitted that if he cut the hair of fellow African Americans, he would lose his white customers. In 1833 a French traveler reported that whites had denied people of color entrance to skilled trades. African Americans found that emancipation failed to open doors to economic advancement.

Four months before emancipation, the first Black newspaper in the United States, *Freedom's Journal,* was published in New York City. It appeared March 16, 1829, four years before

Samuel Cornish (left) and John Russwurm (right)

William Lloyd Garrison issued his famous *Liberator* in Boston and six years before Garrison organized the American Anti-Slavery Society.

It would become the first organized voice of free people of color in the city and the nation. Its editors Samuel Cornish and John Russwurm were highly educated reformers. Russwurm, born a slave, was an immigrant from Jamaica, and in 1826, when he graduated from Bowdoin College in Maine, he became one of the first African American college graduates. Cornish, born free in Delaware, had trained for the ministry and served as a missionary among Black New Yorkers.

Freedom's Journal's first editorial stated its goals:

> We wish to plead our own cause. Too long have others spoken for us. Too long has the publick been deceived by misrepresentations, in things which concern us dearly. . . .
>
> Education being an object of the highest importance to the welfare of society, we shall endeavor to present just and adequate views of it, and to urge upon our brethren the necessity and expediency of training their children, while young, to habits of industry, and thus forming them for becoming useful members of society. . . .
>
> The civil rights of a people being of the greatest value, it shall ever be our duty to vindicate our brethren, when oppressed; and to lay the case before the publick. We shall also urge upon our brethren, (who are qualified by the laws of the different states) the expediency of using their elective franchise; and of making an independent use of the same. . . .
>
> Useful knowledge of every kind, and everything that relates to Africa, shall find a ready admission into our columns. . . .

> And . . . we would not be unmindful of our brethren who are in the iron fetters of bondage. They are our kindred by all the ties of nature. . . .
>
> Our vices and our degradation are ever arrayed against us, but our virtues are passed by unnoticed.[5]

In *Freedom's Journal* Samuel Cornish and John Russwurm called for an end to slavery and advocated equal rights for all. The *Journal* called for unity with white Americans who opposed slavery. The paper solidified New York's Black intellectual class and attracted the attention of intellectuals from other cities. David Walker, who in two years would issue a fiery pamphlet calling for slave rebellions, wrote articles and became *Freedom's Journal*'s Boston agent. From Philadelphia, Bishop Richard Allen, a leader in the African Methodist Episcopal church, contributed articles to its pages.

The paper served as a platform for ideas that would be fully discussed in annual Black national conventions that began in 1830. During its first year *Freedom's Journal* published the earliest statement by an African American woman, "Matilda," on women's rights. Noting the paper had failed to advocate women's education, she insisted that African American women "have minds that are capable and deserving of culture." She wanted mothers to cram "their daughters' minds with useful learning" and to see that they read books. Matilda continued:

> There are difficulties, and great difficulties in the way of our advancement; but that should only stir us to greater efforts. . . . Ignorant ourselves, how can we be expected to form the minds of our youth, and conduct them in the paths of knowledge? There is a great responsibility resting somewhere, and it is time for us to be up and doing.[6]

The two editors soon took divergent paths in their drives to liberate their people. In *Freedom's Journal* Russwurm announced that African Americans should return to the African homeland. In 1829 he left for Liberia, an African nation founded by former

The Weeksville Lady is the symbol of the Society for the Preservation of Weeksville & Bedford-Stuyvesant History. The tintype image was found during the 1968–69 excavation.

U.S. slaves, where he became an educator and a public official. Cornish edited the successor of *Freedom's Journal, The Rights of All,* and then another New York paper, *The Colored American.* In 1833 he was a founding member of the New York Anti-Slavery Society and remained a potent city voice for antislavery and equal rights.

By 1863 the path pioneered by *Freedom's Journal* had been taken up by twelve other Black papers in New York State, including eight in the city.

Weeksville was the first documented Brooklyn community to grow after emancipation in New York. James Weeks acquired part of the vast Lefferts estate in 1838, and in the next decade a small Black village had sprouted on the land near the Hunterfly Road in the present-day Bedford-Stuyvesant area. By 1845 its Bethel A.M.E. Church became Brooklyn's first African American house of worship.

In 1968 this early community was rediscovered and embraced by African American residents of Brooklyn, and a Weeksville Preservation Society was formed to protect and develop the site. The society purchased four historic Weeksville houses, began restoration work, initiated archaeological explorations, and involved local schoolchildren in its educational projects.

By the 1990s an average of three thousand pupils were visiting the restoration site and museum each year to learn about historic Weeksville. The Weeksville Museum newsletter quoted one child, Celeste Lumpkins, eight, with her poem, "A Special Me":

Do you know why I'm special?
Because my family loves me,
And tells me all about who I am,
And my family tree,
That grew in Weeksville,
And is growing through me.[7]

CHAPTER SIX

ABOLITION'S BLACK VANGUARD

U.S. organizations pledging to fight slavery grew from five hundred in 1836 to more than a thousand the next year and more than thirteen hundred in 1838. That year New York became a hub of antislavery activity and boasted more abolitionist organizations than any other state. The state's 274 functioning societies placed it first, ahead of Ohio's 213 and Massachusetts's 145.

Wealthy New Yorkers with economic ties to Southern slave masters used their ownership of leading newspapers to defend bondage and to attack the abolitionists. The abolitionists, in turn, struggled to publicize the evils of slavery, to aid fugitive slaves, and to win equal rights for free people of color.

From 1820 to 1866 African American Thomas Downing became wealthy running the Oyster House, which catered to rich citizens at Broad and Wall streets, and four more restaurants in other parts of the city. In 1835, when a fire raged through more than six hundred city buildings, cider and molasses from his Oyster House helped put out the fire. For twelve years Downing also helped fund the African Free Schools.

While Cornelius Vanderbilt ate dinner at the Oyster House, Downing's son George hid runaways in the cellar among the wine and cider bottles and cheeses. With George often in charge of secret operations, the Downing home served for four decades as a station on the Underground Railroad. Fugitives were provided with food, shelter, and help in reaching Canada. Young George once was arrested for aiding a runaway, but his father's influence won his release.

DALZIEL

In 1828 the Downings were joined in their work by white Quaker Isaac T. Hopper, who had organized the Underground Railroad in Philadelphia. In New York Hopper settled into what is now 110 Second Avenue, with cash provided by two wealthy whites, Arthur and Lewis Tappan. An impoverished tailor, Hopper also spent his own money to aid escapees passing through the city. After he helped a slave named Hughes make his escape, Hopper was expelled by the Society of Friends. However, his efforts never stopped. Hopper also ran an antislavery bookstore on Pearl Street that sold his own *Tales of the Oppressed.* Later Hopper and his daughter began a home for women ex-convicts who needed work. Today, Hopper's home on Second Avenue again serves as a halfway house.[1]

Other Underground Railroad conductors established stations that soon honeycombed the city. Conductors sent passengers through New Jersey, Pennsylvania, New England, and Canada. Reverend Garrett Van Hoesen, another white man, was a conductor on a route from the city along what is now Route 22, destination Bennington, Vermont.

In upstate New York routes passed through North Elba, where abolitionist John Brown's farm served as an Underground Railroad station. In Troy, Reverend Henry Highland Garnet's Presbyterian church became a station. Another line passed through Syracuse, where runaway slave Reverend Jermain Loguen and his wife, Caroline, directed two of the secret railroad's terminals. Because he helped six hundred people escape to Canada, Loguen was called the Underground Railroad King. In Rochester fugitives received aid and comfort from Frederick Douglass, his wife, Anna, and their white friends, feminists Susan B. Anthony and Elizabeth Cady Stanton.

The struggle against bondage in New York was also a battle of words. In 1829 the state's first antislavery tract, *The Ethiopian Manifesto,* had been published anonymously. Its author made veiled, ominous threats against "thou vain bloated upstart wordling of a slaveholder" and used words such as *beware, doomed,* and *death.* "Imperative justice . . . must be obeyed," the *Manifesto* warned, and it ended: "Peace and Liberty to the

Opposite: Aided by the Underground Railroad, fugitive slaves reach Canada and safety in a British antislavery pamphlet.

Ethiopian first, as also all other grades of men, is the invocation we offer to the throne of God."

Also in 1829 an even more menacing pamphlet appeared, David Walker's *Appeal to the Colored Citizens of the World.* He advised enslaved people to "kill or be killed" and openly advocated they begin violent rebellions.

New York City became the center for David Ruggles's antislavery activism. Born free in 1810 in Norwich, Connecticut, he arrived in the city in 1827 and began a grocery. With educators Charles B. Ray and James McCune Smith and writer Philip Bell, Ruggles fought Blackbirders—slave-hunting posses from the South that roamed Northern streets, seizing people they suspected of being escaped slaves whom they intended to return to the South.[2]

In 1835, to aid runaways, Ruggles and his friends formed the New York Committee of Vigilance and he served as the secretary. The committee was able to aid three hundred fugitives in 1836, and in the next year another 366. Ruggles was credited with helping six hundred men, women, and children escape.

When he heard that a fugitive had been seized in the city, Ruggles would appear in court on their behalf. He argued for a trial by jury and insisted on habeas corpus proceedings, which demanded the fugitive be produced in court. He also testified on behalf of defendants. He risked his life many times and once was almost murdered by an angry slave-ship captain.

A man of many talents and broad interests, Ruggles opened the city's first Black bookstore in 1834 at 67 Lispanard Street, near Broadway. Its goal was to aid the "friends of Human rights," and his store sold a variety of abolitionist pamphlets, papers, and books.

The next year Ruggles, finding people of color were denied library privileges in New York, dedicated himself to antislavery education. He lectured on slavery, promoted and wrote for the abolitionist press, and opened his home with its library of African American volumes. Ruggles and Henry Highland Garnet formed the Garrison Literary Society, which attracted 150 Black men under age twenty-one to its first meeting. This society debated African American issues and urged members to cultivate religion, virtue, and literature. It aided the afflicted and challenged slavery in the South and discrimination in the North.

In the summer of 1836 Ruggles defended fugitive slave George Jones, arrested at 21 Broadway. When Jones was jailed, Ruggles issued a fervent appeal:

> In less than three hours after his arrest, he [Jones] was bound in chains, dragged through the streets, like a beast to the shambles. My depressed countrymen, we are all liable; your wives and children are at the mercy of merciless kidnappers.

Saying, "We have no protection in law," Ruggles told fellow Black New Yorkers, "we must look to our own safety and protection from kidnappers."

By the end of the year Ruggles himself had been jailed for antislavery activities and his bookstore had been burned to the ground. Undaunted, he turned his home into a station of the Underground Railroad and sent runaways to Canada. He was jailed several more times.

From 1838 to 1841 Ruggles published his own paper, *Mirror of Liberty,* whose articles mixed humor, wit, and sarcasm to assail bondage and segregation. His paper particularly scorned a hypocritical Christianity that praised virtue and failed to condemn the enslavement of Black women. In 1849, after a seven-year battle against blindness and disease, Ruggles died at thirty-nine.

Ruggles had the distinction of rescuing history's most famous runaway, Frederick Douglass. In 1838 Douglass, twenty-one, fled Baltimore, Maryland, and arrived in New York City. He wrote:

> The flight was a bold and perilous one; but here I am, in the great city of New York, safe and sound, without loss of blood or bone. In less than a week after leaving Baltimore, I was walking amid the hurrying throng, and gazing upon the dazzling wonders of Broadway. The dreams of my childhood and the purpose of my manhood were now fulfilled. A free state around me, and a free earth under my feet! What a moment this was to me!

Fugitive slave Frederick Douglass speaking in London, England.

Douglass made his way to Ruggles's home and was soon reunited with his fiancée, Anna Murray, a free Maryland woman of color. Reverend James W. Pennington married the couple in Ruggles's home.

Douglass became one of antislavery's leading voices. He wrote his autobiography in 1845 and moved to Rochester, where his home became a station on the Underground Railroad. Two years later he began his own abolitionist newspaper, the *North Star.*

In 1848 Douglass was one of the few men—called "Aunt Nancy men" by their detractors—to attend the first Women's Rights convention in Seneca Falls, New York. Elizabeth Cady Stanton, searching for someone to second her daring proposal that women be given the vote, turned to Douglass. He spoke in favor of the resolution, it narrowly passed, and Stanton and the convention had made history.[3]

Unlike Douglass, who secretly learned to read and write in Maryland, Isabella—born a slave in Hurley, New York, and owned by the Dumont family—was illiterate. Beaten repeatedly and sold four times, she became a fervent Christian, believing that God talked to her directly. Isabella had seen her son Peter sold down to Alabama although New York's emancipation law made this illegal. In 1826, as the state moved toward emancipation, the Dumont family agreed to free Isabella, then suddenly changed their mind.

Isabella, by then a tall, gaunt woman, wrote her own declaration of independence. Taking her baby, she fled to a nearby Quaker family, the Van Wageners. They purchased her from the Dumonts and freed her. With their aid, Isabella sued in court and won the return of Peter.

At first, liberty offered no easy path to Isabella. Religious fanatics cheated her out of her savings, furniture, and possessions. She moved to New York City, found a household job, and joined the African Zion Church at Leonard and Church streets.

In 1843 Isabella experienced a religious awakening at the church. (Today a plaque commemorates the event.) She decided to change her name to Sojourner Truth and to preach. A bright, witty, and impelling speaker, she denounced slavery in her own homespun manner. Her tales of bondage, recounted in a stark, gripping language, held audiences spellbound.

Sojourner Truth sought to carry her message everywhere. In 1851 she joined the women's rights movement and befriended its leaders—Lucretia Mott, Elizabeth Cady Stanton, and Lucy Stone. At a women's rights gathering that year she boldly challenged a man who pompously scoffed and joked about equal rights. She silenced him with stories from her sorrowful life as a slave.

Former New York slave Sojourner Truth waged a long campaign against bondage and for women's rights.

With help from a white friend, Sojourner Truth wrote her *Narrative* as an exposure of slavery's cruelties. When the conflict between slave and free states intensified in the 1850s, Sojourner Truth boarded an old wagon with six hundred copies of her *Narrative* and rode and preached along the northern bank of the Ohio River. Each year when the Ohio River froze, slaves from Kentucky and Virginia managed to crawl and skid across the ice to free Ohio. As she sold her *Narrative,* she pleaded with Ohioans to aid the runaways who made it across the river. During the Civil War, Sojourner Truth served as a nurse and distributed supplies in Freedmen's Camps.[4]

Frederick Douglass and Sojourner Truth represented a vanguard of former slaves ready to combat slavery from within African American communities. Their efforts had gained important new support from white abolitionist William Lloyd Garrison of Boston.

In 1831 Garrison initiated his *Liberator* and a program of immediate emancipation. He called for the formation of an American Anti-Slavery Society, and in 1833 New Yorkers Arthur and Lewis Tappan summoned a convention at Clinton Hall in New York City to form a society branch. When a white mob gathered outside, delegates moved to the Chatham Street Chapel. White delegates joined with African American publisher Samuel Cornish and Reverend Theodore Wright to found the New York Anti-Slavery Society.

Until this time white abolitionists in New York and elsewhere favored a gradual process of emancipation. But Garrison, his society, and his black supporters rejected any compromise with slaveholders and sought immediate emancipation without compensation for owners. In Garrison, African Americans found a white man who finally understood their issue. In December 1833 the American Anti-Slavery Society meeting in Philadelphia decided to locate their national headquarters in New York City.

However, New York was still a slave-trading center whose merchants were dependent on Southern slaveholders. Wealthy businessmen had their newspapers stir mob assaults on abolitionist meetings. The home of the Tappans was repeatedly stoned. A white mob ransacked Black abolitionist minister Peter Williams Jr.'s St. Philip's Episcopal Church. In 1834 whites in the city rioted against abolitionism and destroyed hundreds of Black homes. It took the state militia to halt the mayhem.

From their offices on Nassau Street, the American Anti-Slavery Society worked on undeterred. In May 1835, when the society gathered at the Houston Street Presbyterian Church, abolitionist Reverend Samuel May was called aside by a merchant. While admitting slavery was "a great wrong," the businessman insisted abolitionist agitation had to stop. He said:

> The business of the North, as well as the South has become adjusted to it. There are millions upon millions of dollars due from Southerners to the merchants and mechanics of this city alone. . . . We cannot afford, sir, to let you and your associates . . . overthrow slavery. We mean sir, we mean sir, to put you Abolitionists down—by fair means if we can, by foul means if we must.[5]

Abolitionists were not put off by threats. Increasingly, they aimed their message at working white people. In New York, George Henry Evans, labor's leading advocate throughout the 1830s, was not an abolitionist, but he denounced slavery as a danger to the republic and to white workers. In 1831 he was one of very few whites who publicly defended the bloody Nat Turner slave rebellion in Virginia as a blow for American liberty.

Though most white laborers in the U.S. believed slaves were inferior, they still believed all people should be free. In the 1830s the largest number of signers of abolitionist petitions were white artisans. Even those who did not allow Black people in their unions often denounced slavery.

Abolitionists had to withstand fierce attacks. Leading newspapers caricatured them as fanatics and suggested violence as the way to deal with them. The *New York Herald* called them a "few thousand crazy-headed blockheads," who deserved no rights to free speech and assembly.

Words led to action across the United States as rioters broke up antislavery meetings. The 1830s witnessed 115 mob assaults on abolitionist meetings and sixty-four more in the 1840s. In

From his Brooklyn church, Reverend Henry Ward Beecher conducts a "mock" slave auction to dramatize slavery's evil.

James G. Birney

1850 the *New York Herald* called abolitionists "mad people" and "religious lunatics," who would "make our country the arena of blood and murder." It listed the meeting time and place of an antislavery gathering and urged citizens to "go there, speak their views, and prevent it." From Brooklyn the noted children's writer Lydia Maria Child wrote of her fears:

> I have not ventured into the city, nor does one of us dare to go to church today, so great is the excitement here. 'Tis like the times of the French Revolution, when no man dared trust his neighbors. Private assassins from New Orleans are lurking at the corners of streets to stab Arthur Tappan.[6]

James G. Birney was a New York abolitionist who began to change the discussion over slavery. Birney, from Alabama and a founder of the University of Alabama, in 1832 freed his slaves and denounced the institution "absolutely, unconditionally and irrevocably." When he personally befriended African Americans, he was driven from the South. In Cincinnati he edited an antislavery newspaper until a mob ransacked his office and destroyed his press.

In 1835 Birney was welcomed to New York City's abolitionist headquarters. By 1839 he was challenging fellow abolitionists such as Garrison, who had rejected direct political action. To Birney the electoral process was one key way to combat the spread of slavery. He, along with Gerrit Smith and African Americans Reverend Henry H. Garnet, Reverend Samuel Ward, and Charles Ray, broke with Garrison to form the Liberty Party. He also advocated equal voting rights for women and people of color.

In 1840 Birney became the Liberty Party's first presidential candidate and polled seven thousand votes. That year with Lewis Tappan and Black New Yorkers Samuel Cornish, Charles Ray, Reverend Theodore Wright, and Reverend James Pennington, Birney founded the American and Foreign Anti-Slavery Society. In 1844 Birney again ran for president, gained his strongest sup-

Freemen's Ticket.

At the Anti-Slavery Meeting of Lewis County, held at Martinsburgh, Sept. 22, 1840, J. A. NORTHROP, of Lowville, was called to the Chair, and HORATIO HOUGH, of Martinsburgh, apppointed Secretary.

On motion, *Resolved*, That we heartily concur, and hail with pleasure, the organization of the *Freemen's Ticket*, as based on the immutable principles of eternal right, contained in the Declaration of Independence, that all men are created "of one blood," with equal and inalienable rights.

Resolved, That we cheerfully concur, and pledge ourselves practically to support,

FOR PRESIDENT,

JAMES G. BIRNEY,

Of New-York.

FOR VICE-PRESIDENT,

THOMAS EARL,

Of Pennsylvania.

FOR GOVERNOR,

Gerrit Smith,

Of Madison County.

FOR LIEUT. GOVERNOR,

Charles O. Shepard,

Of Genesee County.

Resolved, That we concur in the nomination of STEPHEN CROSBY, of Herkimer County, to represent the *Freemen's Ticket*, in this Congressional District, and of JAMES C. DELONG, of Oneida County, as a candidate to represent the 5th Senate District in the Senate of this State.

Resolved, That LEVI ROBBINS, of Denmark, be Member of Assembly, HORATIO HOUGH, of Martinsburgh, County Clerk, WM. C. LAWTON, of Copenhagen, Sheriff, *George W. Fowler*, of Turin, and *Adoniram Foot*, of Martinsburgh, Coroners.

Liberty Party campaign in New York in 1840.

port in New York State, and received 62,300 votes nationally.

The battle against slavery took many forms. Dr. James McCune Smith, after graduating as a surgeon from the University of Glasgow in Scotland, opened a practice and a pharmacy in New York City. He challenged proslavery senator John C. Calhoun, who used the 1840 U.S. census figures to prove slaves lived happier and longer than free Northern Blacks. Calhoun cited census statistics to prove there was less insanity among slaves than free people.

Smith exposed significant statistical errors in the census figures. For example, Calhoun mentioned nineteen African

Dr. James McCune Smith

Americans in six Maine towns who were insane. Smith showed that only one of the six towns had a Black resident, and he was not insane. Dr. Smith concluded: "Freedom has not made us mad; it has strengthened our minds by throwing us upon our own resources, and has bound us to American institutions with a tenacity which nothing but death can overcome."[7]

Solomon Northup of New York also made an unusual contribution to the antislavery struggle. In 1829 he was seized from a street in Washington, D.C., while visiting there and held as a slave in Louisiana. He could not escape until 1841, but safely back home in New York he wrote a book of his life in bondage that became a weapon in the antislavery arsenal. His *Narrative of Solomon Northup* was one of more than a hundred autobiographies by former slaves that exposed the system's evils to the white readers.

As they waged war against slavery, Black New Yorkers did not neglect their own struggle for equality. In the 1830s few Blacks could vote because of the property qualifications imposed on them. But those who did vote were still able to affect city politics. They defeated the Democrats in the Fifth Ward, and helped Federalists gain three seats in the neighboring Eighth Ward. In 1844 one Democrat warned of Blacks: "Their number in the city of New York was very great, and parties were so evenly divided that it was often sufficient to hold the balance between them."

In New York and other Northern states, "Black Laws" did more than deny people of color voting rights. Black citizens could not legally hold office, serve on juries or in the militia, or give testimony against whites in court. To fight slavery and win full citizenship privileges, beginning in 1830 African Americans in the North began to hold annual national conventions, some in New York. Delegates discussed how to fight the Black Laws and how to reach political and economic equality.

The convention movement debated and gave voice to Black opposition to slavery and discrimination. It also served as a forum that unified an educated and growing intellectual and leadership class.

In 1843 Reverend Henry Highland Garnet of Troy—at twenty-seven, recently ordained a Presbyterian minister and just married to Julia Williams—made his own unique contribution to the antislavery crusade. That year at a national Black convention in Buffalo, he called for massive slave rebellions, shouting, "resistance, resistance, RESISTANCE!"

Offered to delegates as a resolution and opposed by Frederick Douglass, Garnet's call failed to carry by a single vote. But Garnet's militant approach increasingly won acceptance among abolitionists. In 1848 John Brown reprinted Garnet's call for rebellions in a pamphlet that included David Walker's fiery *Appeal.* By the next year Frederick Douglass announced he would be pleased to hear the news "that the slaves had risen in the South."[8]

Drawing support from the convention movement, churches, and newspapers, Black New Yorkers sought to build better lives. By the 1840s African Americans operated two fashionable restaurants in the financial district, two dry goods stores, a hair-dressing shop, three tailor stores, a candy store, a fruit store, and two coal yards.

However, most people of color were held to the lowest jobs. Abolitionist Gerrit Smith described discrimination in the state:

> Even the noblest black is denied that which is free to the vilest white. The omnibus, the car, the ballot-box, the jury box, the halls of legislation, the army, the public lands, the school, the church, the lecture room, the social circle, the table, are all either absolutely or virtually denied to him.

Though slavery ended in the state, discrimination was an ever-present factor in Black lives. Religious services, once open to all, became segregated as white churches instituted "Negro pews" to separate people of color. Some African Americans called for direct action. In 1837 the *Colored American* urged its readers: "Stand in the aisles, and rather worship God upon your feet, than become a party to your own degradation. You must shame your oppressors, and wear out prejudice by this holy policy." In 1845 the city boasted fifteen African American Methodist churches. African American teachers felt the need to organize, and in 1841 sixteen of the city's Black teachers formed an association, issued their own *Journal of Education,* and organized a convention on Long Island to petition for equal voting rights. The teachers, summoning others from Brooklyn and Queens, issued this call:

> Hundreds of children that are now shut out from the blessings of Education, call loudly up to you to come. If there ever was a time that called for united action, it is now. If there ever was a time for colored freemen to show their love of liberty, their hatred of ignorance, and determination to be free and enlightened, it is now. We want union and action.

The Black effort to end voting restrictions at first moved few whites. Finally, in 1846 it won support from Horace Greeley's *New York Tribune.* Greeley published a Black call for equal voting rights and listed it as the first among needed city reforms. But most white citizens remained opposed to equal suffrage.

Along northern boundaries of Manhattan, the community of Harlem had begun to grow. Many of the poor residents were Irish, but by 1832 African Americans had settled around the area of the Harlem Methodist Church. In 1843 members of the African Methodist Episcopal Zion Church had a new brick building on East 117th Street for its sixty-six members. Later that decade Harlem's Bethel A.M.E. Church was started, and by the 1850s a public school had been built.

NEW YORK CITY'S BLACK POPULATION[9]	
1830	14,083
1840	16,358
1850	13,815
1860	12,574

CHAPTER SEVEN

THE CIVIL WAR ERA

In 1850 Congress passed a stringent new Fugitive Slave Act that imposed stiff fines and long jail sentences on those who refused to assist in recapturing runaways. African Americans were not allowed to testify in their own behalf, and judges were paid ten dollars if they ruled an accused fugitive was a slave, five dollars if they ruled he or she was not.

New York County's fourteen thousand people of color, five thousand more in Brooklyn, and white antislavery activists prepared as though for war. Some spoke of a higher law than Congress and urged armed resistance. In Syracuse, Reverend Jermain Loguen declared, "I don't respect this law—I don't fear

An antislavery meeting in New York City is disrupted in 1860. The speaker (center) may be Frederick Douglass.

it—I won't obey it! It outlaws me, and I outlaw it." At a public meeting a runaway, John Jacobs, told his fellow Black New Yorkers to arm and "show a front to our tyrants." He said, "Let them only take our dead bodies," and offered this ominous advice: "My colored brethren, if you have not swords, I say to you, sell your garments and buy one."

New York abolitionist editor Martin R. Delany warned that if anyone from a local sheriff to President Millard Fillmore entered his house in search of a runaway he would "leave a corpse." Frederick Douglass had championed peaceful protest and political action. But now he announced that violence against slave-catching posses was justified. In 1851 *Frederick Douglass' Paper* spelled out his views:

> The only way to meet the man-hunter successfully is with cold steel and the nerve to use it. . . . I have but one lesson for my people in the present trying hour; it is this: "Count your lives utterly worthless, unless coupled with the inestimable blessing of liberty."

Four years later Douglass said: "I would rather see insurrection for the next six months in the South than that slavery should exist there for the next six years."

In September 1851 New York City faced its first case under the new law. James Hamlet, an escaped slave who was working as a porter at 58 Water Street, was arrested by a federal officer and returned to Mary Brown of Baltimore before anyone could do anything. When Brown agreed to sell her slave, some fifteen hundred of Hamlet's friends crowded into the Zion Church on Leonard Street and raised eight hundred dollars to buy him. He returned to New York in triumph.

By the time Hamlet was reunited with his friends in New York, Syracuse's mayor and officials of both parties had dealt the slave catchers a stunning blow. On October 1, fugitive Jerry McHenry was rescued from a Syracuse courthouse by a mob led by Congressman Gerrit Smith and Reverend Samuel May.

During a trial recess, dozens of black and white citizens united to batter down the courtroom doors. They seized deputies and used a crowbar to disarm a marshal who fired at them. The marshal leaped through a second-floor window and fled. McHenry, found lying on the floor in chains and bleeding, was given clothes and money and spirited off to Canada. May and Smith publicly acknowledged their roles and asked to be put on trial. However, only Enoch Reed, an African American, was tried for the crime, and after May's testimony, he was acquitted. The rescuers later heard McHenry found a job making barrels in Canada.

Harriet Tubman saved three hundred people from slavery, and during the Civil War she rescued hundreds more while leading Union armies as a scout in South Carolina.

The McHenry defeat discouraged slave-catching posses from entering New York State until 1860. That year, in Troy, a federal commissioner ordered fugitive Charles Nalle be returned to his owner. His master was Nalle's half-brother and the two men had a similar complexion.

But Harriet Tubman was on hand and had no intention of seeing Nalle returned to slavery. Tubman had been a runaway slave who became the most daring conductor on the Underground Railroad. She left her home in Auburn, New York, nineteen times to travel into the South and liberate three hundred slaves. Despite rewards totaling forty thousand dollars for her dead or alive, she never lost a passenger and was never caught.

Tubman directed the hundreds who gathered outside the courthouse where Nalle was being held. When the master announced he would sell Nalle for fifteen hundred dollars, someone shouted, "Two hundred dollars for his rescue, but not one cent to his master." The crowd roared its approval. When Nalle appeared outside the court, Tubman was ready. A boy sent by her yelled, "Fire."

Reverend James W. Pennington used nonviolent resistance to fight segregation on New York City streetcars.

Confusion spread and Tubman shouted, "Take him!" She threw her own arms around Nalle, pushed aside two officers, and clapped her sunbonnet on his head, so he would be hard to recognize in the crowd. As she tried to wrench him free, lawmen pounded on her head, but her grip on Nalle held until other friends seized him. Still handcuffed and bleeding, the fugitive was whisked away, first by boat and then by wagon to the West. Harriet Tubman and liberty had triumphed once again.[1]

In the decade before the Civil War, New York's fight against slavery and for equality also was reflected in its culture. In March 1852 the Broadway Music Hall featured a play based on Harriet Beecher Stowe's *Uncle Tom's Cabin.* For two years the play's white audiences included not only firm abolitionists but also those who laughed and applauded when overseer Simon Legree whipped old Uncle Tom. After two years *Uncle Tom's Cabin* reopened at the National Theater, which sold seats to African Americans.

On the first night, white rioters rushed the theater to assault people of color. Blacks then counterattacked, and the rioting spilled into the street. New York police arrived, but they dared not swing their clubs at well-dressed whites, for that could lose them their jobs. If they hit the Black servants of the whites, that also might cost them. Instead, police nightsticks fell on the poorly dressed whites, who were largely members of the attending mob. When local papers reported the night's disorder, more people turned out to see *Uncle Tom's Cabin.*

That same year African American entertainers called the Singing Luca Family, after a debut at a New York antislavery convention, strode onto the stage of the city's Old Tabernacle on Broadway and peacefully brought their musical message of liberation to an audience of five thousand.

Using techniques of nonviolent resistance, middle-class African Americans increasingly challenged segregation in the city. On Sunday, July 16, 1854, public schoolteacher Elizabeth

Jennings, an organist at the First Colored American Congregational Church at Sixth Street and Second Avenue, defied the segregated policies of the Third Avenue streetcar line and entered one of its cars. A conductor and a driver wrestled with Ms. Jennings, trying to remove her. At one point she was dangled from the car, her head almost hitting the cobblestone streets. Finally, she was arrested.

The young teacher, though injured in the fight, had just begun her campaign. A church meeting was called to protest her treatment and to hear her sworn statement about the incident. The Black Legal Rights Association hired Chester A. Arthur as her attorney. The next February a white jury awarded her $225 and court costs. The company agreed to serve "colored persons, if sober, well behaved, and free from disease." (In 1881 Chester A. Arthur became president of the United States.) [2]

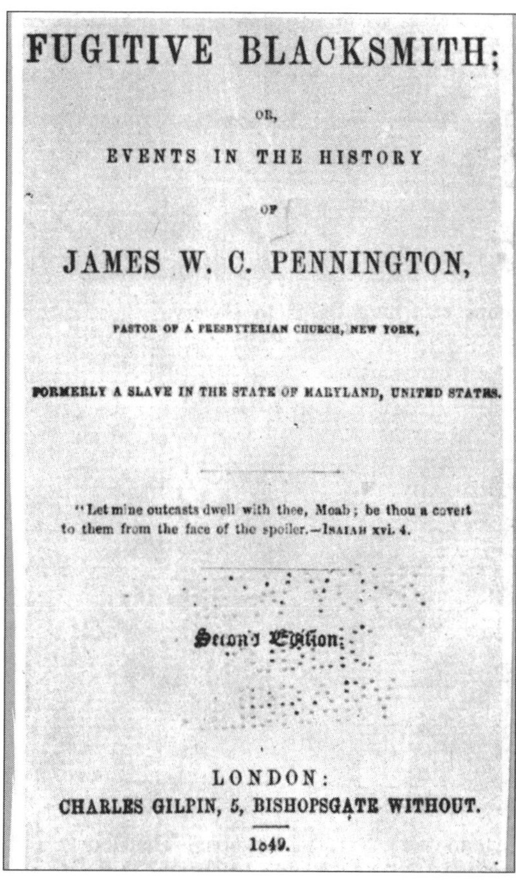

FUGITIVE BLACKSMITH;

OR,

EVENTS IN THE HISTORY

OF

JAMES W. C. PENNINGTON,

PASTOR OF A PRESBYTERIAN CHURCH, NEW YORK,

FORMERLY A SLAVE IN THE STATE OF MARYLAND, UNITED STATES.

"Let mine outcasts dwell with thee, Moab; be thou a covert to them from the face of the spoiler.—ISAIAH xvi. 4.

Second Edition.

LONDON:
CHARLES GILPIN, 5, BISHOPSGATE WITHOUT.

1849.

The reverend James W. Pennington, a former runaway slave, published his autobiography in 1849.

In 1856 Reverend James Pennington, a minister at the Shiloh Presbyterian Church, challenged the policy of Manhattan's Sixth Avenue line. A scholar and activist, Pennington was a runaway slave who had earned a doctorate at Heidelberg University in Germany and in 1841 had written the first Black history textbook. An eyewitness reported that the minister was carried "backward through the car, the doctor apparently making all the resistance in his power." Pennington sued for damages but lost his case.

In the 1850s African Americans paid taxes on real estate valued at a million and a half dollars. That did not include church property valued at a quarter of a million, personal property of almost three quarters of a million, and savings of more than a million dollars.

Manhattan's most stable Black community was Seneca Village near today's Central Park West in the West Eighties. It began around 1825 when Andrew Williams, a shoe shiner, bought three lots for $125. Individuals and churches bought parcels, and by 1850 the village claimed 20 percent of the city's seventy-one Black landowners and 10 percent of its eligible voters. In 1856 the *New York Times* described it as "a neat little village" and noted that families who moved there did not leave. But to make way for Central Park, in 1857 most of Seneca's residents were bought out. Those who remained were driven out by the police.[3]

Throughout the city African Americans mobilized to insure a decent education for their children. In 1857 the New York Society for Promotion of Education Among Colored Children, led by scholar Charles Ray, submitted an educational report to the governor. It stated that the same percentage of Black children attended school as white children. However, Ray pointed to stark racial discrimination in school services. For every dollar spent for an African American pupil, sixteen hundred dollars was spent for a white one.[4]

By this time New York City's board of education had assumed control of city schools for all children. White schools, Ray wrote, were "almost palatial edifices, with manifold comforts, conveniences and elegancies." But African Americans were crowded into old, gloomy buildings, "dark and cheerless, and without the needful facilities." These conditions, Ray concluded, left Black children "painfully neglected and positively degraded." Ray did find that in performances pupils of both races did equally well and that there were committed teachers for both groups.

Ray's report had its impact. Within two years one Black school was moved to a better location on Hudson Street, one on Mulberry Street was replaced by a newer one, and a third school on Laurens Street was remodeled. The report also brought a change in thinking to the African American community. In 1858, to insure their children enjoyed the same benefits as whites, people of color began to demand school integration.

The growing Black intellectual class also renewed its drive for equal suffrage, which meant eliminating the property qualification imposed on African American voters. By 1860 Brooklyn had eighteen Black community suffrage clubs, and forty-eight others were active in Manhattan. But in a referendum that year, white New Yorkers voted overwhelmingly to keep voting a white privilege. Not until 1870, years after the Civil War, were voting rights extended to all men without regard to color.

In the 1850s African Americans also continued their long battle to scale barriers against their entering various trades and professions. An American League of Colored Laborers provided members increased job training and aid in starting businesses.

The Black thrust for decent jobs was an uphill fight since nine out of ten Black city workers still held menial jobs with little chance for advancement. A survey in 1855 found ten or more women and men of color working in each of these occupational categories: carpenters, clergymen, teachers, nurses, musicians, waiters, longshoremen, tailors, butchers, cooks, and dressmakers.

The African American hold on even the lowest-paying jobs began to slip between 1830 and 1860 when five million immigrants, mainly from Europe, entered the country. Many who settled in New York competed with African Americans for low-paying jobs. "Whenever the interests of the white man and the Black come into collision in the United States," wrote an English visitor, "the Black man goes to the wall. It is certain that wherever labor is scarce he is steadily employed, when it becomes plentiful, he is the first to be discharged."[5]

In 1855 Frederick Douglass urged his people to "learn trades," but he noted sadly: "Every hour sees us elbowed out of some employment to make room perhaps for some newly arrived immigrants, whose hunger and color are thought to give them a title to especial favor."

People of color with skills were blocked from membership in white unions. This allowed employers to use Black workers desperate for jobs to replace white laborers who went on strike. This hiring of Black strikebreakers, particularly on the waterfront, stirred a racial animosity in the city. When white longshoremen went on strike in 1855 to protest wage cuts, Black men eagerly took their places. "Of course colored men can feel under no obligation to hold out in a strike with the whites, as the latter have never recognized them," wrote Douglass.

The waterfront became the scene of an unequal seesaw battle for jobs. White longshoremen went on strike; Blacks took their jobs and then were fired after whites returned to work. Irish immigrants were often pitted against African American men for poorly paid, unsteady, and dangerous work on the docks.

Throughout the 1850s people of color relied on their families, churches, and their own self-help organizations for emotional and economic support. In New York City the Dorcas Society had been formed in 1828 for Black women to aid their needy. In 1860 Brooklyn's African American women held a fair that raised fourteen hundred dollars for a Colored Orphan Asylum.

Scholar Dr. James McCune Smith described the conditions facing Black families: "Our lives are much shortened. Look at the preponderance of widows and children among us."

White unions, even those that refused to admit African Americans, often opposed slavery's advance to the West. White laborers saw the frontier lands as their path to economic and social progress and a chance to reach their American dream. If the slaveholders dominated in the West, they reasoned, poorer white people would lose their opportunities for cheap land and a new start. Abraham Lincoln expressed labor's view of slavery: "I want every man to have a chance—and I believe a black man is entitled to it—in which he can better his condition."

White laborers in New York often compared their fate to that of slaves. In 1836, when striking tailors were convicted of conspiracy, they claimed they were on a "level with the slaves of the South." In 1845 twenty-five thousand white workers met in New York under reformers Robert Dale Owen, Arthur Brisbane, and Horace Greeley and denounced slavery in the South and "wage slavery" in the North. White laborers began to join the Free-Soil movement, to oppose the expansion of slavery to the Western territories.

When Southern slaveholders called for the annexation of Texas in 1845, a New York labor meeting denounced this act as a threat to workers. The next year, another workers' meeting denounced the war in Texas as an effort to gain new land for slavery.

The Free-Soil Party attracted laborers and abolitionists. In 1848 James Birney's Liberty Party merged with the Free-Soilers to oppose slavery's expansion. Free-Soil candidates won 10 percent of popular votes and elected five candidates to Congress. The party was able to garner three hundred thousand votes for its presidential candidate, Martin Van Buren, but not enough to win.

By 1852 Frederick Douglass, who had broken with Garrison over the issue of political action, became the first of his race to address a major party when he spoke at the Free-Soil convention. Organized political opposition to slavery increased when the Free-Soil Party merged with the new Republican Party. In 1856 the Republican party nominated Charles Frémont for president. He lost the election by only half a million votes. In the 1860 election, New York City's Democratic Party made race the central issue. The *Herald* warned that a Republican victory meant "the North will be flooded with free Negroes, and the labor of the white man will be depreciated."

The Republican response was also racist. At one city rally Republican senator William Seward called Africans "a foreign and feeble element like the Indian . . . a pitiful exotic unwisely and unnecessarily transplanted in our fields."

Abraham Lincoln defeated a deeply divided Democratic Party to gain the White House, but in New York City Democrats carried the day. The next year eleven Southern states seceded from the United States and formed the Confederate States of America. Of the eleven Southern states that seceded to form the Confederacy, only South Carolina had actually left the United States when Mayor Fernando Wood advanced his plan for New York. Wood, who represented New York City's wealthy, asked the city council to let New York secede from the Union and form a state he wanted to name Tri-Insula. Leading Democrats such as Mayor Wood, his brother Benjamin Wood—who ran the *Daily News*—and the governor, Horatio Seymour, openly opposed Lincoln and favored the Confederacy.[6]

When the Confederate guns opened fire on Fort Sumter in April 1861, most white men in the city tried to avoid military service. But in early 1861 African Americans in the city began military drills in a private hall. The chief of police warned them to stop, saying he "could not protect them from popular indignation and assault."

On July 26, 1861, three African American regiments notified the governor that they were ready for combat. Soldiers promised to furnish their own arms, clothing, provisions, and equipment. Officials rejected the offer, saying this was to be "a white man's war."

From the war's outset, Southern slaves and their sisters and brothers in the North saw the conflict as opportunity. Slaves fled to Union lines, offering to enlist in the army or serve as cooks, construction workers, launderers, and servants. Many were returned to their Confederate masters. In July 1862 New York senator Preston King proposed and Congress passed a law that allowed the army to employ Blacks in "war service." The president, facing mounting labor shortages, signed it.

As late as August 1962, President Lincoln insisted he would not interfere with slavery. Answering a letter from New York editor Horace Greeley, Lincoln said: "What I do about slavery and the colored race, I do because I believe it helps to save the Union. . . ." But as the war dragged on, the president began to reexamine his policy. He knew that Black men and women brought in crops for the Confederacy. This meant that the labor of Black people released Southern whites to join Confederate armies. If plantation life was disrupted, the Confederacy would face disorder and perhaps starvation. White men would fear to leave their Southern families and farms.

By early 1862 sixty thousand U.S. soldiers were killed or wounded each day, a loss equal to twenty-seven regiments a year. The Union had suffered repeated defeats, army morale was low, and desertions soared to tens of thousands. The rising casualty rate among soldiers raised questions. Thousands of slaves who fled to Union lines had volunteered to fight. Why not let them serve?

Lincoln's policy of returning fugitive slaves to their Confederate owners also stirred resentment in Union ranks. The largely Irish American Second Fire Zouave regiment from

New York City watched Confederate owners enter their camp, claim runaways, and beat them. These "desperate and resolute" white New Yorkers, reported an officer, "would go out and rescue the Negro, and in some instances would thrash the masters."

Such actions in the field began to change Union policy. Other units began to rescue runaways. Finally, on January 1, 1863, the president issued his Emancipation Proclamation. By then former slaves had been able to join the Union army, had been trained as soldiers, and some had clashed with Confederates in three Southern states.

In New York, African Americans celebrated Emancipation Day at church and at a massive meeting at Cooper Union, where Reverend Henry Highland Garnet read the proclamation. In Rochester, Frederick Douglass issued a call to arms for his people: "Better die free than live to be slaves," he wrote.

In February 1865 a Black Massachusetts regiment that included New Yorkers liberated Charleston, South Carolina.

> The day dawns; the morning star is bright upon the horizon! The iron gate of our prison stands half open. One gallant rush from the North will fling it wide open, while four millions of our brothers and sisters shall march to liberty.

The 54th Massachusetts Regiment, the first African American unit from the North, was recruited from twenty-two states. Sergeant Robert Simmons of Company B was one of eleven New York volunteers to enlist in the regiment. Simmons hoped to visit his mother in New York on the way South, but the regiment had orders not to enter the city because of racial tensions.

After his first battle, Simmons wrote his mother how "bullets whistled so close that I could feel the wind of them." After another battle he wrote: "God has protected me through this, my first fiery leaden trial, and I do give him the glory, and render praises to his holy name."

Simmons was wounded during the 54th Regiment's gallant charge on Fort Wagner, South Carolina. He was captured and thrown into a dank, dark Charleston jail. Later, in a hot, crowded prison hospital, he was one of 162 Union prisoners without room to lie down. For two days Simmons sat slumped in his blood-soaked clothing. Then he was placed on one of six operating tables in constant use and his arm was amputated. He died days later unaware that he would earn a Congressional Medal of Honor.[7]

More than two hundred thousand African Americans served in the U.S. Army and Navy. Many New Yorkers were among those who distinguished themselves in battle, and 877 lost their lives. Every fourth Union sailor was Black. Navy seaman Joachim Pease of Long Island loaded the number-one gun as part of the integrated crew of 162 aboard the USS *Kearsarge.* In August 1864, near the coast of Cherbourg, France, the *Kearsarge* faced the *Alabama,* a Confederate battleship that had captured or sunk sixty-nine ships. For ninety minutes the two vessels dueled at sea and the *Alabama* was finally sunk. An officer remarked on Pease's "marked coolness, good conduct and . . . courage and fortitude," and saw that he received a Medal of Honor.

CHAPTER EIGHT

FROM THE ASHES OF THE DRAFT RIOTS

On July 15, 1863, as war hero Sergeant Robert Simmons of the 54th Massachusetts Regiment was in a Confederate prison hospital, his life slowly ebbing away, his cousin died in New York, a victim of street rioting that had engulfed the city.

The New York City Draft Riot was the largest urban upheaval of the nineteenth century, and estimates placed the dead and injured from at least twelve hundred people up to triple that number. Crowds sometimes as large as ten thousand tore through the city, killing people of color and any whites who supported them or favored emancipation. No accurate casualty count was ever made since bodies were burned, cast into mass graves, or never found. People of color feared to enter public hospitals, where they might fall into the hands of rioters, though some found a sanctuary at the Jewish Hospital, according to Black scholar M. A. Harris in *The Black Book* (New York: Random House, 1974).

The rampage was triggered by a draft law that did not fall equally on all classes in the population of 813,000. The law allowed a man to avoid service in the armed forces by hiring a substitute for three hundred dollars. For many this turned the Civil War into "a rich man's war but a poor man's fight." But the turmoil had other causes. Lincoln had lost the city by thirty thousand votes. The most influential newspapers in the city supported the Democrats, opposed the war, and denounced

Workers of every race labored along the New York City docks. Harper's Weekly, October 21, 1871.

Lincoln and the draft.[1]

In addition, the foreign born in the city stood at 47 percent and were thrown into daily competition with people of color for the worst jobs. Employers used this competition to provoke violence between whites and people of color, and Democratic papers used it to rally opposition to a war fought against slavery.

Some of New York's leaders carefully stoked the mixture of racism and desperation that drove poor whites into the streets. Mayor Fernando Wood had been ignored in his effort to have New York secede from the Union, and he was defeated in his reelection bid by George Opdyke, another Democrat and a millionaire merchant with friends and business associates in the Confederacy.

In 1863 Wood was elected to Congress as a Peace Democrat. He used his new position of power and his influence over the *New York World* to vehemently oppose the draft and Lincoln's war effort. Writing in the pages of the popular *Daily News* his brother Benjamin warned readers that the draft "would compel the white laborer to leave his family destitute and unprotected while he goes forth to free the negro, who being free, will compete with him in labor." Democratic papers hammered at the theme that freeing slaves meant New York City would soon be inun-dated by former slaves seeking "white jobs."

Even more incendiary was Governor Horatio Seymour, who had already demanded abolition of the draft in the state. He arrived in the city to make a Fourth of July speech, in which he denounced the draft law and warned that revolution "can be proclaimed by a mob as well as by a government." Within a week disorder ruled and reckless mobs commanded many of the city's avenues and streets, but Governor Seymour remained on vacation in southern New Jersey, two hours away.[2]

In the first three days of July, the bloodiest battle of the war raged at Gettysburg, Pennsylvania. Armies under General Robert E. Lee finally suffered a stunning defeat, but this Union victory cost many lives. The *New York Times* reported the "great slaughter" at Gettysburg, and for five days ending with July 10, its front pages listed the Union dead and wounded.

The next day, Saturday, the first 1,236 names of men to be drafted—a majority of whom were poor Irish—were drawn. That night and Sunday, grumbling white laborers met on streets and in saloons to plan resistance to the draft. On Monday between six and seven A.M., at the time men would have been walking to their jobs, they began a rebellion in the streets.

By eight o'clock, railroad, shipyard, iron, and building trade workers surged up Eighth and Ninth avenues. They closed down shops, factories, and construction sites and urged others to join them. After a "no draft" rally at Central Park, the mob divided into two and headed downtown. One column was estimated at twelve thousand, and children began to tag along.

Men cut down telegraph poles and broke into hardware stores to steal weapons. Irish women pulled up the tracks of the Fourth Avenue railway. One crowd marched to Third Avenue and 47th Street, where the draft lottery was to be held that morning. Police officers became special targets. Police superintendent John A. Kennedy was beaten and left bloody in the mud.

Rioters shouted, "Down with the rich men" and "Down with the draft," as they destroyed the files and building where a draft lottery was held. The 2,297 city police and two hundred disabled soldiers were unable to stem the frenzied humanity. When soldiers from the 7th New York Regiment tried to save the draft offices, the mob routed them, seized their guns, and killed their officers. These were the major events of the riot's first morning. New York City's avenues and streets were held by a raging mob.

When police and troops closed off wealthier neighborhoods, crowds began to march on African Americans in Greenwich

During the Draft Riots a man is lynched on Clarkson Street. **<u>Harper's Weekly</u>, July 21, 1863.**

Village. A poor Black community on Thompson Street was burned to the ground. A Black men's club at Seventh Avenue South and Clarkson Street was besieged and a resident hanged from a lamppost. At Sheridan Square, Blacks hid in a basement at 92 Grove Street.

Rioters beat people to death and danced around their bodies. Other Black men were hanged from lampposts. A German store selling to African Americans was set ablaze. Fires consumed a Black boardinghouse and church. Black citizens fled to police stations for protection, and officers, fearing a mob attack, moved hundreds to federal arsenals for safety. An estimated fifty to seventy thousand rioters participated in the mounting mayhem.

By the second day African Americans had become prime targets, and neither rich nor poor, adults nor children were spared. Albro Lyons, a distinguished and well-educated retired sailor, owned a seaman's boardinghouse on Pearl Street. His daughter Maritcha watched in horror as a mob besieged their house, "breaking windowpanes, smashing shutters and partially demolishing the front door." That night Lyons drove off another assault by firing his pistol at an approaching mob.

The next day, when a mob broke into the house, the Lyons family fled over a fence. The police arrived, cleared the premises, and brought the Lyons to the Williamsburg ferry to Brooklyn. The Lyonses reached safety, "tired with only the garments we had on," Maritcha recalled.

Dr. William Powell thought he would be safe. He held a commission in the U.S. Navy and had a son serving as an army surgeon. But Dr. Powell and his family were surrounded in their four-story home. As he led his invalid daughter, his wife, and ten other Black tenants, including two women, to safety on the roof, he could hear his rooms below being plundered.

The Powells were stranded on their roof until a Jewish neighbor appeared with a ladder. First the man rescued Powell's disabled daughter and then handed Powell some rope, which he used to move people "from one roof to the other, until I landed them in a neighbors yard." The Powells hid in a friend's cellar and then went to a police station crowded with seventy "bruised and beaten" African Americans. Later Dr. Powell said: "I thank God that He has yet spared my life, which I am ready to yield in defence of my country."[3]

For days a raging mob—which one eyewitness described as "bare-headed men, with red, swollen faces brandishing sticks and clubs"—ruled Manhattan's East Side. Its men and women fanned out to smash store windows and break into wealthy homes, to steal and to burn buildings. Anyone who favored emancipation was in peril. To save her father and family,

A French paper's artist captures the July 1863 attack on the Colored Orphan Asylum in Manhattan.

Reverend Henry H. Garnet's daughter hacked his nameplate off their front door with an ax.

The home of Sergeant Simmons was set afire. Simmons's mother, his sister, her two children—a baby and her disabled boy—began to flee. Rioters caught the boy, who could not keep up with his mother, and began to smash at him with paving stones and a pistol. He was finally rescued by a white fireman, John McGovern, who brought him to a German immigrant friend of the family.

A large mob gathered on Fifth Avenue between 43rd and 44th streets and prepared to burn the Colored Orphan Asylum for children under twelve. Just before the mob seized the building, director William Davis and his staff of fifty led the two hundred children out a back door. One child, a little girl who hid under a bed, died.

City firemen, including many Irish Americans, helped in the rescue. Frightened children were rushed past Black men dangling from lampposts and trees. Even a police station was not considered safe, and the children were sent to Blackwell's (now Roosevelt) Island in the East River for three months.

With law and order in collapse, some African Americans began to arm for self-defense. At the city's fifth police precinct four hundred African Americans asked for and were issued arms. At the sight of these determined citizens, rioters turned and dispersed. In the largely Black Eighth Ward in Midtown, white crowds fled when Black residents on upper floors showered them with bricks and hot water.

Hundreds of refugees from the rioting in Manhattan and parts of Brooklyn escaped to the Weeksville community, which provided them shelter and food. Others found protection among Black settlements in Flatbush, Carsville, and Flatlands in Brooklyn, and others, according to the *Christian Recorder,* "scattered in the woods and in such places as they could find safety." In Weeksville and Flatbush, the paper reported, Black men "armed themselves . . . determined to die defending their homes."

Governor Seymour relaxed in New Jersey and ignored the urgent appeals of Mayor Opdyke to return and assert authority. Tuesday afternoon, after two full days of murder and mayhem had torn the city apart, Seymour arrived in New York City. The governor, speaking to a crowd that included rioters and murderers, three times referred to his audience as "my friends."

On Thursday, the riot's fourth day, U.S. troops, largely New York units, were pulled from the pursuit of General Lee after Gettysburg and dispatched to New York. These veterans finally ended the anarchy and murder. Forty-three U.S. Army regiments, posted at locations around the city, kept the peace.

Black New Yorkers tried to put the tragedy in perspective. Reverend James Pennington said:

> A part of this country BELONGS TO US; and . . . we assert the right to live and labor here. . . . Our fathers fought for this

> country and helped to free it from the British yoke. We are now fighting to help free it from . . . Jeff Davis and Co.

The riot had a lasting impact on Black lives, he noted:

> The breaking up of families; and business relations just beginning to prosper; the blasting of hopes just dawning; the loss of precious harvest time which will never again return; the feeling of insecurity engendered; the confidence destroyed; the reaction; and lastly, the gross insult offered to our character as a people. . . .

The four days of death and destruction also brought out the best in New Yorkers. Reverend Garnet and other African American leaders organized a committee to aid an estimated ten thousand riot victims. Wealthy whites raised fifty thousand dollars to rebuild the Colored Orphan Asylum and to help its young victims in their recovery.

Middle-class families began to hire Black rather than Irish servants. Citizens began to criticize laws that denied people of color admission to hotels, schools, and streetcars. Some white papers and leaders pointed out that a discriminatory legal system set the stage for and precipitated the violence.

The Fourth Avenue and Eighth Avenue lines still permitted conductors to exclude Black passengers, and the Sixth Avenue line provided segregated cars. But now more whites were prepared to join in the fight against segregation. When abolitionists announced a campaign directed at the discriminatory practices of streetcar companies, two leading white papers joined the effort. After abolitionist threats to sue in court, in February 1864 the Fourth Avenue line admitted African Americans to its cars.

In June 1864 a white conductor and policeman forced a Black woman to leave an Eighth Avenue streetcar. Since her husband, an army sergeant, had died in the Civil War, the *Tribune* described this act as treating "like dogs" those "who are laying down their lives for their country." The officer was reprimanded, the police commissioner ordered his men to refuse to assist

The Union League Club presents flags to the 20th U.S. Colored Infantry at Union Square, March 5, 1864.

conductors, and the Eighth Avenue line ended its segregation policy. A few days later the Sixth Avenue line dropped its discriminatory policy, and New York streetcars were open to all.

The riot aftermath also brought a change in army recruiting. Four months after the rioting ended, New York State began to recruit African Americans as soldiers. White citizens lauded people of color for their patience, courage, and willingness to enlist. Eager African Americans from the city and upstate counties lined up at army recruitment offices in the city.

In early March 1864 the 20th New York Colored Infantry, led by a military band, paraded down Broadway. Thousands of residents cheered from the sidewalks, and an ovation greeted the recruits at Union Square. "A new era has been ushered in," wrote a Black journalist. "All seemed to be one grand jubilee." He ended, "Go to it, Ethiopia!" The only sour note was sounded by an officer of the city's 7th Regiment, who said he'd be damned if he let his men march in front of "niggers."

But the day belonged to the proud men of the 20th Regiment.

It was given a flag designed by whites with special symbols: a conquering eagle, a broken yoke, and Liberty armed. The troops, surrounded by police, marched to a Hudson River pier on 26th Street. Two brass bands, twelve hundred prominent African Americans, and a hundred important white New Yorkers hailed the 20th. The regiment's officers received a scroll filled with New York's exalted names—Astor, Fish, Beekman, Jay, and Wadsworth. The next day the *New York Times* spoke of "a new epoch." A second Black city regiment, the 26th, was formed in March 1864, but efforts to organize a third one did not attract enough recruits.

The Draft Riots changed residential patterns for people of color. More than a few middle-class families moved to Brooklyn, some joining the Weeksville community. In 1866 a Black woman, S. A. Tillman, founded the Brooklyn Howard Colored Orphan Asylum at Pacific Street and Ralph Avenue to shelter homeless children. Its work continued for more than half a century.

The Lyons family left for Providence, Rhode Island, where Albro opened an ice-cream factory. Eventually the family returned to New York, and he lived out his life in Brooklyn. Others settled in San Juan Hill on West 61st, 62nd, and 63rd streets. Some families began to push northward toward Harlem, a suburban area where rich white men rode their horses in the Polo Grounds.

During and after the Civil War, Black New Yorkers made clear their new freedom meant taking a leading role in public affairs. In 1864 at a Black national convention in Syracuse, Frederick Douglass wrote an appeal for the right to vote. In 1866 Douglass and George Downing led a Black delegation to the White House to ask President Andrew Johnson to insure equal voting rights in the South. But Johnson insisted that equality would lead to "a war of the races." He curtly asked them to leave. The meeting was a defining moment, one the president hoped would establish his goal of a second-class citizenship for Black people.

That was also the goal of Governor Horatio Seymour. In 1868 he became the Democratic Party's presidential candidate and advanced the slogan: "This is a white man's country; let white men rule." His bid for the White House was defeated by Ulysses S. Grant.

Douglass, like most African Americans, remained a loyal Republican. He was once quoted as saying, "The Republican party is the ship, all else is the sea." He also continued to champion not only rights for his people, but for all those who faced discrimination—immigrants from China and Europe, Native Americans, and women. His broad view of justice is reflected in his statement: "I can take no part in oppressing and persecuting any variety of the human family." In his last public lecture before his death in Rochester in 1895, he spoke for women's rights.

Edwin P. McCabe left New York City for points west.

Black New Yorkers hoped the 1875 federal civil rights law would end discrimination in the North and South. But when five complaints under the law reached the Supreme Court three of the plaintiffs were Northerners. Bird Gee brought suit because he was not allowed to eat dinner in a Topeka, Kansas, hotel. George Tyler sued when he was denied the right to sit in the dress circle of San Francisco's Maguire's Theater. And William Davis brought suit after being denied the right to attend New York City's Grand Opera.[4]

The Supreme Court majority in 1883, however, declared the 1875 law unconstitutional. Then, in the 1896 *Plessy* case, the high court ruled that when Homer Plessy, a light-skinned Black man, was asked to leave a white railroad car, this act of segregation did not violate the Constitution. Segregation became the law of the land for more than a half-century.

Black New Yorkers tried to win equal rights in a variety of ways. One New Yorker went west, hoping to build a refuge for his people. Edwin P. McCabe left a job on New York's Wall Street and organized thousands of African American families, who fled the South for Kansas in the Exodus of 1879. In Kansas, McCabe was elected state auditor, the first man of color to be elected to state office in the United States, and he was reelected two years later.

In 1889, when the federal government opened the Oklahoma territory for settlement, McCabe promoted a gigantic Black migration. He founded Langston City, began its newspaper, the *Herald,* and sent his agents into the South carrying one-way railroad tickets to Oklahoma. Oppressed tenant farmers and sharecroppers were told of a magical Oklahoma, which offered cheap land and a safe, peaceful life for African American families.

Despite McCabe's efforts, in 1907 Oklahoma entered the Union as another segregationist state. He had helped his people to establish thirty all-Black towns in Oklahoma, but he left the state soon after that and died in poverty in Chicago in 1920.

By then New York had become a sanctuary for some African Americans discouraged with the ability of the West to provide them opportunities. In February 1892, 78 adults and 122 children in tattered clothing with their bedding and baggage arrived from Arkansas to seek a ship for Liberia, Africa, as their final refuge. Their children lacked shoes, and the refugees wandered through cold, wet Manhattan streets and took rooms in cheap hotels. A Methodist mission in Brooklyn took in and boarded many families.[5]

African American families who left Arkansas await passage to Liberia, Africa, at a Black Brooklyn church. Frank Leslie's Illustrated Newspaper, April 24, 1880.

New Yorkers organized two public fund-raising meetings for the refugees. In March fifty people finally sailed to Liberia. Some, unable to book passage, headed west again, but many stayed on, seeking their American dream in Brooklyn and Manhattan. These exiles from oppression reached the city just as wave upon wave of European exiles began to pass the new Statue of Liberty in New York Harbor.

In a segregated United States, people of color found the pursuit of happiness a frustrating effort. But some found ways to improve their lot through sports. In 1870 "Black Sam" Small, the first known wrestler of African descent, made his debut at New York's Owney's Bastille. Still in his teens, New York's Bud Fowler in 1872 became the first Black major league baseball player when he joined the white New Castle, Pennsylvania, team.

In 1885 in Babylon, Long Island, Frank Thompson, a headwaiter at the fashionable Argyle Hotel, organized the first U.S. Black baseball team by recruiting his waiters. A white man took over, named the team the Cuban Giants, paid pitchers and catchers eighteen dollars a week, infielders sixteen dollars, and outfielders twelve dollars. In two years Black ball clubs formed a seven-team league. By this time players of color had been banned from professional baseball leagues.

As a boxing center, New York City drew no color line and often attracted Black contenders. In a 1891 bout, African American George Dixon won the bantamweight title. Joe Walcott, a boxer known as Caveman because of his short neck, dazzled audiences with his ability to duck blows. He managed to defeat tall boxers and in 1901 won the welterweight title. Asked about his ring career, Dixon once said: "We had to beat a white man half to death to get a decision."

Black dancers, actors, and directors had always been drawn to New York. In the late nineteenth century vice was no longer confined to the Five Points section but reached virtually every neighborhood. On Leonard, Thompson, Church, and Duane streets in Greenwich Village, there were Black dance halls and gambling joints ruled by gangsters such as No-Toe Charley,

Bloodthirsty, and Black Cat.

By the 1890s the city's Marshall Hotel on West 53rd Street became the heart of "Black Bohemia," a meeting place for Black theater people seeking to launch careers as composers, singers, and actors. The Marshall also attracted famous Black jockeys such as Isaac Murphy, members of the Black Cuban Giants baseball team, and the Memphis Students, an early jazz band. The hotel served as home for poet Paul Laurence Dunbar and writers Bob Cole and Will Marion Cook, whose theater productions would thrill audiences.[6]

Black jockeys were well known on all U.S. racetracks, such as this one in Jerome Park, Fordham, the Bronx, in 1867. Frank Leslie's Illustrated Newspaper, June 15, 1867.

Black actors tried to challenge the highly popular minstrel shows that had whites in "blackface," offering stereotypes of slow-moving, word-slurring Blacks who lied, stole chickens, and ate watermelon. Black performers challenged these caricatures with their own humanistic sketches. By 1885 James A. Bland, who wrote the state anthem of Virginia, was the first African American to achieve success as a dignified minstrel. In 1892 a classy young tap dancer named Bill Robinson made his first appearance on a New York stage in a minstrel show.

Black performers began to blaze a path in the theater as well. In 1891 Sam Jack, a white man, dressed sixteen beautiful Black women in beguiling costumes for *The Creole Show.* This paved the way for the 1894 stage hit *Black America*, Broadway's first extravaganza with a Black cast. Two years later *Oriental America* strutted onto a Broadway stage with African American chorus girls, buffoons, clowns—and music from *Faust, Rigoletto, Carmen,* and *Il Trovatore.* In 1898 the musical *Clorindy,* by Will Marion Cook with lyrics by Paul Laurence Dunbar, introduced a new art form, the Broadway musical, and a new dance, the cakewalk.

Comedian Bert Williams and dancer George Walker produced a string of stage hits in New York in the early part of the twentieth century: *Sons of Ham* (1900), *In Dahomey* (1902), and *Bandana Land* and *In Abyssinia* (1908).

Williams, a strange and moody man who lived quietly with his wife in New York, asked to perform in blackface in order to dispel the white stereotypes. He used his characters to bring his audiences to tears and laughter. In 1910 he became the first African American to appear in the popular Ziegfield Follies, where his antics delighted audiences and stole scenes. He refused to perform in the South, and he would not appear alone on stage with a white woman.

The cakewalk became a dance craze in the 1890s.

By his death in 1922, Williams earned a staggering fifty thousand dollars a week. He also had become the first actor since Ira Aldridge who was permitted to portray sympathetic Black stage roles before white audiences. "Bert Williams was the funniest man I ever saw and the saddest man I ever met," said comedian W. C. Fields, who starred with him in the Ziegfield Follies.[7]

Since African Americans remained stalwart Republicans in the overwhelmingly Democratic New York, they were awarded few political jobs. Democratic Tammany Hall picked some as street cleaners, assistant janitors, and laborers. One man became a street inspector and another a garbage inspector.

The Democratic Party ignored Charlotte E. Ray, twenty-two, who in 1872 became the first Black woman to graduate from a law school, and later the first to practice law. But in 1897 the

Police brutality, particularly toward people of color, was a well-publicized city problem by 1874. Thomas Nast made this sketch for *Harper's Weekly*, July 11, 1874.

Republican Party urged the appointment of James Carr, a Black graduate of Rutgers and Columbia universities, as an assistant district attorney. He was told his "time had not come" and instead a Black messenger was hired.

Democrats had ignored Black people as politically unreachable, and the Republicans saw them as sewed up. Then, in 1898, a United Colored Democratic club formed, although white Democratic bosses selected its leaders and kept it segregated. The club failed to develop much of a following, since its members were generally ostracized as traitors by Black neighbors. Several members of the United Colored Democracy finally received appointments, and a patient James Carr eventually became an assistant district attorney.

Far more devoted to racial progress was the National Association of Colored Women, organized at 9 Murray Street in 1896 by the activist Mary Church Terrell and a former slave named Booker T. Washington, who was just achieving a reputation as a leader.[8]

CHAPTER NINE

TURNING INTO A NEW CENTURY

At the end of the nineteenth century, thousands of African Americans lived all over Manhattan and parts of Brooklyn, Queens, and Long Island. Manhattan had a Black home for the aged and a host of churches and Sunday schools.

A thriving middle class lived in Brooklyn. By 1892 there were two Black police officers walking the beat there, and by 1898 three people of color had served on the local board of education. In 1904 St. Phillip's Church, the dream of Mrs. Esther Reese, had its own building at 1610 Dean Street between Troy and Schenectady avenues in the Weeksville section. In 1907 it charted a Boys' Brigade of America, a forerunner of the Boy Scouts.

New York City's Black population increased by twenty-five thousand in the last decade of the century and tripled in the twenty years that ended with 1910. By 1890 most African Americans had left Greenwich Village for the rough Tenderloin section that spread out from the Hudson River in the west to Seventh Avenue (some claimed all the way to Sixth or Fifth Avenue) in the east, and from the Twenties to the Fifties. Between the Twenties and Forties some people called the neighborhood African Broadway.

Some artists of color lived in a Black bohemia around 53rd Street near Sixth and Seventh avenues, where the Marshall Hotel and the nearby Maceo and Waldorf attracted Black actors, writers, jockeys, prizefighters, composers, musicians, and their followers.

By the 1890s others had pushed into San Juan Hill, a new neighborhood north of the Tenderloin, stretching from West 61st Street to 64th Street between Tenth and Eleventh avenues.

Paul Lawence Dunbar

Some said San Juan Hill was named for Black soldiers who fought in the Spanish-American war. Others claimed San Juan Hill meant an urban combat zone for its different ethnic groups.

As they had back in Five Points, African Americans often shared poor, dilapidated neighborhoods with Irish Americans and other immigrant groups. Crumbling homes, poor schools, and massive unemployment did not promote intergroup peace.

In August 1900 the Tenderloin was the scene of another New York riot. It began when Robert Thorpe, a white plainclothes police officer on West 41st Street, told African American May Enoch she was "soliciting." Her escort, Arthur Harris, unaware that Thorpe was an officer, came to her defense and fatally stabbed him with a penknife.

Following Thorpe's funeral thousands of his fellow officers and friends sought revenge. For two steamy nights his supporters attacked African Americans in the Tenderloin from 34th and 41st streets between Eighth and Ninth avenues. One of those beaten as he walked down a street was the noted Black author Paul Laurence Dunbar, at the height of his career and busy on his third novel.

Black people, not even safe in their homes, began to fight back. The *New York Sun* reported that every white volley of stones and clubs was answered in kind by a volley from the roofs of Black homes.

Police led the rioters. They not only failed to restrain whites, but clubbed people of color who sought their protection. Only Blacks were arrested. An angry white judge finally said, "I'd like to see some of the people who really started this riot in court."[1]

After the mayhem ended, sympathetic whites organized a fund-raising meeting in Carnegie Hall for the victims. Those assaulted brought suit in court for $250,000 in damages, but no officer was indicted. A police department investigation stated that no white person in uniform or out had been at fault.

In December of 1901 the most noted African American scholar of the day, Dr. W. E. B. Du Bois, wrote the first thorough study of the city's people of color for the *New York Times.*

Half of African American heads of families, Du Bois found, were "country bred" people undergoing "the strain of city life." One in four mothers was a widow, a percentage exceeded only by Irish families and far ahead of the 16 percent average for other whites. Two-thirds of young men and five-eighths of young women of color could not afford to marry.

Du Bois discovered that 99 percent of African Americans and 90 percent of white men held jobs, but Blacks earned less than a third of the wages of whites. Some 10 percent of workers of color held skilled jobs as barbers, tailors, and builders. Five and a half percent ran their own businesses, chiefly real estate, drugstores, catering, funeral parlors, hotels, and restaurants.

Du Bois reported ten attorneys, twenty physicians, and ninety civil service workers, who were largely mail carriers. There was one principal, thirty-seven classroom teachers, and in integrated schools "no complaint of the work and very little objection to their presence has been heard."

Summarizing their economic status, Du Bois said fifteen thousand African Americans had good jobs and thirty thousand

Breakfast time at the Blackwell's Island prison, where Black inmates comprised a large part of the population. Harper's Weekly, December 18, 1875.

In 1872 this fancy dress ball on Seventh Avenue put a Black upper class on display.

were servants and day laborers. He further noted that "a substratum of 15,000" might be called "God's poor, the devil's poor, and the poor devils." These people, he insisted, "had not yet succeeded and . . . New Yorkers have helped [them] to fail." This class, he learned, lived in crowded homes and paid high monthly rents, at least a dollar or two more than whites. This he called "an excess rent charge . . . [of] a quarter of a million dollars annually" based solely on race.

Black New Yorkers, Du Bois said, created their own protected world. "They live and move in a community of their own kith and kin and shrink quickly and permanently from those rough edges where contact with the larger life of the city wounds and humiliates them." He concluded: "Here, then, is a world of itself, closed in from the outer world and almost unknown to it, with churches, clubs, hotels, saloons, and charities; with its own social distinctions, amusements, and ambitions."[2]

In 1903 a *New York Sun* article, "New York's Rich Negroes," told how the city's wealthy African Americans hired white servants and sent their sons to Howard University or European colleges. The *Sun* discovered a snobbish "400 club," open only to men of color born in the city, and interviewed a smug member, Ward McAllister: "The colored club simply recognizes this self-evident truth. It is not for all; it does not pretend to be for all; it is for the chosen and fortunate few."

Some people were able, with community aid, to pull themselves into the middle class. In 1900 Jessie Sleet, a trained nurse, became the first woman of color hired as a temporary public health nurse and given a permanent appointment. In 1906 the National League for the Protection of Colored Women was established in New York to help new arrivals from the South. It soon had branches in Baltimore, Philadelphia, and Norfolk.

One New Yorker scaled ancient barriers to achieve success. Susan Maria Smith of Weeksville, Brooklyn, had eleven sisters and brothers. In 1870 the young woman graduated from New York Medical College as valedictorian of her class. Ms. Smith was the first Black woman medical graduate in the state and the third in the country. In 1888 she completed postgraduate work at Long Island Medical College Hospital, the only woman in the college.

Dr. Susan Smith McKinney Steward. Schomburg Collection.

Dr. Smith helped found the Women's Hospital and Dispensary at Myrtle and Grand avenues in Brooklyn. When her first husband died, she married Dr. Theophilus Steward, an army chaplain, and accompanied him to remote outposts in Nebraska and Montana. The doctor also delivered a paper at the famous London interracial conference organized by Dr. Du Bois in 1911. At her death in 1918 in Brooklyn, Dr. Du Bois delivered her funeral oration.[3]

Other Black New Yorkers also demonstrated scientific and technical skills. In 1880 inventor Granville T. Woods arrived in the city and began to devise dozens of inventions, including a system of telegraphy between moving trains. For the next thirty years he worked alone

Inventor Granville T. Woods

or for Thomas Edison and Alexander Graham Bell and developed patents for two dozen mechanical devices. He died in virtual poverty.

Another New York inventor, Lewis H. Latimer, was the son of a fugitive slave. In 1876, when he was twenty-eight, he drew each part of the original telephone for the patent by Alexander Graham Bell. In 1881 Latimer himself patented a filament for the first electric lightbulb, and in 1890 he wrote the first book on the use of electricity. He served as a chief draftsman for General Electric and Westinghouse and supervised installation of the electric lighting systems of New York, Philadelphia, and London. Latimer became the only African American member of the famous Edison Pioneers. In 1968 a Brooklyn public school was named in his honor.[4]

Black New Yorkers at the outset of the new century celebrated the victories of Jack Johnson, the first African American boxing champion in the United States. In 1908, after he defeated the white heavyweight champion Tommy Burns in fourteen rounds, promoters began a frantic search for "a white hope."

Johnson had to contend with a hostile white media, particularly after he married a white woman. His ring triumphs triggered riots. In 1910, when Johnson defeated Jim Jeffries in a heavyweight bout in Nevada, furious whites in New York started what the *New York Herald* called a Reign of Terror, which left six African Americans dead. The *New York World* explained that Johnson's victory gave "a shock to every devoted believer in the supremacy of the Anglo-Saxon race."

Jack Johnson with his wife in May, 1912.

Johnson's New York followers often lacked good-paying jobs and had little chance to become a champion of anything. In the United States, some 102 trades still refused to hire people of color. Only a handful were admitted to the growing labor unions, such as the Knights of Labor, and even fewer were able to join unions of the American Federation of Labor.

Of two million U.S. workers enrolled in U.S. unions in 1905, only 5 percent were African American. In 1906, 1,386 people of color (5 percent of the 27,039 total local membership) were members of unions in New York City. They were largely asphalt workers, teamsters, rock drillers, tool sharpeners, cigar makers, bricklayers, waiters, carpenters, plasterers, firemen, letter carriers, and sheet metalworkers. In her 1910 New York study, Mary White Ovington found "colored men are in few skilled trades. There are no machinists, no structural iron workers, no plumbers, no garment workers."

George E. Haynes of the National Urban League. Courtesy Mrs. George E. Haynes.

Low pay, underemployment, and poverty left most urban African Americans in a precarious existence. The once sparkling, cultural Black bohemia in the West Fifties became a slum and a red-light district. On a single block on 53rd Street, five thousand Black people were packed into dilapidated, cold-water flats. Two babies out of seven on this street died before their first birthday. By 1910 New York's population soared to 3,132,532, including hundreds of thousands of immigrants and 69,700 African Americans. Black enclaves could be found in San Juan Hill near Columbus Circle and from Central Park West westward to Tenth Avenue between 60th to 64th streets. That year Black sociologist George E. Haynes found Black neighborhoods were multiclass.

> The Negro population was solidly segregated into a few assembly districts, thereby confining the respectable to the same neighborhoods with the disreputable. This population is made up mainly of young persons and adults of the working period of life, attracted to the city largely from the South and the West Indies, principally by the thought of better industrial and commercial advantages. Single persons predominate and the percentage of the aged is low.

Fewer than one in four Blacks in Manhattan were born in the city, and thousands said they were recent immigrants from the West Indies. Black businesspeople and their customers spoke in accents from the American South; the British possessions; the islands of the French, Danish, and Dutch Caribbean; the Portuguese of Brazil; and the Spanish spoken in Latin America.

Haynes found shocking levels of overcrowding: "Largely because of high rents and low incomes, lodgers made up of married couples, parts of broken families and individuals seriously interfere with normal family life."[5] Noted writer George Schuyler was a young man who found it almost impossible to land a good job.

> Day after day I tramped the streets answering advertisements out of the newspapers. Day after day I was met with refusal. Sometimes I was frankly told that no colored help was wanted. More often I was met with evasions, excuses or profuse apologies.
>
> [A while later] I sought only restaurant and hotel jobs. Even here I found my color against me in many instances. Some establishments hired no colored help. No Negroes were wanted as counter-men or cashiers. . . .
>
> I have found that more and more factories, plants and industries cater to Negro labor, but generally for Negro unskilled labor.

Discrimination ruled the day. In 1911 an investigation uncovered the "custom of refusing to colored people seats in the orchestras of the theaters has been growing in New York City." It noted "the colored people of the city are confronted every day of their lives with the most galling conditions, are subjected to insult, are refused service and courteous treatment. . . ."

The dispersion of the Black population throughout the city kept it from electing its own representatives. But there was political progress for some. Charles W. Anderson, a Republican, was appointed chief of the state treasury. In 1914 Anderson used his influence with the new Republican governor Charles Whitman to gain more jobs for his people, and in 1916 a Black man sat in the city council. In 1922 President Warren Harding appointed Anderson a New York tax collector.

Black Democrats also became more active. In 1910, as fifty thousand Black New Yorkers voted, the United Colored Democracy tried to win their loyalty with a leaflet:

An African American couple make their way along Seventh Avenue in 1891. W. A. Rogers, artist, *Harper's Weekly*, June 20, 1891.

We want Colored Policemen.
We want Colored Firemen.
We want garbage removed from our streets before noon.
We want crooks driven out of tenements. . . .
We want work for our boys and protection for our girls.
We want our civil rights as citizens in theaters and restaurants.
We want a colored regiment in the National Guard.

In 1916 the United Colored Democracy installed a powerful new leader, Harvard graduate Ferdinand Q. Morton. In 1917 Morton saw his candidate Edward Johnson gain a state assembly seat, and four Black Democratic assembly candidates also won seats in the next decade. Morton repaid his white bosses by delivering 17 percent of the Black vote to Mayor John Hylan in 1917 and increasing that to 75 percent four years later.

Morton was appointed as a civil service commissioner but, like Anderson, could do little more than manipulate the politics of patronage. He handed out small jobs, dogmatically pursued old

Dr. Du Bois (second from right, middle row) at the Niagara Conference in 1905.

issues, and in the end was unresponsive to new leaders.

In 1924 James Weldon Johnson said of New York: "The Republican party will hold the Negro and do as little for him as possible, and the Democratic party will have none of him at all." It would take the Great Depression, a time of experimentation, to dislodge both Morton and Anderson. Truly independent Black political power in the city would have to wait until World War II and the dynamic figure of Adam Clayton Powell Jr.

People of color in the city watched the unfolding controversy between Booker T. Washington and W. E. B. Du Bois. In 1895 Washington, a former slave and director of Alabama's Tuskegee Institute, outlined his vision of racial peace at the Atlanta Exposition. "Cast down your bucket where you are," he told his people in the South, urging pursuit of economic advances.

Washington urged African Americans to be patient, learn a craft, work hard, and depend on the good whites of the South. He urged his people to reject trade unions and strikes, forgo higher education, and not demand equal rights. His ideas were heartily approved by white supremacists, and he received a great deal of financial aid from wealthy whites.

Dr. W. E. B. Du Bois, the first African American to earn a doctorate in history at Harvard, applauded Washington's emphasis on self-help and economic progress. But he insisted African Americans had to enjoy their full constitutional rights, including the vote. He urged that a "talented tenth"—the best educated—lead the Black fight for equality. In 1903 his monumental *The Souls of Black Folk* articulated this vision.

In January 1904 Washington invited Du Bois and his associates to a reconciliation conference at New York's Carnegie Hall. Andrew Carnegie, the millionaire industrialist, told the delegates of Washington's virtues. But Du Bois's followers arrived armed with excerpts of Washington's speeches "so he can face his record in print." Du Bois spoke of Washington's views:

> We did not object to industrial education, we did not object to his enthusiasm for its advancement, we did object to his attacks upon higher training and upon his general attitude of belittling the race and not putting enough stress upon voting and things of that sort.

When a unity committee grew out of the conference, Washington, used to having his way, dominated it. "There was no use trying to cooperate with a man who would act like that," concluded Du Bois. Their rancorous debate continued. In cities such as New York, Boston, and Philadelphia "the talented tenth" often supported the scholar. But for 90 percent of African Americans, trapped in poverty in a white-ruled rural South, Washington at least provided some chance of hope for a better day.

T. Thomas Fortune, a former slave and famous editor, tried to navigate through the troubled waters of the Washington–Du Bois debate. An independent Republican willing to support Democrats, he urged his people not to "confine ourselves to the narrow limits of either political party."

In 1890 Fortune helped found the National Afro-American

Booker T. Washington

League, an early civil rights society that lasted two years. In 1898, in Rochester, he organized a National Afro-American Council, but it was soon torn apart by arguments over Washington. By 1900 Fortune had become the most militant and the most highly respected African American journalist. At his death in 1928, he was lauded as "the best journalist that the Negro race has produced in the Western World."

Booker T. Washington continued to visit New York and arrived in 1911 to give a lecture. As he was standing at 53rd Street, in a former Black slum, Henry Ulrich, a white man, accused the educator of insulting his wife and began smashing him with a cane. Washington needed sixteen stitches in his head. Ulrich tried to have him arrested, but once Washington established his identity, he had Ulrich arrested for assault. Eight months later a judge exonerated Ulrich saying, Dr. Washington "had no business . . . in a white neighborhood."

In November 1915 Washington returned to New York City. He became ill and entered St. Luke's Hospital for more than a week of medical tests. Then he left with his wife and his doctor, saying, "I expect to die in the South." A few days later at age fifty-nine and at home in Tuskegee, Alabama, Washington died.[6]

African Americans continued to flock to a rising northern neighborhood called Harlem. The Harlem Dispensary, begun in 1868, served three thousand people a year. In 1887 Harlem Hospital, with its twenty beds, was opened on 120th Street and the foot of the East River, and by 1907 it had moved one block north. Three years later the Hotel Theresa was built on 125th Street in the western center of a thriving community.

CHAPTER TEN

MOVING TO HARLEM

Africans had had a close relationship to Harlem since the days of Dutch rule in the 1600s. Some had been runaway slaves who sought a refuge in its woods. Others had built the first Dutch road to reach Harlem. In 1853 the Third Avenue horse-drawn streetcar line connecting 53rd Street with Wall Street opened a route northward to reach Harlem. Except for this new venture, the streetcars relied on steam engines. The trip from Wall Street took an hour and a half.

By the 1890s Harlem was known as Manhattan's first wealthy suburb. Isolated from the crowding and squalor of downtown, families of successful entrepreneurs were drawn to its farmlands and solidly built large houses. Harlem became a community for prominent judges, politicians, merchants, and immigrants who "made it" in the city. "Harlem had become the rural retreat of the aristocratic New Yorker," wrote a visitor. Men on horses played polo in the Polo Grounds, and Commodore Cornelius Vanderbilt rode his trotter on Harlem Lane.

Working people began to arrive. In the 1890s poor Italian immigrants settled on Harlem's east side from 110th to 125th streets. African Americans moved in as domestic servants and laborers for wealthy families. There was even one music teacher.

By the 1890s middle-class African Americans resided on 125th and nearby streets, in two apartment houses at Broadway and 125th Street, in less expensive apartments at 146th Street, and on 130th Street. This sprinkling of settlers gave birth to a Black political club and a Knights of Pythias, and churches held baptisms in the Harlem river on the east side.

The transformation of Harlem began in the early years of the new century, and one man, Philip A. Payton Jr., deserved the credit for its rebirth as a Black community. He was a well-dressed, smooth-talking real estate agent whose passion from 1900 to his death in 1917 was to build a haven for his people uptown.

In 1904 Payton formed the Afro-American Realty Company, capitalized at half a million dollars and boasting a Black board of directors. Its prospectus defined Payton's lofty mission: "The idea that Negroes must be confined to certain localities can be done away with. The idea that it is not practical to put colored and white tenants in the same house can be done away with."

By appealing to Black pride, Payton hoped to fill Harlem apartments. He could not have picked a better moment. A new subway line was started in October 1904 at City Hall, and it took only minutes to reach a distant 145th Street in the north. The next year an economic downturn forced white people to move out. The prices of Harlem housing dropped and a migration of eager Black families began to fill the newly available apartments.

But first Payton had to contend with wealthy whites who warned about the arrival of "black hordes." They formed a Harlem Property Owners Protective Association and spoke in menacing military language: "The Negro invasion . . . must be vigilantly fought until it is permanently checked or the invaders will slowly but surely drive the whites out of Harlem."

However, while some whites raised cries of racial purity, others looked forward to profits from African American buyers and renters. Payton's company failed in 1908, but another Black firm, Nail and Parker, leaped into the breach. The exodus of African American families to Harlem continued.[1]

Leading African American churches arrived with accumulated capital and purchased Harlem real estate. Baptist, Methodist, Seventh-Day Adventist, Roman Catholic, and evangelical churches bought land; others rented. Then the congregations followed their churches to Harlem.

St. Philip's Protestant Episcopal Church, the most exclusive and elegant black church in the city, set the pace. Founded in

1809 in Five Points, it opened its wooden building in 1819 on Center Street. In 1856 it moved to Mulberry Street and in 1889 to West 25th Street. In 1910 St. Philip's Reverend Bishop sold the church's downtown property, bought houses in Harlem without telling his congregation, and then surprised them with the news. By the next year the church owned ten apartment houses on 135th Street worth $640,000. At the time, this complex near the present-day Schomburg Center amounted to one of the city's largest private real estate purchases.

Between 1905 and 1918 the African American real estate boom in Harlem gave birth to 39 churches of 8 denominations, 44 saloons, 3 public schools, 10 groceries, 10 restaurants, an oyster house, a laundry, 9 hairdressers, 11 barbershops, 4 undertakers, 6 coal and wood dealers, 4 express businesses, and 6 tailoring establishments.[2]

In 1910 sociologist George E. Haynes wrote of the growth of Harlem in these words: "There has been a decided shifting from the parts of Manhattan between 25th, 42nd streets, 6th and 8th avenue, into Harlem between One Hundred and Thirtieth, One Hundred and Fortieth streets, Fifth and Eighth avenues during the past five years. . . ." The new arrivals found some earlier African American residents living there well and happily.

In 1910 Harlem was already the home of the famous vaudeville star Bert Williams. Noted ragtime composer Scott Joplin arrived in 1907. Joplin's *Maple Leaf Rag* had sold a million copies and forever changed popular music. The "King of Ragtime" hoped to see his opera *Treemonisha* performed, and in 1915 he was finally able to summon a special audience to hear it, with him at the piano. People were unimpressed, and a heartbroken Joplin entered a mental hospital the next year and died in 1917.

Joplin's ragtime would soon be called "jass" or "jazz" and seize public acclaim in New York and the world. W. C. Handy, whose "St. Louis Blues" introduced an infectious, soulful strain to jazz, arrived from Memphis, Tennessee, to settle in Harlem.

Jazz's first famous bandleader was Jim Europe of New York, a skilled organizer of musicians and the man who introduced the saxophone to dance music. In 1914 he conducted Carnegie

Hall's first evening of African American music. He also began the first effective black musicians' union. Ballroom dancers Irene and Vernon Castle taught the world the fox-trot, but they admitted it was Jim Europe who taught it to them. (And he credited Handy with teaching him the steps.) Europe was also the first Black bandleader to receive a major recording contract.

Some of Harlem's most successful Black residents stood ready to fight to open the community to their race. In 1913 the Black Equity Congress brought legal suits against restrictive agreements in Harlem. The congress also formed the United Civic League to conduct a "civic, industrial, political and educational campaign among members of the race." Its hundred wealthy Harlem members bought a thirty thousand–dollar stone building.

John M. Royall, a real estate agent, ran for the Board of Aldermen in 1913, saying to his voters he was "a black man first, a black man last, and a black man all the time." Though he lost the election, he gained half of the Black vote. By then whites had learned African Americans were in Harlem to stay.

The previous year Harlem gained new prestige when an enormously successful businesswoman, Madame C. J. Walker, forty-four, bought three lots at 108 West 136th Street and built a castle made of Indiana limestone. With "two dollars and a dream," Madame Walker had created a vast empire based on selling beauty secrets, facial creams, and hair products to women of color. Above all, her sales force of women taught Black women to think of themselves as beautiful.

Madame C. J. Walker, first American woman millionaire.

Walker's saleswomen also taught hygiene and health to millions. She became the first American woman to earn a million dollars. In 1917 she moved into a quarter-million-dollar mansion overlooking the Hudson River that she built in Westchester. When she died two years later, her will left large cash grants for the education of her people. Mrs. A'Leila Walker Robinson, her only daughter, inherited her financial empire and her mansion and would soon make her own mark on Harlem.[3]

From Brooklyn and elsewhere in the city, other wealthy

Black families began to arrive. The community boasted sturdy buildings, large windows, and small gardens. By 1914 *Outlook* magazine reported that Black Harlem had grown to the size of Dallas, Texas, or Springfield, Massachusetts.

> If one stands on the corner of One Hundred and Thirty-Fifth Street and Fifth Avenue, in four directions can be seen rows of apartments or flat houses all inhabited by Negroes. This is virtually the center of the community. The houses are in good repair; windows, entrances, halls, sidewalks, and streets are clean, and the houses comfortable and respectable inside to a degree not often found in a workingman's locality. . . .
>
> In the professions this Negro community has some twenty physicians who received their medical training at various universities and colleges [from Harvard, Yale, and Columbia to Oxford, England].
>
> In the legal fraternity there are fifteen lawyers from Harvard, Yale, Syracuse, Columbia, New York Law School, and Northwestern University. One of these men is a deputy Assistant District Attorney for New York County, and one is Assistant Corporation Counsel for the city of New York.
>
> There are eight dentists from Howard and New York Dental Colleges, two architects from Cornell University, four registered pharmacists from Columbia and the New York College of Pharmacy . . . and 25 registered trained nurses. . . .
>
> The thoroughgoing business attitude of a majority of the community is witnessed in the small percentage of saloons. . . .
>
> Of public institutions run for and by Negroes the community possesses an old folks' home, a day nursery, a home for graduate nurses, a house for boys which is the headquarters for sixty Boy Scouts and their major, a union rescue home for girls, and a music school settlement.

New civil rights organizations born in the early twentieth century established national headquarters in New York. In 1909 the city was host to a national conference "to revive the spirit of the abolitionists." Out of its deliberations came the National

In 1916 NAACP leaders met for a crucial conference in Amenia, New York.

Association for the Advancement of Colored People (NAACP) and its headquarters at 70 Fifth Avenue at 13th Street.

Dr. W. E. B. Du Bois moved from Atlanta to New York to become the NAACP's director of publicity and to research and edit its *Crisis* magazine. He remained in the city for the next quarter-century. Some of the time, he resided at Harlem's upper-class Strivers' Row or in the fancy Dunbar apartments.

In 1910 the National Urban League was created by leading American reformers in New York. Reflecting the African American march from rural to city life, the league merged with the National League for the Protection of Colored Women. It fought for Black acceptance in trade unions and industry and demanded better jobs and advancement possibilities for people of color. Its *Opportunity* magazine, like the *Crisis,* called for resistance to discrimination and racism, and published creative writing by young African Americans.

World War I completed the African American domination of Harlem. The massive war effort required millions of new workers. The danger of the Atlantic crossing in wartime and European governments had virtually ended the flow of emigrants to America. In the single year between 1914 and 1915, immigration to the United States fell by 90 percent.

To fill the void, Southern farm families, black and white, poured out of the rural South and into cities such as Chicago, Detroit, New York, and Los Angeles. Only one in twenty Southern Blacks earned more than three dollars a day, while standard pay in the North began at three dollars and steelworkers earned $4.50 daily.

In 1915 and 1916 droughts and the ravages of the boll weevil on Southern cotton crops drove many others northward. James Weldon Johnson wrote: "I witnessed the sending North from a Southern city in one day a crowd estimated at 2,500 on a train in three sections, packed in day coaches with all their baggage. . . . The exodus was on."

The war opened opportunities for people of color, including women, but African Americans still faced racist stereotypes. In 1919 a writer in *Industrial Management* spoke of the "natural laziness . . . of the colored race." He wrote, "I have found the Negro as a class possess less muscular coordination than the white in that they seem to be most susceptible to strain."

Black Harlem continued to grow during and after the war. By 1920, 118,792 white residents had left the community (though some also stayed on) and were replaced by 87,417 African Americans. Some 164,566 people of color called Harlem home. In 1923 the federal census bureau tabulated the city's African American

The first issue of the <u>Crisis</u>, official voice of the NAACP.

THE CRISIS

A RECORD OF THE DARKER RACES

Volume One — NOVEMBER, 1910 — Number One

Edited by W. E. BURGHARDT DU BOIS, with the co-operation of Oswald Garrison Villard, J. Max Barber, Charles Edward Russell, Kelly Miller, W. S. Braithwaite and M. D. Maclean.

CONTENTS

Along the Color Line	3
Opinion	7
Editorial	10
The N. A. A. C. P.	12
Athens and Brownsville By MOORFIELD STOREY	13
The Burden	14
What to Read	15

PUBLISHED MONTHLY BY THE

National Association for the Advancement of Colored People

AT TWENTY VESEY STREET — NEW YORK CITY

ONE DOLLAR A YEAR — TEN CENTS A COPY

population at 183,428, but the United Hospital Fund put the figure at 300,000. Whatever the exact figure, it was clear that at least two-thirds of Black New Yorkers lived in Harlem.

Originally built for a white elite, Harlem boasted some of the architecturally strongest buildings in the city. But this advantage passed almost unnoticed because people of color were seeking not an elite neighborhood but a safe one, free of hostility.

Churches continued to pioneer in Harlem's development. In 1920 the Abyssinian Baptist Church purchased lots on 138th Street between Seventh and Lenox avenues, and by 1923 it opened the largest Baptist church in the nation. The church's sanctuary sat two thousand parishioners, and boasted one large lecture room, fourteen smaller ones, a gym, and facilities for teaching nursing, sewing, and cooking. Its minister, Adam Clayton Powell Sr., presided over Harlem's first large community and recreational center, and in 1926 the church had built a home for the aged.

That year Harlem's 150 blocks boasted more than 140 churches, though only forty-four had regular buildings. "They are anywhere and everywhere," wrote sociologist Ira De A.Reid of Harlem's religious institutions. They also dominated the community's social life.

Previous African American communities were only a few blocks in size, but Harlem had grown into a Black world. Its main thoroughfare in 1920 was 135th Street between Lenox and Seventh avenues. St. Philip's Protestant Episcopal Church owned a block of houses and stores on its north side. One store was home to both the *New York News,* a community paper, and Harlem's first bookstore. George Young, a former Pullman porter who had collected books during his travels, offered a wide selection of Africana and African Americana.

By the end of the 1920s, Harlem boundaries stretched from 110th to 145th streets and from Fifth to Eighth avenues. In 1925 New York City's population density was 223 people per acre, but in Harlem the figure stood at 336. White landlords were able to overcharge African Americans, who were limited in the areas that would accept them, so Harlem rents skyrocketed to double the city average. In 1927 apartment rents for 48 percent of Harlem residents, noted an Urban League report, were more than twice as much as comparable apartments downtown. Yet most Harlem residents earned lower wages than whites.

World War I put Harlem on the map. African Americans entered World War I, "the war to make the world safe for democracy," with mixed feelings. In 1913 President Wilson had restored segregation to federal offices and curtly dismissed a Black delegation that protested his action. Wilson advocated self-determination for colonial people but believed in white supremacy. Radical street orators warned their Harlem listeners not to sacrifice their lives to help imperialist powers keep dividing Africa into European colonies.

In 1917 the United States entered the war against Germany, and the Wilson administration's war propaganda flooded the country. People were stirred into action. "Yes, we are loyal and patriotic," said Reverend Adam Clayton Powell Sr. from his Harlem pulpit. W. E. B. Du Bois asked his readers in the *Crisis* to "close our ranks shoulder to shoulder with our own white fellow citizens." But he also called for Black voting rights and an end to lynchings and racist laws.

However, in July 1917, as the first U.S. troops prepared for battle in France, whites in east St. Louis besieged the Black ghetto, killing two hundred and driving another six thousand from their homes. Two weeks later Du Bois and the NAACP led a "Silent March" of fifteen thousand men, women, and children down New York's Fifth Avenue. Tramping to muffled drums, they carried placards that read: "Mr. President, Why Not Make America Safe for Democracy?" and "Mother, Do Lynchers Go to Heaven?"

During the war, more than two million African American men registered for the draft, and more than three hundred thousand entered the armed services. In New York six thousand African Americans donned uniforms. The most famous Black U.S. Army unit was a part of New York's National Guard 15th Regiment. But in France it was known as the 369th U.S. Infantry, or the Harlem Hellfighters.

Dr. Du Bois (on right with cane) taking part in the 1917 Silent March down Fifth Avenue.

The Hellfighters first drilled in an old dance hall and without rifles. They were shipped to the front lines in France to keep them from fighting with bigoted white troops on Long Island. In France they were placed under French command and became the first U.S. unit to battle the German enemy.

As African Americans died bravely in the war, a secret U.S. Army memo warned French officers to "prevent degeneracy" by seeing that Black soldiers did not associate with white women. U.S. orders also demanded the French "not eat with [African Americans] . . . not shake hands or seek to talk or meet with them outside of the requirements of military service."

With their New York flag held high, the Harlem Hellfighters became part of the 8th French Corps. They set a record by fighting for 191 days without relief and never lost a foot of ground. In all, some eighty thousand African Americans saw service overseas, but only fifty thousand were combat troops. The rest served in labor and engineering battalions. More African Americans buried the white dead than had a chance to shoot at Germans.

Jim Europe, asked to form a forty-eight-man band for the regiment, said he would only if he could have the best one in the army. He hoped his band would contribute to racial progress, and he recruited a number of talented Black Puerto Rican clarinet and saxophone players. Since the French treated the African Americans as equals, sharing supplies and companionship, Europe's band, with its superb reed section, returned the favor. They traveled two thousand miles to the front to entertain audiences of French, British, and American troops and French civilians with the first jazz heard on foreign soil.

World War I hero Sergeant Henry Johnson (holding flowers) being welcomed home to New York City. National Archives.

At the front northeast of Paris, two Hellfighters, Henry Johnson and Needham Roberts, virtually destroyed a German raiding party of two dozen soldiers. Johnson and Roberts, who suffered disabling wounds, became the first Americans granted the French Croix de Guerre. Neither they nor any other Black heroes were awarded the U.S. Congressional Medal of Honor.

The Hellfighters returned with an astounding seventy-one French medals and honors. More than one hundred African Americans earned French decorations, and the 369th was one of four Black regiments to earn French Croixes de Guerres.

The African American veterans returned home to find a bold new tone in a *Crisis* editorial by Du Bois:

> We return.
> We return from fighting.
> We return fighting.

The Harlem Hellfighters return to New York from France in 1919. National Archives.

> Make way for democracy! We saved it in France, and by the Great Jehovah, we will save it in the United States of America, or know the reason why.

One Hellfighter reflected the new mood: "We're going to keep on fighting for democracy till we get our rights here at home. The black worm has turned."[4]

The Harlem troops received a huge Fifth Avenue ticker-tape parade in February 1919. On a corner Ben Katz, a white high school student, stood and watched in wonder:

> There was something odd about this parade right from the start. Most of the other parades came down Fifth Avenue—this one was moving uptown!

We soon saw why. Back from the Rhine to get the applause of their city of Harlem were the troops known in France as the 369th U.S. Infantry, but known in New York as the Harlem Hell Fighters.

. . . The 369th was marching in a formation unfamiliar to most American troops, and certainly to the public until that day. Because the 369th had been segregated from the rest of the American forces and had served under French command, they were marching in the extraordinarily dramatic Phalanx formation of the French Army. Shoulder to shoulder, from curb to curb, they stretched in great massed squares, thirty-five feet wide by thirty-five feet long, of men, helmets, and bayonets. . . .

Then we heard that music! Somewhere in the line of march was Jim Europe and his band that the French had heard before we ever did. . . . My school friends and I stepped out into the middle of the street with great hordes of other spectators, and swung up Fifth Avenue behind the 369th and the fantastic sixty-piece band that was beating out those rhythms that could be heard all the way down at our end of the parade.[5]

In the months following the World War I victory parades, whites in twenty-six cities attacked Black neighborhoods. Men of color, some still in uniform, were slain during this "red summer" of 1919. Lynchings in the South also had increased. However, white rioters met a new Black spirit. In Chicago, Washington, D. C., and other cities, white invaders were fired on by armed African Americans. In that turbulent year this spirit of resistance was dramatically captured by Harlem poet Claude McKay.

If we must die, let it not be like hogs
Hunted and penned in an inglorious spot. . . .
Pressed to the wall, dying, but fighting back!

CHAPTER ELEVEN

MARCUS GARVEY CAPTURES HARLEM

When Marcus Garvey left Jamaica for Harlem in 1916, he was not the first Black radical activist to make New York's Harlem his base. Dissident socialists, Marxists, and nationalists had preceded him, just as others would follow in his footsteps.

The grandfather of Black New York radicalism was self-educated Hubert Harrison, born in the Virgin Islands in 1883. He joined the Socialist Party in 1909, became Harlem's best-known street orator, and wrote about racial injustice. He told his people that white violence had to be met by violence and called for a separate Black region of the United States.

In 1912 Harrison found an ally in Jamaican immigrant Claude McKay, at twenty-two a radical and author of two books of poetry. McKay served as an editor of the *Liberator,* which published his famous poem "If We Must Die." In the 1920s he traveled to Germany and spoke at a Communist international conference in the Soviet Union. The two men joined the paramilitary African Blood Brotherhood (ABB), which advocated armed resistance to lynchings and white rioters and claimed five thousand members in fifty posts around the world.

As World War I fever gripped white America, radical orators mounted their soapboxes at Harlem's Speakers Corner at Lenox Avenue and 135th Street to recount tales of European nations that long had divided and exploited Africa and crushed its dreams of independence. White Americans were moved by British propaganda stories of German atrocities in Belgium, but not Harlem. The *New York Age* reminded its readers how King Leopold ordered his Belgian troops to massacre thousands in the Congo. "The German's ain't done nothing to me," said one Harlem resident, "and I ain't doing nothing to them."[1]

This 1919 cartoon from A. Philip Randolph's Messenger applauded the violent Black response to white rioters.

In the 1917 election for mayor, 25 percent of Harlem voters cast ballots for Morris Hillquit, an antiwar Socialist. One of Hillquit's strongest supporters was Harlem's radical editor A. Philip Randolph. Briefly arrested during the war for obstructing the draft law, Randolph resumed his antiwar talks after his release. His *Messenger,* "a magazine of Scientific Radicalism," proclaimed: "Revolution must come. . . . The capitalist system must go and its going must be hastened by the workers themselves." To J. Edgar Hoover and the Justice Department, Randolph was "the most dangerous Negro in America." Hoover's agents kept him under surveillance.

But the radical who turned Harlem on its head was Marcus Garvey, a small, self-taught man, born to a British West Indies family in Jamaica. Garvey early defined his political and economic goals, saying he intended to marshal people of African descent to retake Africa and take their rightful place in the world. In 1914 his mission came to him in a series of questions he posed: "Where is the black man's Government? Where is his King and his kingdom? Where is his President, his country, and his ambassador, his army, his navy, his men of big affairs? . . . I could not find them," he said, and decided to help make them.

In Jamaica, Garvey incorporated his Universal Negro Improvement Association (UNIA). Inspired by Booker T. Washington's self-help philosophy, the Jamaican planned to visit the educator in Alabama, but Washington died before Garvey reached the United States. Instead, the young man visited thirty-eight states to study the conditions of people of color. He reached New York in March 1916 with little cash and a big plan. He moved into a building at 235 West 131st Street, and the next year moved across the street to 238 W. 131st Street.

On a bright spring day in 1916, Garvey found his way to Speakers Corner, where A. Philip Randolph was standing on a short ladder lecturing about socialism. He stepped aside and introduced the Jamaican to the evening crowd. Garvey had found his career. He became a master of soapbox oratory and a mainstay of Speakers Corner.

From the outset, Garvey's words were not aimed at the hopeful, upwardly mobile people Randolph and Du Bois excited with talk about racial equality. His audience was the poor, struggling peasants from the rural South and recent immigrants from Caribbean islands. His listeners, concerned with surviving in a hostile culture, viewed civil rights and integration as neither obtainable nor necessary. They felt dispossessed from society, had no desire to live near whites, and had no interest in debates about constitutional rights. Their goals were simple: to keep a job, pay the rent, feed the family, and avoid economic disasters.

Garvey's message found responsive crowds in Harlem's churches. He told descendants of Africa to take pride in their past, study their history, rejoice in their blackness, and build sturdy economic and social institutions in their communities. For the first time Harlem heard from one of its own that European world rule was dying and the days of the white man were numbered. Sounding like an ancient drum, Garvey was an impelling, even spellbinding voice that sounded a wake-up call for the oppressed. He predicted the doom of European colonialism and called for a massive return to Africa.

Garvey told his audiences he had been chosen to lead a movement to reclaim Africa, and in May 1918 he incorporated the

UNIA in New York. A month later he began publication of his weekly newspaper, the *Negro World.* Printed in English, French, and Spanish, his *Negro World* sold two hundred thousand copies each week. It refused to print ads that demeaned people of color by telling them to straighten their hair or to whiten their skin. In 1920 Hubert Harrison signed on as the *Negro World*'s editor.

Marcus Garvey in the 1920s led America's largest Black nationalist movement.

The movement's main offices were at 2305 Seventh Avenue. The next year the UNIA purchased Liberty Hall at 120 West 138th Street to hold rallies. "Up, you mighty race," Garvey shouted to rallies of as many as six thousand at Liberty Hall, "you can accomplish what you will."

Garvey brought a global approach to problems of race. He sent two delegates to the Versailles Peace Conference to advocate liberating Africa from European rulers. His enthusiastic followers on five continents organized UNIA branches to carry forth his message. A West Indian immigrant, Hugh Mulzac, the first African American to earn the rank of master sailor, was chosen to captain the *Frederick Douglass,* the first ship in Garvey's famous Black Star Line, designed to take the faithful to the African motherland.[2]

Among the dynamic women enlisted by the UNIA crusade was Audley Moore. In Louisiana she organized a small army to guard Garvey's right to speak in New Orleans. She moved to New York to work in his UNIA and began a long career as "Queen Mother" Moore. She recruited domestic workers in the Bronx into a union and assisted tenants dispossessed from their apartments.

In 1919 an angry follower rushed into Garvey's new 135th

Street headquarters and fired a shot that grazed his forehead. Blood steaming down his face, Garvey rushed defiantly into the street. Many of his followers were convinced nothing could stop him from saving his people.

In 1920 Garvey launched a full-month extravaganza known as the first International Convention of the Negro Peoples of the World. Black men armed with guns and followed by nurses marched through New York under banners of red, black, and green, the colors of a new "Negro nation." A Harlem motorcade car carried the sign THE NEW NEGRO HAS NO FEAR. An estimated twenty-five thousand people packed into Madison Square Garden to hear Garvey. A master showman, he energized the first night's audience with a fervent internationalism: "We believe Ireland should be free even as Africa shall be free for the Negroes of the World. Keep up the fight for a free Ireland."

Garvey was the first major African American leader to publicly scoff at white claims of superiority and to call on his people to honor their color, their homeland, and their past. He would be Africa's savior: "The glorious continent of Africa stands to be redeemed. A mighty nation must be built in Africa."

Garvey soon made enemies. He insisted that light-skinned and middle-class people of color imitated whites. His belief that "wealth is power, wealth is influence, wealth is justice, wealth is liberty" upset his radical and socialist supporters. Black middle-class intellectuals scorned his ideas and his lower-class followers. One called him the Jamaican Jackass. Du Bois praised his self-help programs but said Garvey lacked the training and temperament for leadership.

Garvey was blithely unconcerned when foes appeared at every side. He expected opposition, never expressed a fear of controversy, and relished a vigorous debate. He saw his message as broadly useful for African Americans and whites as well:

> We love all humanity. We are working for the peace of the world which we believe can only come about when all races are given their due.

> We feel there is absolutely no reason why there should be any differences between the black and white races, if each stops to adjust and steady itself. We believe in the purity of both races. . . .
>
> We believe the black people should have a country of their own where they should be given the fullest opportunity to develop politically, socially and industrially. The black people should not be encouraged to remain in white people's countries and expect to be Presidents, Governors, Mayors, Senators, Congressmen, Judges and social and industrial leaders.

Garvey was also the first leader to touch the fifty thousand Harlem people from the Caribbean who spoke French or Spanish or whose English came with a British accent. Even some who first denounced his vision became converts. New York journalist John E. Bruce, known as Bruce Grit, first described Garvey as "a little sawed-off and hammered-down Black Man, with determination written all over his face, and an engaging smile that . . . compelled you to listen to his story." In 1922 Bruce described the Garvey spell:

> His street corner audiences were larger than those of the Socialist orators on the other corners a few blocks away, and they stayed longer. The people hung upon his words, drank in his messages to them, and were as enthusiastic and earnest about this business as their doughty little Black Orator. . . .
>
> Garvey is neither a rum drinker, user of tobacco in any form, a social bug, nor a grafter. He is scrupulously honest in the handling of the funds of the Organization. . . . Garvey is relentless with crooks and fakers, and he is the idol of the masses of the common people, of whom he is one.

Garvey's Back to Africa notions drew broad derision. A. Philip Randolph said that the UNIA could not liberate Africa "in a raging sea of imperialism" and warned that "Negro exploiters and tyrants are as bad as white ones." Randolph denounced him as a "clown and imperial buffoon" and a "little half-wit Lilliputian."

However, Garvey's star, despite increased criticism, continued to rise. In the eyes of his followers, he could do no wrong. Some found in his words the ring of ancient prophecy: "No one knows when the hour of Africa's Redemption cometh. It is in the wind. It is coming. One day, like a storm, it will be here." They chortled with glee as Garvey punctured white arrogance: "The white man fixed the Bible to suit himself."

In 1921 Garvey claimed four million UNIA members out of a Black population of ten million, and he later raised the figure to six million. The fast-growing Ku Klux Klan also claimed four million members drawn from tens of millions of white Protestants in the U.S. population.[3]

Like other fraternal societies of the day, Garvey wrapped his in mystical names, rituals and symbols. He anointed himself Provisional President of Africa and chose a host of dukes, duchesses, knight commanders, and an African Legion. Generals in resplendent green-and-black uniforms commanded his brigades. His African Motor Corps symbolized huge potential power. His Black Star Line promised to carry people to their ancestral homeland.

Garvey created a religion with a Black God and, like Moses, was prepared to lead his people through a sea of white hate to a new destiny. At a moment when Black people had not had a single representative in the U.S. Congress for twenty-seven years, African Americans ruled his vast business empire, wrote for his newspaper, and taught in his schools.

From the pages of the *Negro World* and from UNIA teachers, children learned about the struggles of their people and Black heroes who did not appear in school texts. They read of ancient African emperors, Hottentot and Zulu leaders, and Black rebels such as Nat Turner, Denmark Vesey, and Gabriel Prosser. Jesus Christ and Mary were celebrated as Black figures.

In a few years Garvey had mobilized the largest number of Black people in American history, raised more money than any other Black leader, and issued the best-selling paper in the African diaspora. By 1922 his business empire sprawled across Harlem, between 135th and 145th streets and along Lenox

Avenue. Among UNIA enterprises were a grocery store at 646 Lenox Avenue, a laundry and dressmaking shop at 62 West 142 Street, a restaurant at 120 West 138th Street, a bakery at Seventh Avenue and 145th Street, and a publishing house at 2305 Seventh Avenue. More than just community services, they represented examples of self-determination and achievement.

Garvey welcomed the attention of white racists who favored his Back to Africa campaign and his brand of segregation. When President Warren Harding denounced "Racial amalgamation," the Jamaican heartily agreed, but some followers were not happy.

In 1922, as his UNIA reached its peak, Garvey strolled into a political minefield. He attended a Ku Klux Klan summit meeting, met a rabidly racist senator, and courted officers of a white supremacist society. In North Carolina, he ridiculed African Americans while speaking at a white supremacist public rally. He even invited his new allies to speak at Liberty Hall.

Garvey defended his actions in language his followers understood. Klan members and other white supremacy societies, he said, were "better friends of the race than all the groups of hypocritical whites put together. . . . You may call me a Klansman if you will," he continued "but, potentially, every white man is a Klansman . . . and there is no use lying about it." But when he pointedly added the NAACP and Urban League to his list of racists, even zealous followers wondered if he had gone too far.[4]

Garvey also viewed U.S. Blacks through the eyes of a Jamaican culture, where a white elite hired light-skinned Black people to carry out their policies. To him light-skinned people or those economically dependent on whites were guilty of racial disloyalty. He failed to understand that racists in the United States applied a "one drop of blood" rule, which drew a circle of exclusion around African Americans no matter how light their skin color or how high their class. Garvey's critics insisted he was dividing the race.

As his errors multiplied, even ardent supporters began to ask questions. Would Klan funds be used to pay the rent on UNIA buildings, to help subsidize Black Star ships, or to pay wages for teachers who brought Africa's legacy to Black children?

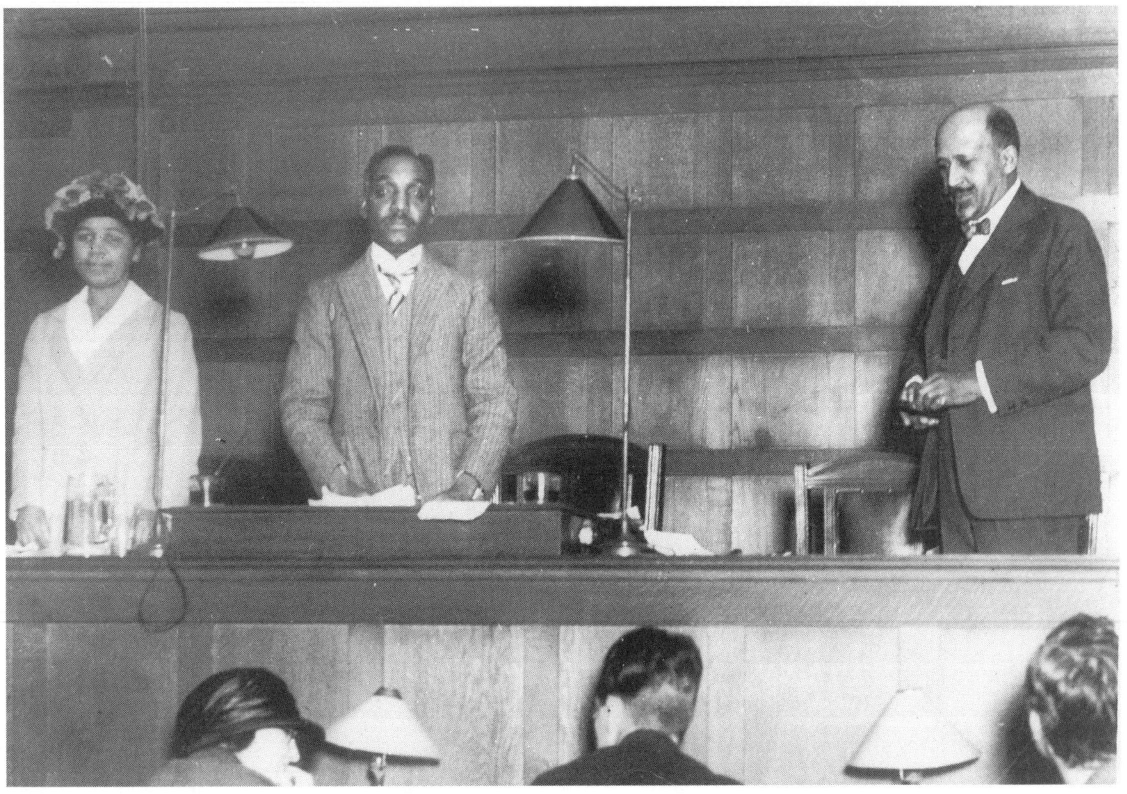

Dr. Du Bois (right) had urged Pan-Africanism at international conferences since 1900. Here he participates in a 1923 London meeting of people of color from around the world.

Garvey's worst enemy was the U.S. Department of Justice. Attorney General A. Mitchell Palmer and his young assistant in the Justice Department, J. Edgar Hoover, feared that any kind of African American agitation might trigger Black violence. During the war, Hoover ordered his agents to begin a secret surveillance of Black leaders and their publications and organizations. Federal agents even monitored sermons in Black churches.

After the Communist revolution in Russia, Black figures who voiced admiration for Communism became prime surveillance targets. Hoover soon decided that the two greatest threats to America were Communism and the rise of a "Black Messiah" who might lead his people to revolution. Hoover's agents confronted Dr. Du Bois at the NAACP's offices and asked about NAACP goals. "We're fighting for the enforcement of the Constitution of the United States," Du Bois replied coldly.

Palmer and Hoover were shocked at the militancy that appeared in Black papers. The *New York Age* wrote:

> Every day we are told to keep quiet. Only a fool will keep quiet when he is being robbed of his birthright. Only a coward will lie down and whine under the lash if he too can give back the lash. America hates, lynches and enslaves us, not because we are black but because we are weak. A strong, united Negro race will not be mistreated.

In 1920 the attorney general's report "Radicalism and Sedition among the Negroes as Reflected in their Publications" found fifty Black periodicals that "openly expressed demands for social equality." Justice Department officials were upset to find highly educated Black editors who wrote in "fine, pure English, with a background of scholarship" and were "defiantly assertive of . . . equality."

To J. Edgar Hoover, Garvey was the "Black Messiah" he worried about, a man capable of leading his people to revolution. Garvey became Hoover's first high-profile Black target. He sent four secret operatives into the UNIA seeking evidence of criminal acts. In 1923 federal agents arrested Garvey for mail fraud in advertising for his Black Star Line.[5]

Garvey hired a white attorney but insisted on conducting his own defense. Lacking knowledge of U.S. legal procedures, he tried to put his philosophy on trial. Despite his many talents, he lacked training as an attorney. Bad news on his finances and ships began to seep out. Court testimony established that Garvey's wife kept loose books on the cash collected from forty thousand stockholders and that some high UNIA officials were embezzlers. Garvey said the Black Star Line had $750,000 in the bank when actually it had $6,000 and owed $200,000.

Garvey was convicted and sentenced, but he appealed his case, and his followers, more loyal than before, raised twenty-five thousand dollars in bail. Then they raised enough for another ship—the *Booker T. Washington.* Journalist T. Thomas Fortune, who had long criticized Garvey's segregationist views, agreed to serve as editor of the *Negro World.*

T. Thomas Fortune, considered Black America's foremost journalist, became editor of the <u>Negro World</u>.

Garvey still carried enormous political clout. In 1924 Republican Calvin Coolidge welcomed his support in his presidential race. Democratic governor Al Smith and mayor John Hylan eagerly agreed to speak at Liberty Hall. But Garvey's star had begun to fall. In 1925 his case came before the Supreme Court and he lost. When he was handcuffed and brought to an Atlanta prison, Harlem residents mourned a fallen champion.

In 1927 President Coolidge pardoned Garvey and deported him to Jamaica. Back home he tried to revive his flagging crusade, but his efforts were stalled by the Great Depression. As savings and jobs dried up for his supporters, he moved to London where he lectured and remained hopeful.[6]

But Garvey mostly found indifference. In 1934 he wrote, "It would have seemed almost impossible for such a movement to wane, but the unexpected happened. The movement did wane. . . ." Worse was ahead. The next year, when Mussolini's Fascist armies invaded Ethiopia, Garvey's criticism of emperor Haile Selassie alienated many. In 1940, as Nazi armies smashed Belgium, Holland, and France and stood poised to enter Paris, Garvey died in obscurity at his London home. He was fifty-two.

Garvey failed to raise the economic level of his people or to free Africa. But his efforts had restored hope and dignity to millions. His wisdom, ringing oratory, and his educational messages struck off the mental shackles whites imposed on his people.

Garvey's world movement educated people about their own innate beauty and past glories. Once his followers uncovered their true heritage, he reasoned, they would strengthen their families, solve their problems, build communities, and be able to triumph over their foes. His crusade had not made anyone richer, but it had better prepared his people for the future.

Garvey cast a spell over generations. He was, said Dr. Martin Luther King Jr., the first of his race to give his people "a sense of dignity and destiny." In the 1960s Malcolm X told his enthusiastic young followers, "You know that Garvey is alive!"

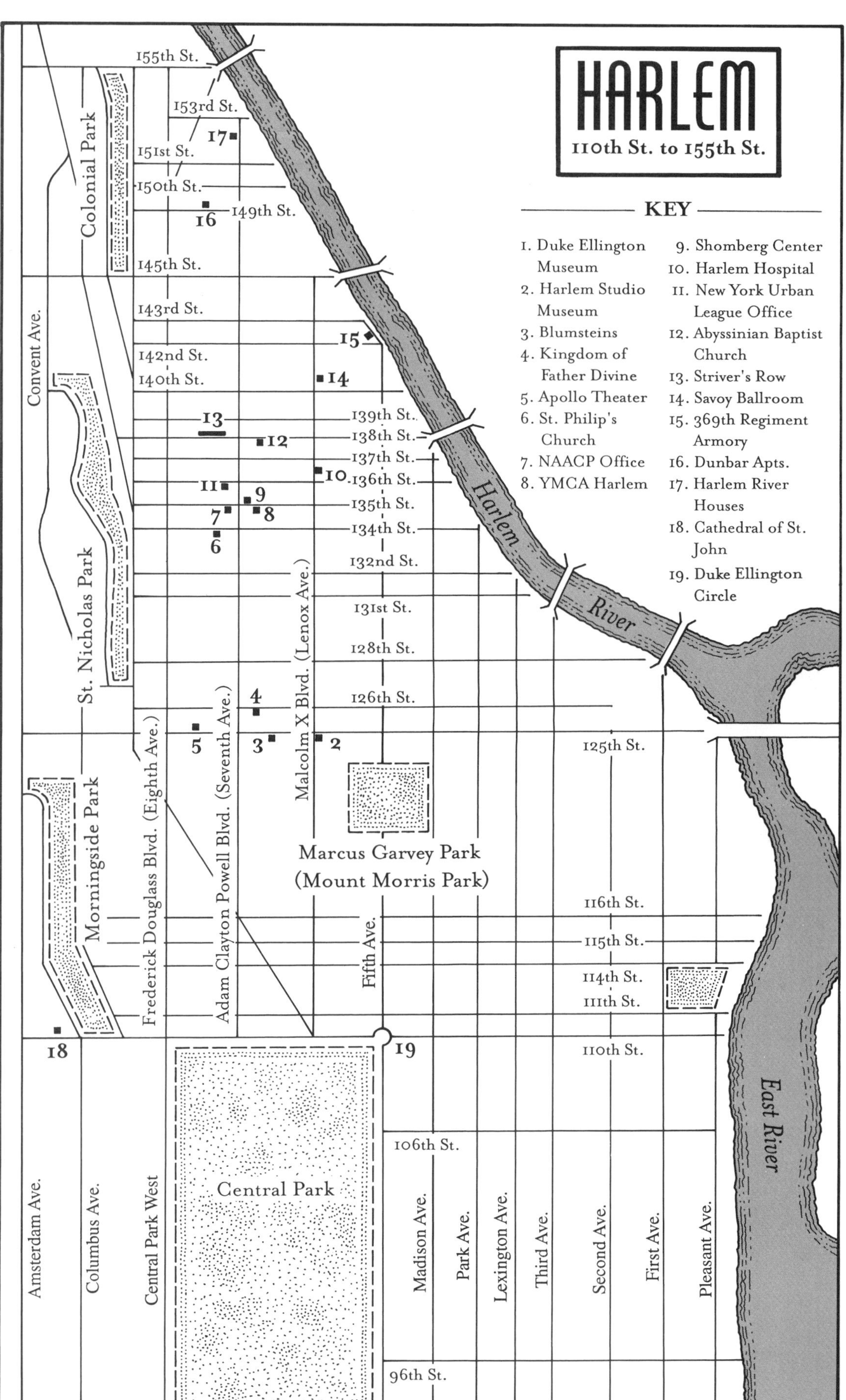

HARLEM
110th St. to 155th St.
KEY
1. Duke Ellington Museum
2. Harlem Studio Museum
3. Blumsteins
4. Kingdom of Father Divine
5. Apollo Theater
6. St. Philip's Church
7. NAACP Office
8. YMCA Harlem
9. Shomberg Center
10. Harlem Hospital
11. New York Urban League Office
12. Abyssinian Baptist Church
13. Striver's Row
14. Savoy Ballroom
15. 369th Regiment Armory
16. Dunbar Apts.
17. Harlem River Houses
18. Cathedral of St. John
19. Duke Ellington Circle
155th St.
153rd St.
151st St.
150th St.
149th St.
145th St.
143rd St.
142nd St.
140th St.
139th St.
138th St.
137th St.
136th St.
135th St.
134th St.
132nd St.
131st St.
128th St.
126th St.
125th St.
116th St.
115th St.
114th St.
111th St.
110th St.
106th St.
96th St.
Colonial Park
Convent Ave.
St. Nicholas Park
Morningside Park
Frederick Douglass Blvd. (Eighth Ave.)
Adam Clayton Powell Blvd. (Seventh Ave.)
Malcolm X Blvd. (Lenox Ave.)
Fifth Ave.
Marcus Garvey Park
(Mount Morris Park)
Harlem River
East River
Central Park
Amsterdam Ave.
Columbus Ave.
Central Park West
Madison Ave.
Park Ave.
Lexington Ave.
Third Ave.
Second Ave.
First Ave.
Pleasant Ave.

CHAPTER TWELVE

A CULTURAL RENAISSANCE

For more than a decade beginning in the early 1920s, Harlem experienced a cultural flowering that gave birth to novels, plays, poems, paintings, sculptures, and musical compositions. This "Harlem Renaissance" celebrated Africa's contribution to the world and to the Americas. In a world that taught that white was better than Black, it sang the praises of blackness. One leading participant, writer Arna Bontemps, said the Harlem Renaissance gave Black artists an understanding of how to become better poets, painters, or singers.

Long before Garvey arrived from Jamaica, Black scholars had begun to rescue a glorious African past from white neglect and slanders. Many were inspired by W. E. B. Du Bois's scholarly work; others were by Dr. Carter G. Woodson, a Harvard graduate, who in 1915 began the Association for the Study of Negro Life and History. The next year in the pages of his *Journal of Negro History,* he invited a host of scholars to research and write about a maligned or little-known heritage.

Dr. Carter G. Woodson, father of modern African American history.

The shepherd of the Harlem Renaissance was sociologist Charles S. Johnson, editor of the Urban League's *Opportunity.* With the path to voting and education for his people blocked, he opened roads to publishers, art galleries, and concert stages. Poems, plays, books, sculptures, and paintings, he reasoned, might serve his people as a cultural polling booth for equality.

Johnson's *Opportunity,* founded in 1923, raised thousands of dollars in literary prizes for the talented, and he rounded up white sponsors who would help pay their rent. By the late 1920s he was a cultural senior statesman for his people.

As James Weldon Johnson looks on, singer Roland Hayes receives the praise of noted conductor Walter Damrosh.

James Weldon Johnson, no relation, was another leading force in this Black awakening. In 1900, for Lincoln's birthday, Johnson wrote the song and his brother, Rosamond, wrote the music for "Lift Every Voice and Sing," known as the "Negro National Anthem." In 1914 he'd left Florida for New York, and from his apartment at 138 West 135th Street, he carried on a career in music, drama, poetry, fiction, and history and became the first poet

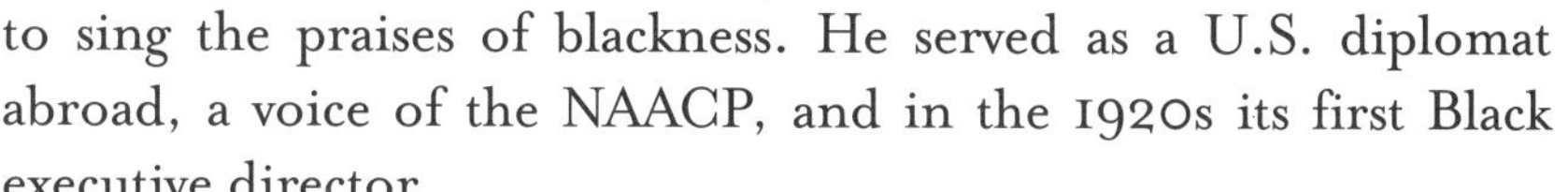

to sing the praises of blackness. He served as a U.S. diplomat abroad, a voice of the NAACP, and in the 1920s its first Black executive director.

Dr. Du Bois was vital to the new movement as his people's philosopher knight and elder statesman. Walter White, also of the NAACP, served as the movement's master of publicity, introducing deserving artists to literary agents, Broadway producers, and book publishers. Dr. Alain Locke, the first Black Rhodes scholar, edited *The New Negro,* which in 1925 served as the movement's bible and trumpet.

Charles S. Johnson, James Weldon Johnson, Du Bois, White, and Locke tried to turn the shared beauty of art and letters into a bridge of understanding between races. If artists and poets could inspire the world, they reasoned, others might see the folly of hate and discrimination. Since the five saw little else to be hopeful about, said one critic, they "promoted poetry, prose, painting, and music as if their lives depended on it." This civil rights high command, wrote poet Claude McKay, made themselves "a Ministry of Culture for Afro-America." "They thought," recalled Langston Hughes, "the race problem had at last been solved through art."[1]

The ministry was well able to gain the support of a white intellectual elite, which included sociologist Horace Kallen, educator John Dewey, and playwright Eugene O'Neill. After a word from Charles S. Johnson, Walter White, or James Weldon Johnson, an unknown author would receive a phone call saying a major publisher was ready to read her or his manuscript.

The banker of the Harlem Renaissance was Julius Rosenwald, a son of Jewish immigrants. Born in Abraham Lincoln's Springfield, Illinois, house, Rosenwald was the millionaire owner of Sears Roebuck. But his great passion was Black education, and from 1917 to 1924 he gave four million dollars to finance 5,000 Southern elementary schools, 195 teachers' homes, 103 workshops, and 5 industrial high schools. Rosenwald's cash awards for artists and writers provided wings for the creative to fly.

Some experts trace this enormous cultural flowering to an earlier time and a music called jazz and give the birthing credit to Jim Europe. In 1918, Europe and a two-hundred-piece orchestra boarded a chartered train with dancers Vernon and Irene Castle to tour thirty-two U.S. cities. This trip announced "the jazz age." Another legendary jazz figure who arrived in the city that year was W. C. Handy, the father of the blues. He came to New York City to make a record and stayed on at the fancy section known as Strivers' Row between Seventh and Eighth avenues and 138th and 139th streets, near dancer Bill Robinson, composer Eubie Blake, and record promoter Harry Pace.

Europe and Handy were only a few of the musicians seeking to turn New York into a jazz center rivaling New Orleans and Chicago. Black jazzmen blew forth at Harlem's Crescent and Lincoln Theaters between Fifth and Lenox on 135th Street or Seventh Avenue's Lafayette and Alhambra Theaters.

In 1920 vocalist Mamie Smith sang "Crazy Blues" into Okeh's New York recording equipment, and this first recorded blues number sold a million copies in six months. A blues craze soon made millions of dollars, mostly for white companies that sold recordings to the public as "race records."

Many staid sponsors of the Harlem Renaissance refused to take jazz seriously. Its first champions were Europeans—a Belgian critic, Robert Goffin, and French critic Hugues Pennassie, whose books extolled jazz as a dazzling spontaneous art. But highbrows of both races in the United States condemned it as a discordant folk art based on chaotic rhythms. It also had the wrong parents: It was born in New Orleans bordellos to instrumentalists who could not read music. By 1920, however, jazz sounds had transformed urban cultural life. Jazz and blues formed the background music to the Harlem Renaissance and helped define this exciting and creative age.

Some critics traced the Harlem Renaissance's origins to World War I Broadway plays. In 1917 three different dramas with African Americans opened at the Garden Theater to critical acclaim. Black shows captivated Broadway throughout the twenties. Eugene O'Neill's *Emperor Jones,* starring Black actors, began a four-year run in 1920. The next year Eubie Blake's sparkling musical *Shuffle Along* left audiences singing "I'm Just Wild About Harry." In 1922 Paul Robeson, a football star turned baritone, stepped onto the stage as an actor. The next year Roland Hayes sang in Town Hall and then gave sixty-eight concerts in fifty-four other cities. By then African American performers had won Broadway's heart.

The earliest jazz records in 1917 featured not the Black New Orleans musicians who created it but a white "Original Dixieland Jazz Band," who recorded for a white company. Saying whites "were not recording the voices of Negro singers and musicians," in 1921 Harry H. Pace started his Black Swan Phonograph Company with financial aid from Dr. Du Bois and other Black investors. His recording operation began in his basement on 138th Street. Ethel Waters became Black Swan's first recording artist, and in six months her first disc sold half a million copies.

Pace began to issue a new Waters disc each month, and she went on to make 259 other recordings. When Black Swan records were selling seven thousand a day, Pace opened a big plant in Long Island City. Then in 1923, a new invention, radio, made its appearance, and that, Pace noted sadly, "spelled doom for us." By then Columbia, Victor, and other major companies recorded Black jazz and blues artists on their "race records."[2]

New York began to make jazz history. In 1923 blues star Bessie Smith came to New York to make her first record—"Gulf Coast Blues" and "Downhearted Blues"—at Columbia's studio on Columbus Circle. She stayed in Harlem, and over the next eight years, she returned to create the most important collection of blues recordings ever made.

In 1924 Louis Armstrong joined Fletcher Henderson's New York band and recorded his first dynamic and unique cornet solos. In 1927 Armstrong's New Orleans mentor, Joe "King" Oliver, turned down a Cotton Club date. Instead, the management hired a young pianist, Edward "Duke" Ellington, twenty-seven, and his ten-piece band. They stayed for six years, and he became a musical legend.

In 1928 the lindy hop, which would dominate social dancing for a generation, was introduced at the Manhattan Casino. When top jazzmen began to drop in after hours so they could play until dawn at Connie's Inn, "jam sessions" were born.

The Harlem Renaissance drew young artists from all over to the city. Some were encouraged by the literary contests, and others arrived to display their talents no matter the personal price.

Oscar Micheaux left a homestead in South Dakota for Harlem, wrote a host of novels based on the Black western experience, and by 1919 had made New York the home of his Black movie company. Operating on a tiny budget and with great speed, he turned out plots for thirty movies with Black themes. Micheaux's films gave his people a first chance to see themselves on the silver screen as doctors, pioneers, lawyers, detectives, and pilots.[3] In 1924 his *Body and Soul* introduced Paul Robeson to silent screen audiences. When sound came to movies, he went bankrupt, but he managed to bounce back with talkies in the 1930s.

Filmmaker Oscar Micheaux

Bill Robinson, born in Virginia in 1878, settled in Harlem. From 1929 to 1943 his unique translations of African American folk dance styles into light, breezy tap dance steps earned him parts in ten Hollywood feature films. He also starred in independent Black films. In 1935, in *The*

Harlem's Black Jews, photographed in 1929. James VanDerZee collection.

Little Colonel, Robinson delighted movie audiences as he taught child star Shirley Temple to dance up a staircase. By then he was known as "the mayor of Harlem."

At age nineteen, in 1905, James VanDerZee, with little more than a fascination with photography, settled in Harlem. He was an elevator boy and waiter who snapped pictures when he had the time. In 1918, from his studio on 135th Street, he stood ready to capture the grandeur of the Harlem Renaissance on film. He became the official photographer for Garvey's UNIA. VanDerZee's photos reveal a vibrant community grappling with its burdens.

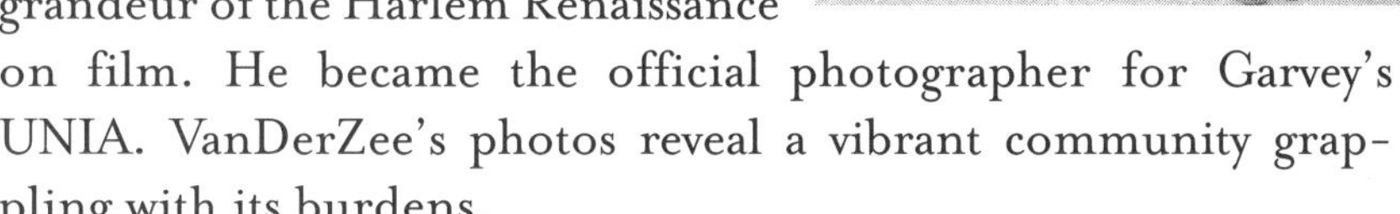

For poet Countee Cullen, New York City was home. Born in 1903, he graduated from New York public schools where he had begun to write poetry. One of a few Black students at the De Witt Clinton High School, he was vice president of its senior class and editor of its *Clinton News* and of its literary magazine. By graduation, Cullen held honors in Latin, English, history, and French, and one of his poems had earned a coveted prize. He went on to NYU, where he won one poetry prize after another, and then to Harvard University and the Sorbonne. He lived at 234 West 131st Street.[4]

Langston Hughes left Missouri to arrive in Harlem by subway on a September morning in 1921. He took a room at the Harlem YMCA on 135th Street for seven dollars a week and immediately visited the Public Library's collection of Black history and literature. He spent his first evening listening to a blues singer, perhaps Bessie Smith, at the Lincoln Theater.

When he had saved enough for a ticket, Hughes went to the Broadway musical *Shuffle Along.* After a stint at sea and in Paris, he returned to New York in 1925 to find "the Negro Renaissance was in full swing." He described its frenetic pace:

Arna Bontemps, poet and historian

> Countee Cullen was publishing his early poems, Aaron Douglass was painting, Zora Neale Hurston, Rudolph Fisher, Jean Toomer and Wallace Thurman were writing, Louis Armstrong was playing, Cora La Redd was dancing, and the Savoy Ballroom was open with a specially built floor that rocked as the dancers swayed. . . . Art took heart from Harlem creativity. Jazz filled the night air—but not everywhere—and people came from all around after dark to look upon our city within a city, Black Harlem.[5]

To writer Arna Bontemps, Harlem seemed a rare time and place for artists:

> [There] was something special about being young and a poet in Harlem in the middle twenties. We couldn't quite explain it. . . .
>
> Up and down the streets of Harlem untamed youngsters were doing a wild dance called the Charleston. They were flitting over the sidewalks like mad while their companions, squatting nearby, beat tom-tom rhythms on kitchenware. . . .
>
> Through us, no less, America would regain a certain value that civilization had destroyed.
>
> The idea intoxicated us. We went to work zealously, and some Americans saw the things we did. . . .
>
> The young intellectuals who came to Harlem in the middle twenties made a wonderful discovery. They found that it was fun to be a Negro under some conditions. Those who, like myself, had grown up in mixed or predominantly white communities even found that some segregation can be fun, when it's completely voluntary.

Countee Cullen, Langston Hughes, and Zora Neale Hurston often gathered at fellow writer Wallace Thurman's large apartment at 267 West 136th Street. Hurston mockingly named it, in honor of the assembled talent, the "Niggerati Manor."

If the Harlem Renaissance meant anything to artists and scholars, it meant a time to explore anything connected with Africa or their blackness. For the first time, an African American vanguard in music, art, dance, and writing had the financial support necessary to complete their work and reach the public.

Poet Countee Cullen

This cultural flowering was never confined to one piece of uptown Manhattan real estate, and it was too short for a Renaissance. But its torrent of talent forever changed American culture. "Our group," wrote Bontemps proudly, "came within an inch of giving America . . . at least a certain new aesthetic value."[6]

The Harlem Renaissance welcomed a host of talented African American women such as Zora Neale Hurston, a native of Eatonville, Florida. She arrived in January 1925 with $1.50, knowing no one, having high hopes but no job. At Columbia University she studied anthropology with Dr. Franz Boas, and with help from a wealthy white sponsor she began to study Eatonville's folkways. In *Their Eyes Were Watching God,* she told of a young Florida woman (like herself) who loved life and was determined to succeed. Hurston went on to write a host of novels, sociological studies, and plays.[7]

Hurston was one of many Black artists who clashed with their white sponsors. Though generous and well-meaning, upper-class, educated patrons sometime looked down on the impoverished artists they helped. Poets and painters often received less money and more advice than they wanted. In 1926 Langston Hughes issued their personal declaration of independence:

> We younger Negro artists who create now intend to express our dark-skinned selves without fear or shame. If white people are pleased we are glad. If they are not, it doesn't matter. We know we are beautiful. And ugly too. . . . We build our temples for tomorrow, strong as we know how, and we stand on top of the mountain, free within ourselves.

Writer Zora Neale Hurston

The Renaissance also gave Harlem an upscale reputation that drew wealthy African Americans to its stately homes. By the early twenties, Harlem housed two-thirds of Manhattan's Black pop-

Langston Hughes meets some of his young readers.

ulation, and it was still growing.

The On to Harlem movement grew until virtually all major African American institutions had a headquarters in Harlem: fraternal orders such as Odd Fellows, Masons, Pythians, Elks; the YMCA and YWCA, NAACP, National Urban League, and Black churches. Harlem's paper, the *New York Age,* suddenly faced competition from the *Amsterdam News.* Black music schools, dance academies, acting studios, and labor unions found new homes. Night schools, reading rooms, and community centers mushroomed.

African America's poet laureate, Langston Hughes, celebrated his love for the people of his community:

The night is beautiful,
So the faces of my people.

The stars are beautiful,
So the eyes of my people.

Beautiful, also, is the sun.
Beautiful, also, are the souls of my people.

James Weldon Johnson announced that Harlem would be "the greatest Negro city in the world." It soon claimed a cosmopolitan population that included 54,753 men, women, and children who had been born in the Caribbean. Another forty-five thousand Puerto Ricans made their home in nearby East Harlem.

In 1928 *Home to Harlem* by Claude McKay became the first book by a person of color to reach the best-seller list. McKay saw Harlem as "drawing Afro-americans together into a vast humming hive." His vibrant images celebrated Harlem, but some intellectuals felt *Home to Harlem* was a humiliation because it had so many disreputable characters and ugly scenes. After reading it, Du Bois said, "I feel distinctly like taking a bath."

Claude McKay, poet and novelist

For European tourists and wealthy whites from downtown, northern Manhattan became the place to visit at night. The curious took the subway uptown to see those who created jazz and the blues. Whites were drawn to Harlem for different reasons: Some were in personal rebellion against a dull, complacent life and wanted to explore an exotic nightlife. Some sought to break through society's constraints and saw Black artists as voices for freedom. To writers such as Sinclair Lewis, Eugene O'Neill, and Theodore Dreiser, who warned of the emptiness of white middle-class life, Harlem represented freshness and diversity.

But mostly for whites, Harlem was an escape valve. Wealthy visitors sometimes referred to their visits as "slumming." They traveled uptown knowing they could loosen their ties and collars. Those who feared to "strut their stuff" watched others glide and swirl on the glistening dance floors.

Harlem's fanciest nightclubs featured scantily clad, light-skinned dancers—and catered only to whites. From 1923 to 1929, Black people could not enter the Cotton Club at 644 Lenox Avenue. W. C. Handy was turned away from the door as whites danced to his blues tunes. Connie's Inn at Seventh Avenue and 131st Street long maintained a "whites only" policy.

White money was welcomed in the community, but some residents feared it would elbow aside their intellectuals and corrupt their artists. "Harlem," insisted Claude McKay, "is an all-white picnic ground with no apparent gain to the blacks." Many residents agreed with the poet.

But at least the doors to Small's Paradise at Seventh Avenue and 135th Street was open to all who wanted to enjoy its waiters on roller skates. And Leroy's at 2250 Seventh Avenue had a policy that barred *white* patrons.[8]

Harlem's cultural heroes attended the exciting, lavish parties at 80 Edgecomb Avenue, the regal home of the millionaire heiress A'Leila Walker Robinson. Unknown poets, novelists, and per-

Bessie Smith

formers mixed with the well-known Langston Hughes, Eugene O'Neill, Paul Robeson, white royalty, and stock exchange executives. The parties made the newspapers, but the hostess spent her money on food and decor, not on struggling creative artists.

Singer Bessie Smith tried to bring her community to its racial senses. For a scheduled appearance at the Apollo, the singer arrived with her own chorus line—stocky, dark-skinned women called Ma Raineys in honor of the legendary entertainer who first trained her to sing the blues.

The Apollo's white owners insisted Smith drop the Ma Raineys. Their policy was to hire only light-skinned dancers. Smith glared. "If you don't want my girls, you don't want me." She performed with her Ma Raineys. The singer's victory spread through Harlem, and crowds filled each performance. "You never saw people give applause like they did for us girls—we broke it up," one of the Ma Raineys later remembered. For two years Bessie Smith and her chorus performed in Harlem and in other New York nightclubs.[9]

In 1926 residents of Harlem welcomed the Savoy Ballroom, which opened its doors and stretched along Lenox Avenue from 140th to 141st streets. It boasted a huge lobby, a marble staircase, a blue-and-orange dance hall with two bandstands, and a 250 by 50 foot dance floor made to accommodate four thousand at a time. It drew no racial lines. On opening night, Fletcher Henderson's band received a standing ovation and ended the evening with a soaring finale. Each night hot jazz, happy hearts, and dancing feet celebrated the Savoy's conquest of Harlem.

But the Harlem community's greatest source of pride was the Branch Public Library on 135th Street near Lenox Avenue. It offered a huge collection of African American books, making it Harlem's nerve center and intellectual heartbeat. The collection was formally started in May 1925 with a special dedication ceremony attended by its founder, Puerto Rican–born bibliographer and writer, Arthur A. Schomburg.[10]

Supervised by librarian Ernestine Rose, the Branch featured

lectures by such leading scholars as W. E. B. Du Bois, Carter G. Woodson, and anthropologists Franz Boas and Melville J. Herskovits. Its educational forums, poetry readings, and literary activities drew enthusiastic crowds. Sometimes heated arguments stretched into the night and spilled out onto Lenox Avenue as the building closed.

The collection, to be named after Schomburg in 1938, was a fine, lasting, and profound example of the cultural revolution that gripped Harlem in the 1920s. The Harlem Renaissance provoked laughter, dancing, and literary parties. But it unrelentingly powered an interest in education for young and old. In 1917 only 2,132 African Americans attended college. In 1927 the figure stood at 13,580, including 105 Phi Beta Kappas, and 39 people of color earned doctorates at various universities.

In the short span of a single decade, Harlem had spawned a cultural output that included twenty-six novels, ten volumes of poetry, five Broadway plays, hundreds of essays and short stories, three ballets and concerts, and untold paintings, sketches, and sculptures. This flowed from residents who still remembered that in slavery days their kinfolk had been denied the right to read a book, write a sentence, or sit in a schoolroom.

A media revolution largely centered in New York City in the 1920s gave the Harlem Renaissance a global audience. Black faces might be stopped at the door but recordings and radio sent Black music and voices soaring over mountains and oceans. Paul Whiteman had called himself "the King of Jazz," but the public began to learn about Black jazz artists and blues singers. Talented men and women in Harlem touched white artists, musicians, dancers, composers, writers and entertainers.

As New York became a world entertainment capitol of staggering power, U.S. culture was both integrated and transformed by the Harlem Renaissance. Black men and women changed creative expression into something less European and more African, and a new media scattered its seeds everywhere.

In 1930 James Weldon Johnson looked at his community's future and saw "greater and greater things." But hard times were about to bring down the curtain on Harlem's moment in the sun.

CHAPTER THIRTEEN

HARD TIMES HIT NEW YORK

By the end of the 1920s, Harlem was economically doomed. The community's nightclubs sparkled brightly for tourists on weekends, but residents were no richer on Monday morning. Harlem was a colony owned by absentee white landlords who controlled 80 percent of its businesses, buildings, and profit-making establishments and left a fifth of small businesses to local owners. Local loan sharks feasted on community needs and misery.

Few white entrepreneurs in Harlem employed people of color, and those who did consigned them to menial positions. Local residents did not control the community's finances. Harlem's A & P chain had twenty-four branches and hired nine people of color—as errand boys. Thirteen United Cigar stores branches hired no people of color. Undertaking, Harlem's most profitable business, remained in local hands only because whites were unwilling to do it. The largest store, Blumstein's, refused to hire Black elevator operators until forced by community protests, then hired a token few. Another store, Koch's, closed rather than integrate its staff. The money made in Harlem by whites was carted off to suburbia.

Langston Hughes described a community that could not stand on its own economic feet:

> It was not even an area that ran itself. The famous night clubs were owned by whites, as were the theaters. Almost all the stores were owned by whites, and many at the time did not even (in the very middle of Harlem) employ Negro clerks. The books of Harlem writers all had to be published downtown, if they were to be pub-

lished at all. Downtown: *white.* Uptown: *black.* White downtown pulling all the strings in Harlem. . . . Negroes could not even play their own numbers with their own people. And almost all the policemen in Harlem were white. Negroes couldn't even get graft from themselves for themselves by themselves. Black Harlem really was in white face, economically speaking. So I wrote this poem:

Because my mouth
Is wide with laughter,
And my throat is deep with song,
You do not think
I suffer after
I have held my pain
So long?

Because my mouth
Is wide with laughter
You do not hear
My inner cry?
Because my feet
Are gay with dancing
You do not know
I die?[1]

Even worse for local people, some of Harlem's most lucrative enterprises were owned by Mafia bosses. During this era of Prohibition, they owned its nightclubs and 90 percent of its vice, gambling, and prostitution rackets.

The Harlem that whites visited at night may have sparkled like a star, but as Langston Hughes pointed out, it was a hard place to make a decent living or find a job. Harlem's wages were lower, rents higher, and jobs fewer. "I could not eat the poems I wrote," Hughes recalled. Most residents who had jobs took the subway down to the white world of Midtown Manhattan.

Economic desperation led to novel and creative solutions. Apartment tenants, to meet monthly rent payments, held "rent parties." For a twenty-five-cent admission, a host offered danc-

P.S. 89 on 135th Street and Lenox Avenue as students leave at dismissal.

ing, food, and drink beginning around midnight. Parties featured Southern-style delicacies such as black-eyed peas with rice and bacon, chitterlings, and pig snouts. Music was usually provided by a lone piano virtuoso. In an effort to make up for other instruments, these pianists developed a "stride" style, or "boogie-woogie." Two hands kept the rhythm and created the melody and feel of a full-blown jazz band. Some white tourists, bored with the fancy exterior Harlem had painted especially for them, began to turn up at these authentic parties of the poor.

To seek their pleasure, residents also visited their own speakeasies—small, crowded nightclubs bearing exotic names such as Glory Hole, Air Raid Shelter, Blue Room, and Basement Brownie's Coal Bed. White visitors, seeking the "real Harlem experience," also learned to seek out these tiny clubs.

Most residents agreed that the community disgrace was an antiquated, run-down public school system. It had old buildings, crowded classes, and too many overage pupils. Schools were built to fail. Pupils did not graduate with many skills or much hope. Few were instructed in more than the basics of reading, writing, and math. Students who showed signs of slow learning were assigned to classes for the mentally retarded. A city agency that investigated this classification found individual pupils suffering from a sense of "subordination, of insecurity, of lack of self-confidence and self-respect."

Some of the community's greatest cultural heroes got discouraged and left for Paris. But even these, like Langston Hughes, came back after a while. "Harlem was like a great magnet for the Negro intellectual, pulling him from everywhere," he wrote.

In 1929 the New York stock market crashed and triggered a global depression. Banks and businesses closed, and people lost their savings and jobs. Unemployed men and women lined up before outdoor charity kitchens for warm soup and a crust of bread. Charities handed out milk to mothers with babies and children. In Harlem the Great Depression completed the long process that had been grinding a proud community into a slum.

By 1935 half of Harlem's families received city relief. Fifty percent of these relief recipients were families that included a husband, wife, and their children, a higher family rate than other cities. About a fourth of relief families were headed by women.

As the last hired and the first fired, African Americans lost their jobs faster than other New Yorkers. Few had savings accounts to fall back on. When rehiring took place, people of color stood last in line. For African Americans during the economic decline, hardship was no stranger requiring a great deal of adjustment: It was an old and familiar neighbor.

To support their families before the hard times, 60 percent of Black women worked—four times higher than the percentage of white women. With mounting joblessness, whites who asked people of color to clean their homes stopped hiring. Housework rates, always low, fell sharply.[2]

In the quarter of a century that ended in 1932, Harlem's population had increased more than 600 percent to about

350,000. Its density per block was almost double the rest of Manhattan. A study by scholar E. Franklin Frazier found a sharp decline in Harlem income. Median earnings of skilled workers fell by half, from $1,995 in 1929 to $1,003 in 1932. Semiskilled and unskilled laborers suffered a 43 percent fall in wages. Black white-collar workers and professionals lived with a 35 percent decline, proprietors 44 percent, and clerical workers 37 percent. Some Harlem doctors had to seek relief. As elsewhere in American cities, men and women joined cats and dogs in foraging for food, sometimes in piles of garbage.

By 1935 living conditions for Harlem's poor were dismal. They lived on wages that were 46 percent lower than the white poor. A mayor's commission investigation discovered that more than ten thousand people of color lived in dank basement apartments or in dirty cellars with water leaks but without running water. People used packing boxes for furniture and had slits for windows.

Winter winds and cold brought a special misery to homes that were not adequately heated. Flush toilets in many apartment buildings did not work, and janitors had to guard coal deliveries from thieves. Families helped pay landlords by renting "hot beds" to lodgers in eight-hour shifts. In 1936 Charlie Green, Bessie Smith's favorite trombonist, was found frozen to death on the steps of a Harlem tenement.

In Harlem during the hard times, rents devoured 50 percent of wages while rents for whites downtown took only 25 percent of salaries. A Langston Hughes rhyme voiced this heartache:

I wish the rent
Was Heaven sent.[3]

Hard times generated other problems. TB, sexual diseases, and death rates, usually double the white average, rose even faster among African Americans than whites during the Great Depression. Harlem Hospital had a mortality rate of 11.2 percent compared to a downtown hospital, Bellevue, which had a 5.7 percent rate. Juvenile arrests of African Americans rose from 12 percent of the city total in 1930 to 25 percent in 1938.

Racial hiring policies practiced by New York companies further depressed living standards. The New York Gas Company announced: "We do not assign Negroes as stenographers, clerks or inspectors." The telephone company stated it did not "employ such persons" except as menials.

Bigoted union officials aggravated hiring problems. In 1936 twenty-four city international unions excluded African American members. Of sixteen New York unions that responded to a questionnaire, thirteen admitted imposing racial bars. African American nurses and doctors were denied training at white hospitals and could not join white professional organizations. In Harlem Hospital, seven of fifty-seven staff doctors were African Americans.

In 1927, a Black policeman at 135th Street and Lenox Avenue.

The Great Depression sent Harlem nightclubs downtown in pursuit of their white customers. Connie's Inn moved from 131st and Seventh Avenue to 48th Street near Broadway and soon became known as the Latin Quarter. On 52nd Street other jazz clubs blossomed, the first being the Famous Door in 1935. These clubs soon heard newer Black voices such as Billie Holiday.

Adding to Black New York's economic distress during the massive joblessness, city relief was not equally distributed. In 1936, though people of color formed 21 percent of the city's relief rolls, the Home Relief Bureau gave them only 9 percent of work relief jobs. The bureau paid recipients eight cents a meal for food. For a male over sixteen, a two-week welfare allotment for food was $3.30 in 1934, $3.55 in 1935, and $4.15 in 1936. It was not nearly enough to feed, clothe, and house a family.

With little work and less hope, it was hard to get up in the morning and search for jobs. It took an act of courage to dress, put on a good face, and pursue slim possibilities. On Jerome Avenue and 167th Street in the Bronx, jobless Black women congregated at eight in the morning hoping to be chosen as a housecleaner for a white housewife with some pennies to spare,

Early 1930s protest in Harlem.

and some stayed past noon hoping for a job.

Naomi Ward, a widow of forty with a daughter to support, recalled her household job: "Our wages are pitifully small. I doubt if wages for domestics average higher anywhere than in New York City; and here $45 a month is good for a 'refined woman, good cook, and fond of children.'"

As they struggled to survive the hard times, African Americans tried to preserve their neighborhoods and protect their children. Loften Mitchell remembered the neighborhood of his youth being "crowded with togetherness, love, human warmth, and neighborliness."

> In this climate everyone knew everyone else. A youngster's misbehavior in any house earned him a beating there plus one when he got home. . . .
>
> The child of Harlem had the will to survive, to "make it". . . . This Harlem child learned to laugh in the face of adversity, to cry in the midst of plentifulness, to fight quickly and reconcile easily. . . . From his African, Southern Negro and West Indian heritage, he knew the value of gregariousness and he held group consultations on the street corners to review problems of race, economics, or politics.
>
> He was poor, but proud. He hid his impoverishment with clothes, pseudo–good living, or sheer laughter. Though he complained of being broke, he never admitted his family was poor. . . .
>
> I know it. I felt it. We had a will to survive, for bloody street fighting bruised our bodies and a sadistic school system attempted to destroy our hearts and minds.[4]

In the 150-block area of Harlem, 140 religious institutions with seventy thousand congregants and ninety million dollars in property investments opened their doors to take care of the needy. They fed people for a few pennies and sometimes for free. Hard times also had opened the community to dozens of "faith healers," medicine men and religious quacks who preyed on the sorry, the demoralized, and the disheartened.

At the outset of the depression, Reverend Adam Clayton Powell Sr., of the Abyssinian Baptist Church on West 138th Street, was the community's most powerful voice. Attorney Paul Zuber credited him "with getting more Negroes jobs with the city than any other man alive or dead."

In 1933 Reverend Adam Clayton Powell Jr. succeeded his father. Under his pastorage, the church increasingly pursued an activist course against the hard times. In 1936 James Yates from Chicago heard young Powell preach a sermon:

> Is it right, in the eyes of God, for white people to own stores in our own community, and not employ a single one of our young people as clerks? Is it right, in the eyes of God, for white people to come to Harlem, to swarm all over Harlem, seeking to amuse themselves in clubs that slammed their doors upon Black faces? Is it right that we don't have jobs, are barred from the city's hotels, are denied the best in medical facilities? . . .
>
> Maybe Blacks should organize picket lines before the clubs and hospitals and hotels that won't admit them. . . .
>
> We're not going to the river and lay our burdens down. We're going to look upon our shoulders and dump the burdensome white man off our backs.[5]

Father Divine and some of his flock.

Perhaps the most unusual Harlem-inspired cleric of the Great Depression was George Baker, who arrived from Savannah, Georgia. He called himself "God" or Father Divine, his wife Mother Divine, and their storefront mission chapels "kingdoms." Parishioners were called "angels."

Divine's kingdoms earned a reputation for feeding generous meals to the starving for only pennies. By 1935 Father Divine had enrolled a large interracial congregation, including many white women. His headquarters was at 455 Lenox Avenue, and his membership soared to an impressive half a million nationally. Father Divine said it stood at two million.[6]

"God" and his "angels" raised enough money to purchase fifteen "divine kingdom" buildings in New York City alone. Others sprouted in Jamaica, Brooklyn, White Plains, New Jersey, Connecticut, Washington, D.C., and in Seattle, Washington. With faith, effort, and cash, members published a paper, *The New Day,* in seven languages. In 1935 Harlem novelist Claude McKay described Father Divine's potent magnetism:

> Father Divine is God! With that one phrase Father Divine stands out above all other leaders and their cults. God, who was invisible to all before, is now personified in Him. He has created "Kingdoms" of Heaven in Harlem and elsewhere. "He is sweet, so sweet," chant his "angel" followers, "God, so sweet, Father Divine." According to them Father Divine is the source of all things. He gives his angels work, health, food, happiness, prosperity—everything. Accepting nothing, he gives all, being God.

Americans fought against the hard times in a variety of ways. Many joined industrial unions that in 1935 formed the Congress of Industrial Organizations (CIO). Others that year followed A. Philip Randolph, who convened Harlem's first Negro Labor Conference and called for solidarity between all workers, an end to child labor, and a thirty-hour work week. Across the country, people took direct action. Across lines of race, men and women entered markets and seized food for their starving families.

In Harlem, Father Divine and his flock, armed with a worldly outlook, sallied into the protest politics of the day. His Peace Mission demanded freedom for all and an end to "the mistreatment of the Jews in Germany and all other countries." His "angels" joined picket lines, and he said he was "always willing to cooperate with Communists or any group that was fighting for international peace."

Activist Salaria Kee served as a nurse in the Abraham Lincoln Brigade in Spain.

One teenager launched a direct challenge to segregation in Harlem. In 1933 Salaria Kee, a nurse at Harlem Hospital on 135th Street, was appalled by conditions of overcrowding and understaffing. She watched helplessly as ill people were turned away for lack of beds and patients died from lack of adequate care.

As an obstetric nurse, Kee was placed in charge of the hospital's maternity-nursery unit. She had no staff for fifty babies. Unable to change that, she challenged segregation in the hospital cafeteria. One day Kee and five young nurses took seats at a dining table "reserved for whites only." When they were refused service, Kee later wrote, the six "rose quickly, caught up the corners of the tablecloth, threw it and everything on it to the floor. Everyone in the dining room was upset. We demanded to see the Superintendent of Nurses. She arrived shortly, much excited."

Kee gained support from the doctors and carried her campaign into that year's mayoral contest. When the mayor opened an investigation, Kee wrote, segregation "was abolished in one day." Her social activism had just begun.[7]

For W. E. B. Du Bois, the hard times required new approaches. In 1934, in the *Crisis,* Dr. Du Bois, an ardent integrationist, urged a "voluntary segregation" so African Americans could pool their economic resources. "I am not worried about being inconsistent," said Du Bois. "What worries me is the truth. I am talking about conditions in 1934 and not 1910." As a result, Du Bois lost his post at the pro-integrationist NAACP.

Du Bois's dissent was only part of a political ferment that questioned past wisdom. In April 1935 Langston Hughes spoke to four thousand at the first American Writers Congress in New York. In words only Marxists used, he called for unity among "blacks and whites in our country . . . on the solid ground of the

Roy Wilkins (left) and others in New York in 1934 demanded an anti-lynching law.

daily working class struggle to wipe out, now and forever, all the old inequalities of the past." Hughes was elected president of a pro-Communist League of Struggle for Negro Rights.

That year, teacher Williana Burroughs, writing in the *Unemployed Teacher,* attacked the New Deal program of reforms advocated by President Franklin D. Roosevelt and "Rich New York" for denying a decent education to Black pupils.

> Surveys here disclose old unsanitary buildings, firetraps in some cases, overcrowded classes, few up-to-date laboratories or workshops, swimming pools or playgrounds. . . . No nursery schools have been placed by the N.R.A. management in Negro Harlem, and teachers in such a school in Spanish Harlem were instructed not to admit dark Puerto Ricans.

In March 1935 Harlem exploded in a violent protest. A Black high school student, Lino Rivera, was arrested for stealing a ten-cent pocketknife at a Kress store on 125th Street. False rumors spread that police had beaten Rivera to death. In a few hours ten thousand angry residents, reacting to a long record of police brutality, rampaged through the streets, particularly the main shopping area on 125th Street.[8]

Claude McKay wrote, "The crowds went crazy like the remnants of a defeated, abandoned, and hungry army." Looting of white-owned stores was "brazen and daring," he wrote, but whites on the street were not molested.

By night an overwhelming police presence arrived in Harlem: five hundred uniformed officers, two hundred in plainclothes, and mounted police. Officers in fifty police cars drove onto sidewalks, and officers mounted on horses charged into street crowds. But roaming mobs grew in size and determination. A white Merchants' Association demanded Governor Herbert Lehman send the National Guard, but he refused.

When the smoke on 125th Street had cleared, two hundred stores had been destroyed and property losses stood at two million dollars. Three African Americans had been slain, thirty more hospitalized, and a hundred had been arrested.

Claude McKay saw the riot as arising from urban desperation aggravated by the Depression: "A considerable part of the population can no longer cling even to the hand-to-mouth-margin." Reverend Powell Jr. termed the mayhem "an open, unorganized protest against empty stomachs, overcrowded tenements, filthy sanitation, rotten foodstuffs, chiseling landlords and merchants, discrimination in relief, disfranchisement, and against a disinterested administration."

E. Franklin Frazier, sociologist and historian

Mayor La Guardia named a study commission led by Black sociologist E. Franklin Frazier. Its hearings on Saturday afternoons on 151st Street drew intense crowds ready to testify. An eyewitness described the scene:

> Often emotional and incoherent, some timid and reticent, some noisy and inarticulate, but all with burning resentment,

they registered their complaints against the discriminations, the Jim-Crowism, and all the forms of oppression to which they had been subjected.

Mayor La Guardia suppressed his commission's report as inflammatory because it included so many grievances by residents. The *Amsterdam News* published the text of the report and added this note:

> While one, in view of the available facts, would hesitate to give Communists full credit for preventing the outbreak from becoming a race riot, they deserve more credit than any other element in Harlem for preventing a physical conflict between whites and Negroes.

The uprising in Harlem was only one part of a massive political change gripping African Americans. After decades of voting solidly Republican, people of color in Harlem were switching to the Democratic party. Though they appreciated the Communist effort, they voted overwhelmingly for President Franklin D. Roosevelt. They saw him as a friend and his New Deal programs as helpful to all Americans. And many identified with his wife, Eleanor, who befriended African Americans and openly opposed racism.

Eleanor Roosevelt visits an orphan home in Riverdale, New York.

The Communist Party also vied for Black support by demanding federal unemployment insurance and an end to segregation. Communists helped those who were dispossessed for not paying their rent to move back into their apartments.

In 1931 the party attracted attention by its spirited defense

"Scottsboro Boys" mothers prepare to march in a 1930s' New York City May Day parade.

of nine innocent Black youths jailed in Scottsboro, Alabama, for the rape of two white women. Even when one of the women admitted the charge was a lie, the youths were not released. Vaughn Love, who arrived in Harlem from Ohio three years earlier, was one of seventy-four Black Communist Party members in 1932. Though inexperienced, he told how "we would organize until finally all of Harlem was out there on the Scottsboro case." The NAACP joined the legal defense of the nine, but the last Scottsboro defendant was not released until 1950.

Love became a member of the League of Struggle for Negro Rights and then joined the Convulsionaries, a popular interracial vaudeville troupe that blended political humor and satire. Years later he said, "Harlem gave me a certain outlook. I was through with the system. I knew it didn't work, and I was thinking in terms of changing society—to change the world."

In 1932 the Communists chose New Yorker James Ford as the party's vice-presidential candidate, the first time in the century a Black had been selected to run for the second highest office. In 1936 Ford was again nominated, and the Communist platform included a special appeal to people of color: "The Negro people suffer doubly. Most exploited of working people, they are also victims of Jim-crowism and lynching. They are denied the right to live as human beings."

Love began to enjoy his work: "We could get things done. We could have a meeting and have thousands of people." During Ford's campaign, Audley "Queen Mother" Moore joined the Communist Party, two years later she was its candidate for state assembly, and in 1940 she ran for city council. By 1942 she was chosen as secretary of the New York State party.

The Communists championed the slogan "black and white, unite and fight," but laborers achieved little unity because of union discrimination. The Communists failed on other counts. Their idealization of Stalin and the USSR meant little to most people of color. Some who visited the USSR reported it was free of racism, but Black nationalists derided the party's love for Russia.[9]

Black union membership rose from two thousand in 1930 to six thousand in 1935. The new Congress of Industrial Organizations (CIO) called for the organization of workers regardless of color and attracted many Blacks. That year the Harlem Labor Center and the Negro Labor Committee, which began in 1933, had forty thousand Black members.

For years the leading Black union was A. Philip Randolph's Brotherhood of Sleeping Car Porters and Maids. He organized it in 1925 in an Elks hall at 160 West 129th Street with five hundred in attendance. At that time a porter's average salary was sixty-seven dollars a month plus tips. But by 1927 only half of the thirty-five hundred eligible workers had signed up, and the hard times slowed its growth.[10]

By using the Wagner Act and other New Deal laws to aid labor, the Brotherhood finally compelled the Pullman Company to accept the union as bargaining agent for its employees. For years Randolph spoke at American Federation of Labor (AFL) con-

Mayor La Guardia greets members of the Brotherhood of Sleeping Car Porters Union in the 1930s.

ventions as Black labor's voice, demanding that unions drop discriminatory policies and lead the fight for equal justice.

In this activist decade, May Day labor celebrations drew more people than Easter parades. Black ministers urged their congregations to take part in elections and to protest conditions. Reverend Lorenzo King of St. Mark's Episcopal Church expressed the new mood among clerics: "We're tired of religion that puts us to sleep. We've got to put religion to work—for us!" By 1937 Black protest began to achieve important victories. Randolph joined with Reverend Adam Clayton Powell Jr. to lead "Don't Shop Where You Can't Work" campaigns. Picket lines became commonplace in Harlem. Doctors, attorneys, and artists joined workers on picket lines.

To compel Consolidated Edison to hire people of color, Powell declared Tuesday "black-out night" and told residents to turn off their lights and use candles. His followers then organized a Bill Payers parade to the Edison offices at 32 West 125th Street to pay

Black and white New Yorkers at a May Day parade in 1937.

their bills in pennies and nickels. A mass meeting protested the company's refusal to hire qualified African Americans. Mayor La Guardia praised their bold venture and was photographed with Randolph and his Brotherhood.

Powell next led a "Don't Shop Where You Can't Work" campaign in front of large white-owned stores on 125th Street. His campaigns attracted hundreds of ordinary church members, supporters of Marcus Garvey's ideas, and radicals. By 1938 most Harlem storeowners agreed to hire at least one-third of their employees from the community. The next year, Powell focused public attention on the World's Fair in Flushing Meadows, Queens, and its failure to hire people of color. After he led picketers before the Fair's Empire State Building headquarters, hundreds of people of color were hired. Powell, by then a major political force in Harlem, had just started.

New York also was host to an important first effort to unify Black women. In December 1935 Black educator Mary McLeod Bethune, an adviser to Franklin Roosevelt and a friend to Eleanor, greeted women delegates from fourteen Black organizations at the YWCA branch on 137th Street, where they founded the National Council of Negro Women (NCNW). This was the first Black umbrella organization in the United States. One of its first official acts was to denounce Nazi Germany's anti-Semitic laws.

For two decades Bethune served as NCNW president and was a driving force in battles against discrimination in housing, employment, and advancement. During World War II, the council sold thousands of U.S. bonds and helped to launch the *Harriet Tubman* Liberty ship, the first U.S. vessel named after a woman of color. Under Dorothy Height, the council continued for more than half a century and did not end until 1992.

Ralph Ellison (1913–1994)

During the 1930s New York continued to attract young Black writers. In 1936 Langston Hughes met an aspiring young writer named Ralph Ellison at the YMCA on 135th Street and lent him some books. Hughes taught Ellison how to let others "buy you lunch," and the young man delivered manuscripts for the poet. Ellison also met writer Richard Wright and later served as the best man at his Chicago wedding.

James Yates of Mississippi also arrived in the city that year with one dollar. At a Father Divine soup kitchen, he spent fifteen cents for a large meal and still had enough to attend the Savoy Ballroom that night. Yates joined New York's Pullman Union, then found a government job laying bricks on the West Side Highway and drifted into radical protest movements.

Agitation by African Americans in New York led to an increase in appointed officials. Mayor La Guardia named one African American as a tax commissioner, two others as judges, and one as a civil service commissioner. In 1936 a Black woman was appointed a school principal, and a Black man became director of the Central Harlem Health Center. La Guardia also asked Randolph to join his commission on racial problems.

Political pressure led to community improvements. La Guardia saw that Harlem had new playgrounds, a housing project, a recreational center, a sports field, tennis courts, and a concert stadium. He saw that 435 antiquated buildings were replaced with money supplied by the federal and city government.

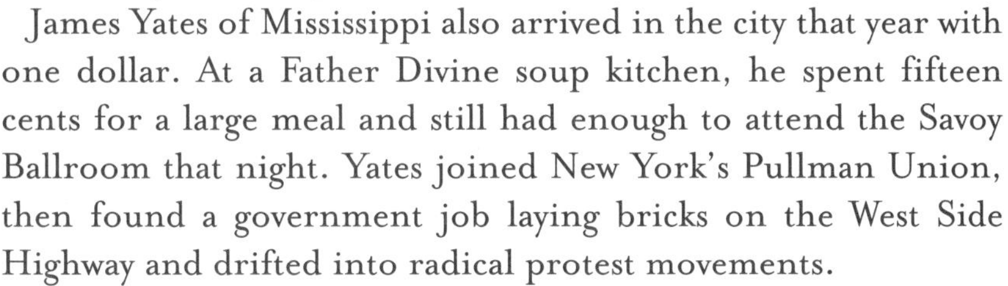

NEW YORK CITY POPULATION BY DECADES[11]

Year	Total City Population	Blacks
1900	3,437,202	60,666
1910	4,766,833	91,709
1920	5,620,048	152,467
1930	6,930,446	327,706

CHAPTER FOURTEEN

FIGHTING FOR THE DOUBLE V

In the 1930s Black New Yorkers found themselves increasingly drawn into the battle against world fascism. Hitler in Germany and Mussolini in Italy had begun the imperialist march that would end in a new world war. In 1935 Mussolini's Fascist troops invaded Ethiopia, an African nation ruled by emperor Haile Selassie. Ethiopia was the oldest kingdom in Africa, and a country many saw as an African Jerusalem destined to liberate Africans everywhere. When Mussolini's pilots boasted of bombing Ethiopia's civilians, African Americans wanted to do something. Emperor Selassie asked the League of Nations to save his nation, but no country helped.

Langston Hughes interviews Lincoln brigadier Crawford Morgan in Spain in 1937. Abraham Lincoln Brigade Archives, Brandeis University.

In spite of this, African Americans were ready to come to his aid. Efforts to recruit troops for the emperor's army led to a mobilization of a thousand in New York and another seventeen thousand in other cities. Americans who left for Ethiopia faced a loss of citizenship, a three-year prison term, and a two-thousand-dollar fine.

John Henrik Clarke, eighteen and from an Alabama sharecropping family, arrived in Harlem in 1933. In Georgia he had been a shoe-shine boy and a golf caddie for General Dwight Eisenhower. He took menial and odd

Paul Robeson entertaining the troops at University City, Madrid. Paul Robeson Archives.

jobs, living in a small room with his many books piled under the bed, and he joined Arthur A. Schomburg's Harlem History Club. He recalled:

> During Mussolini's invasion of Ethiopia we debated the issues on Lenox Avenue and Seventh Avenue. We raised money and built an Ethiopian World Federation. This gave us a Pan-African awakening we never would have had—out of our concern to save Ethiopia.

Communists, Garveyites, and others in Harlem united to form the Provisional Committee for the Defense of Ethiopia.

Activist Salaria Kee, who had organized the protest at Harlem Hospital, led a group of nurses, who raised enough money to send tons of medical supplies and a seventy-five-bed hospital to Ethiopia. Marcus Garvey's Black Legion built a training camp for three thousand volunteers in upstate New York. But there was too little time to reach the war zone. By May 1936 the small nation was overwhelmed by Mussolini's Fascist forces.[1]

That same year General Francisco Franco led an army revolt against the newly elected Republican government in Spain. Hitler's Luftwaffe flew Franco's troops to Spain from Morocco and provided air support for their march on Madrid. Mussolini sent in fifty thousand troops fresh from his Ethiopian campaign.

Spain asked the world for help, and forty thousand men and

When Joe Louis defeated Max Baer, Harlem residents celebrated.

women from fifty-three nations volunteered to try to stop Fascism's march in Spain. Harlemites Salaria Kee, Vaughn Love, James Yates, Crawford Morgan, and others were among ninety African Americans who went to Spain. "It ain't Ethiopia," one said, "but it'll have to do!" Eventually twenty-eight hundred Americans formed the Abraham Lincoln Brigade.

Black churches and societies raised money, collected medical supplies, and sponsored rallies for the Spanish Republic. Harlem's Musician's Committee for Spanish Democracy, which included W. C. Handy, Fats Waller, and Cab Calloway, held benefit concerts. Paul Robeson left his home in New York City to sing for the international brigades. James Baldwin was twelve and a public-school pupil when his first published short story appeared, and it was about Spain's battle for democracy. Dr. Arnold Donowa, Harvard graduate, former dean at Howard University, and a Harlem Hospital dental authority on facial wounds, established two hospitals on Spain's war fronts.

In Spain the volunteers were not able to defeat Fascism, but they slowed down Hitler's timetable by three years. They also demonstrated the kind of unified effort the United Nations would use to finally ensure the defeat of world Fascism.[2]

By the late 1930s the boxer Joe Louis, Detroit's "Brown Bomber," did more than stir millions in Black communities. His victories in the ring, said writer Loften Mitchell, were seen in Harlem as blows against racism and Fascism. He explained:

> Our biggest celebrations were on nights when Joe Louis fought. The Brown Bomber, appearing in the darkness when Italy

invaded Ethiopia and the Scottsboro Boys faced lynching, became a black hero the history books could not ignore. . . . [He] was there, and he knew I was there. When he won a fight I went into the streets with other Negroes and I hollered until I was hoarse. Then, Joe would come to Harlem, to the [Hotel] Theresa, and he couldn't say what he felt when he saw us hollering at him. And he didn't have to.

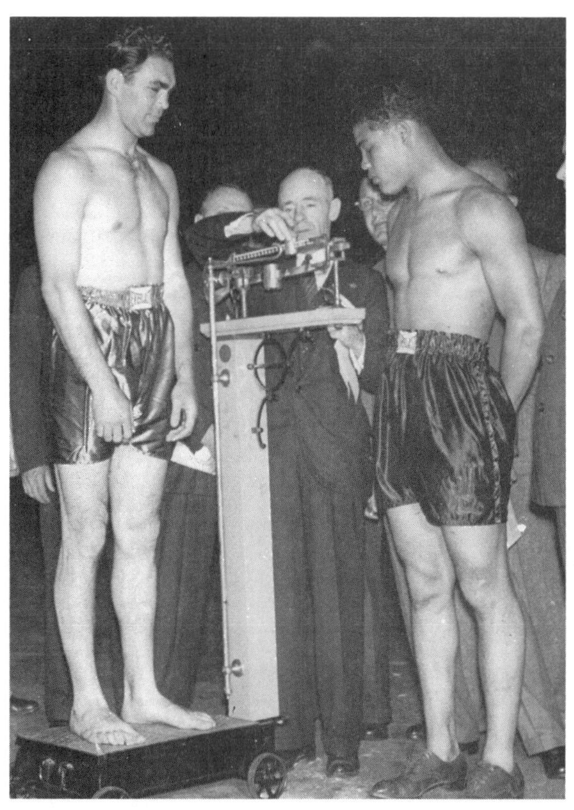

Max Schmeling and Joe Louis weigh in.

On June 22, 1937, in Madison Square Garden before forty-five thousand fans, Louis defeated James Braddock in the eighth round and won the world's heavyweight crown. Writer Richard Wright captured the moment in Harlem:

> The eyes of these people were bold that night. Their fear of property, of the armed police, fell away. There was in their chant a hunger deeper than that for bread as they marched along. In their joy, they were feeling an impulse which only the oppressed can feel to the full. They wanted to fling the heavy burden out of their hearts and embrace the world. They wanted to feel . . . that the earth was theirs as much as anybody else's. . . . They wanted a holiday.

In 1938 Joe Louis was drawn directly into the fight against Nazism when he was pitted against Germany's champion, Max Schmeling. Two years before the men had fought and Schmeling had defeated Louis in the twelfth round. This time Schmeling said Louis came from "an inferior race and country," and Nazi propaganda echoed his view.

For the first time, Louis, a calm, calculating boxer, was angry. By the second minute of the first round, he had knocked Schmeling to the floor twice and had been declared the winner.

President Roosevelt called Louis "a credit to his race—and I mean the human race."

Nazi racism and imperialism continued to draw an angry response from Black New Yorkers. Vaughn Love's League of Struggle for Negro Rights called the Nazi's Nuremberg Laws against Jews "death to us darker races." At rallies in Madison Square Garden, Walter White of the NAACP, Mayor La Guardia, and other city notables denounced anti-Semitism and Fascism's threats to peace.

As the nation prepared for war in 1941, people of color found they were rarely hired by defense industries. The NAACP launched protest demonstrations in twenty-three cities. Then in March, A. Philip Randolph planned a march on Washington by ten thousand Blacks, to demand defense jobs.

> There are some things Negroes must do alone. This is our fight and we must see it through. If it costs money to finance a march on Washington, let Negroes pay for it. If any sacrifices are to be made for Negro rights in national defense, let Negroes make them. . . . Let the Negro masses speak!

In June Mayor La Guardia and Eleanor Roosevelt, at the request of the president, asked Randolph and Walter White to City Hall to discuss calling off the march. Next Randolph and White met at the White House with Secretary of the Navy Frank Knox, the president, and other members of his cabinet. Convinced of Randolph's determination to march, two days later Roosevelt issued an executive order opening defense jobs to all. A week before it was scheduled, the march was called off.[3]

Executive order 8802 was the first presidential decree since the Emancipation Proclamation aimed at people of color. Roosevelt also appointed a Fair Employment Practices Commission (FEPC) to implement it. Roy Wilkins of the NAACP saw it as a sign "that we get more when we yell than we do when we plead."

But the Youth Division of the Negro March Committee meeting in New York was disappointed the march had been called off.

Its members were unenthusiastic about an FEPC with a small budget and staff that could hold hearings but lacked enforcement powers. This rancor did not end when the Japanese attacked Pearl Harbor in December 1941 and the United States entered the war.

In June 1942 Randolph presided over a Madison Square Garden meeting of eighteen thousand people. For five hours speakers issued new calls for the federal government to end job discrimination. New York actor Canada Lee drew the greatest applause in a skit in which he played a man who told his draft board: "I want you to know I ain't afraid. I don't mind fighting. I'll fight Hitler, Mussolini and the Japs all at the same time, but I'm telling you I'll give those crackers down South the same damn medicine." In October 1942 more than half of Black New Yorkers surveyed still said a march on Washington would accomplish some good.

Although in New York Black people didn't, prior to Pearl Harbor, show much enthusiasm for the war—because they saw it as European nations fighting over who would control colonies of dark-skinned people—the attack on Pearl Harbor united Americans as never before. "Your ancestors came to America on the *Mayflower* while mine came here on a slave ship," said NAACP director Walter White. "But we're all in the same boat now!" Alice Godwin, a New York high school student, spoke for many people of color when she called the conflict "a war for liberty for everybody. . . . It is for a new world tomorrow, isn't it?"

African Americans fought under the slogan "the Double V"—victory over Fascism abroad, and liberty at home. Some three million African Americans registered for the draft, and 701,678 served in the army, 165,000 in the navy, and 5,000 in the coast guard. In 1943, for the first time, the Marine Corps opened its ranks to people of color and seventeen thousand enlisted. Some four thousand Black women enrolled in women's branches of the armed forces, and half a million Blacks were sent overseas.

Black women and men served in segregated units. Using the Lincoln Brigade as his model, Reverend Adam Clayton Powell Jr. suggested an interracial brigade to be called the Crispus Attucks Brigade. In his *People's Voice* newspaper, he also advocated launching a destroyer with a mixed crew and naming it *Joe Louis.*

Inside the armed forces, people of color had to "fight for the right to fight." Their assignments kept most in noncombat jobs doing heavy work behind the lines. The army asked Dr. Arnold Donowa, dental surgeon and veteran of the Lincoln Brigade, "what is the lowest position" he would accept. Black combat units were considered a "progressive experiment."

Finally, Black New Yorkers went ashore on Omaha Beach, flew air force combat missions over Europe as part of the 332nd Fighter Group, and served in the Pacific fleet. The "Black Panther" 761st Tank Battalion helped liberate Nazi concentration camp prisoners. Because Eleanor Roosevelt and General George Patton strongly defended the record of the 761st, the unit's members were called "Patton's Pets" or "Eleanor's Niggers."

New Yorker Captain Hugh Mulzac, at fifty-five, had served thirty-five years as a professional sailor, been a chief mate in World War I, and then commanded Marcus Garvey's three ships. In early 1941 Mulzac called thirty government and private organizations to seek appointment as master of a U.S. vessel. He received no responses. There were at the time no Black officers in the U.S. Merchant Marine. The National Negro Congress took up his case and in 1942 he finally was asked to command the *Booker T. Washington* and offered an all-Black crew. "I think we should get crew members without any regard to their color," he said. "Do you ask white captains to get all-white crews? Of course not! The union would forbid it. . . . Give me an appointment the same as you would any other man." In California Mulzac found a union willing to recruit his mixed crew.

For the next two and a half years, Mulzac and his crew made twenty-two successful wartime voyages. They carried eighteen thousand troops, delivered supplies to U.S. troops in France, Africa, and Italy, and returned with enemy prisoners. On the home front, Mulzac also lectured on behalf of the war effort. In 1945 his eleventh voyage from Europe returned with the Japanese American heroes of the 442nd Regiment. He completed twenty-two voyages, but three years after the war Mulzac and some two hundred other Black officers had employment problems.[4]

Even though African Americans helped to defeat Fascism abroad, they still had to battle racism at home. Black troops trained in segregated Southern camps, ate in segregated mess halls, watched movies in segregated theaters, and sat at the back of the bus. The U.S. Army's blood-plasma program to save lives of soldiers was pioneered in 1939 by a Black surgeon, Dr. Charles Drew of New York's Columbia Presbyterian Hospital. But Dr. Drew and others had to mount a long fight to end the segregation of blood by the race of the donor.

One of the longest battles for equality was waged by Mabel K. Staupers, executive secretary of the National Association of Colored Graduate Nurses (NACGN). The NACGN had defended the rights of Black nurses since its formation in 1908, and in 1934 established a headquarters in Rockefeller Center near major nursing societies.

Staupers was the first paid executive of the NACGN. Born in Barbados, West Indies, in 1890, she migrated with her family to New York in 1903, earned her degree in 1917, and became a private-duty nurse. She helped organize the first facility in Harlem where Black doctors could treat their patients, and for twelve years she led the Harlem Committee of the New York Tuberculosis and Health Association.

Staupers traveled thousands of miles as a lecturer, enrolled Black nurses, and brought pressure on the American Nurses' Association to admit women of color. Before Pearl Harbor, she made friends with Eleanor Roosevelt and battled to prevent Black nurses from being barred from the Army and the Navy Nurse Corps. But General George C. Marshall continued "the custom" and treated integration as a "danger to efficiency, discipline, and morale."

After Pearl Harbor, Staupers campaigned to abolish color quotas established by the War Department base hospitals. She carried her complaints to Eleanor Roosevelt and objected to assignments of Black nurses to Nazi prisoners of war rather than U.S. soldiers. The Red Cross, she said, solicited Black applicants only to turn them down by saying the army had no place for them.

In early 1945, at a press conference at New York's Hotel

Walter White (left) and other New York NAACP members picketing the Stork Club in the 1940s.

Pierre, Surgeon General Norman Kirk announced that shortages might mandate a draft of nurses. Staupers was on her feet: "If nurses are needed so desperately, why isn't the Army using colored nurses? Of 9,000 registered Negro nurses the Army has taken 247, the Navy takes none." The media carried her words, and within two weeks Kirk announced that the army would enroll nurses of color. A few weeks later the first Black navy nurse was accepted. In 1951 Staupers dissolved her NACGN, saying it had fulfilled its aims.[5]

The war years did bring cultural advances to New York City. Dr. Louis T. Wright, after a long battle against bigotry in the medical profession, became director of surgery at Harlem Hospital. Dean Dixon, twenty-six, of Harlem's Symphony Orchestra, made history when he conducted the New York Philharmonic. In 1943 Paul Robeson's 296 performances as Othello set a record for a Shakespearean production on Broadway. The next year Dizzy Gillespie, who began a musical revolution in 1934 at Monroe's Uptown House on 134th Street, initiated a "bebop" revolution at the 52nd Street's Oynx Club.

Bernice Robinson, who came from South Carolina, was delighted with a New York City where "you could go to the theater and sit anywhere you wanted to sit . . . get on the bus and sit anywhere you wanted." During the war she ignored the "subtle segregation" at some exclusive restaurants and instead took her daughter to hear Dean Dixon and Duke Ellington and to concerts at Carnegie Hall and Town Hall. She recalled:

> New York really prepared me to live in an integrated society. Even the work in the garment industry contributed because there you had Armenians, you had Germans, you had Jews; we *all* worked

side by side on those machines. . . . We would go to lunch together, and we would get together some evenings for movies.[6]

Dramatic political changes also took place. In 1941 a four-week city bus boycott forced the hiring of the city's first Black drivers. That same year Adam Clayton Powell Jr. was elected to the New York City Council from Harlem.

A war being conducted with a segregated army did little to ease racial tensions. So many whites came to dance at Harlem's Savoy ballroom that in 1943 New York police temporarily closed it down for encouraging "racial mixing." That summer Harlem exploded again. A white police officer argued with Margie Polite, a local resident, at 126th Street and Eighth Avenue and then shot a Black soldier who intervened. In the mayhem that followed, hundreds of stores were wrecked. Some eight thousand National Guard troops joined city police and fifteen hundred Black volunteers to restore order. Property damage amounted to five million dollars. Five residents were killed, four hundred injured, and five hundred arrested, including one hundred women.

Langston Hughes found crucial changes followed the riot:

> Chocolate and vanilla teams of policemen appeared on uptown streets walking together. Squad cars became more integrated. And a white policeman would often grant his Negro colleague the courtesy of making the arrest, if an arrest had to be made.

Witnessing a peaceful arrest, Hughes heard a Harlemite say: "You see—since the riots, they sure do arrest you politely. Now his head won't be cracked, till they get him down to the precinct house."[7]

The war against Nazi racism and the Harlem riot served to encourage the drive for African American political power in New York, and Reverend Adam Clayton Powell Jr. was ready. He had received degrees from Colgate in 1930 and Columbia University, and in 1933 he had assumed command of his father's

Reverend Adam Clayton Powell Jr. addressing his congregation in 1942. Library of Congress.

huge Abyssinian Baptist Church. At twenty-two he organized job campaigns, ran a relief center from his church, and was known for leading picket lines in Harlem and downtown Manhattan.

With his church congregation as a base of support, in 1941 Powell was elected to the city council and reelected in 1943. One year later Harlem voters sent him to Washington, the first person of color to represent New York in Congress.

Powell's choice for his city council post was the popular Harlem attorney Benjamin J. Davis, a Communist. During World War II, Powell had said: "There is no group in America, including the Christian church, that practices racial brotherhood one-tenth as much as the Communist party."

Davis, born to a college-educated, conservative Republican family in Atlanta, arrived in New York in 1935. Under his leadership, Harlem's party membership grew to twenty-eight hundred by 1938. In 1943 Powell asked Davis to run for the city council. Davis, who sometimes attended thirty meetings in an evening, was cheered in both Black and Jewish neighborhoods and had the support of stars such as Lena Horne, Paul Robeson, and Joe Louis.

Davis won his city council seat by 43,334 votes. Since twenty-three thousand whites voted for him, he considered himself "the representative of all the people." Mayor La Guardia, whom Davis had met while leading protest delegations, insisted on swearing him in. Davis noted, "City Hall did not fall down."

In the council, Davis focused public attention on police brutality, major league baseball's color line, discrimination in city housing and the fire department, and conditions in Harlem Hospital, whose four hundred beds served more than half a million people. Davis introduced 175 bills and fourteen became law, including one to celebrate "Negro History Week" in New York public schools. He won another term in 1945 with 63,498 votes, the second highest in Manhattan. With Congressman Powell, Davis organized a march on Washington, seeking passage of an anti-lynching bill, an anti-poll tax bill, a new fair employment law, and enforcement of the Constitutional Amendments. The two politicians drew six hundred supporters to the capital from thirty states.[8]

The legislative efforts of Powell and Davis reflected the growing potency of the Black vote. They highlighted an agenda that would be followed by civil rights activists of the 1960s.

African Americans also continued their cultural liberation during the war. New York singer Lena Horne brought her dazzling glamour and sultry voice to many movies. Although she appeared with white stars, Hollywood directors only placed her in special musical numbers. She also starred in two all-Black

In the late 1940s the Committee for the Negro in the Arts challenged negative Black images in the media and included (from right) Ernest Crichlow, Viola Scott, Frank Silvera, Janet Collins, Charles White, Ruth Jett, and Walter Christmas. Ben Katz photograph.

musicals, *Stormy Weather* and *Cabin in the Sky,* which featured such performers as Duke Ellington, Louis Armstrong, and Bill Robinson.

By the end of the war, Hollywood studios began to offer films that seriously treated issues of race. One aspiring actor who tried unsuccessfully to make it in New York after the war was a gangly teenager named Sidney Poitier. He arrived from Florida with twenty-seven dollars and a thick West Indian accent that he learned to bury.

Author Richard Wright came from Chicago and hoped New York's Greenwich Village would welcome or at least ignore his family. Instead his neighbors protested their presence. When he visited novelist Sinclair Lewis, he was barred from the elevator and had to walk up the stairs. A Fifth Avenue store prevented his daughter from using the rest room. In 1947, following other racial affronts, Wright moved his family to Paris.

Jacob Lawrence was born in Atlantic City and moved to Harlem in 1929 with his family when he was twelve. At twenty-one he painted thirty-two pictures of Frederick Douglass and thirty-one of Harriet Tubman. Lawrence's series of paintings of families like his own, who settled in Northern cities after World War I, became highly acclaimed. He recalled:

> I remember people used to tell us when a new family would arrive. The people in the neighborhood would collect clothes for the newcomers and pick out coals that had not completely burned in the furnace to get them started.

Lawrence's later series "Harlem" was filled with details of city life and marked by sweeping movement.

Lawrence became the most venerated African American artist of his generation, and his canvases placed his people in the thick of the global battle for human rights. In 1970 he became the first artist to win the NAACP's Spingarn Medal, awarded to the outstanding Black figure of the year.

Ella Fitzgerald and Sarah Vaughan sang their way to victory in amateur night contests at the Apollo Theater. Vaughan was hired

Paul Robeson (center) and W. E. B. Du Bois (right) meet at a Paris peace conference in 1949.

by bandleader Earl Hines. Elizabeth Catlett taught sculpture to ordinary working men and women at the George Washington Carver School in Harlem. "We have to create an art for liberation and for life," she said. By the 1990s she was considered the greatest living African American sculptor.

The Red Scare that followed World War II had a profound impact on Black New York. In 1949 Communist councilman Benjamin Davis was defeated when both major parties united behind a single candidate. In the mounting hysteria over Communism, Davis was jailed, released, jailed again, and in 1962 indicted again only to die two years later.

The State Department seized the passports of Paul Robeson and W. E. B. Du Bois, depriving them of the right to travel abroad and cutting them off from world audiences.[9] At eighty-three, Dr. Du Bois was arrested as a foreign agent, handcuffed, and tried in federal court in New York. The charge arose from his Peace Information Center, which circulated a petition calling on the two major powers to end the nuclear arms race.

In 1948 A. Philip Randolph (right) prepares to testify before Congress, urging desegregation of the U.S. armed forces. Speaking is Grant Reynolds, a Republican who agreed with Randolph.

Though he was acquitted, the trial bankrupted his center.

In 1950 the NAACP investigated Communist infiltration of its branches and began to "clean house" of "red influences." The NAACP banned groups and individuals suspected of Communist views from their civil rights meetings. Anti-Communist Black leaders such as A. Philip Randolph continued his work on behalf of his League for Nonviolent Civil Disobedience Against Military Segregation. He threatened a march on Washington if the army was not desegregated, and in July, 1948, President Harry Truman issued executive order 9981 that finally eliminated segregation in the U.S. armed forces.

The Red Scare ended the forty-year sailing career of Captain Hugh Mulzac. He had fought for world peace, West Indian welfare, and civil rights. In 1951, at age sixty-five, Mulzac was questioned about what papers he read, whom he talked to in his union, and what he thought of the USSR. He later wrote:

> My interrogators presumed to be in possession of information which they refused to reveal to me. There were no witnesses against me. I was not told the source of the Coast Guard's derogatory information. . . . It could have come from a neighbor who disliked me.

Labeled a security risk, Mulzac had to find jobs as a delivery boy, elevator operator, hotel clerk, and short-order cook. "These were bad years for me. The higher McCarthy soared the lower I sank," he wrote. Finally, he and others sued their union for blacklisting them and won. At seventy-six, he was still strong: "Fight . . . join the common struggle. Fight for the liberation of the oppressed everywhere. . . . Thus does life become worth living."[10]

CHAPTER FIFTEEN

MALCOLM X IN NEW YORK

World War II created new opportunities for African Americans. In 1944 an African American who ran for the New York state assembly lost but garnered a thousand votes. In 1953 attorney Walter Gladwin, a native of British Guiana, was elected to the state assembly, from a district that was 45 percent Black, 40 percent Jewish and 15 percent Puerto Rican. After four years in the assembly, Gladwin became a city magistrate.

Ivan Warner, born in 1920 to West Indian immigrants in New York, followed Gladwin to Albany. He had been a high school dropout, a shoe-shine boy, and had pushed handcarts in the garment district. In high school, college, and law school, he worked to pay for his expenses, then diligently threaded his way through the various levels of the Bronx Democratic Party.

From 1940 to 1957, African Americans in the Bronx increased by 315 percent, largely in neighborhoods located on a direct subway line from Harlem. There they turned factional fights within the party to their advantage to win election to local offices. Between 1950 and 1953, for the first time Bronx voters sent people of color to the Court of General Sessions, the New York State Assembly, and the Senate. Julius A. Archibald from the Bronx became the first of his race elected to the New York State Senate. In 1957 J. Daniel Diggs became Brooklyn's first African American city councilman.

The first sizable African American community in the borough of Queens began to grow along the subway line from Harlem in the South Jamaica area and then in St. Albans. The completion of the Triborough Bridge in 1936 linked Harlem to Corona,

Dr. Ralph Bunche mediating the Middle East crisis of 1948 for the United Nations. UN photo.

Queens, and Corona's African American population rose. In 1964 Kenneth Brown became the first African American from Queens elected to the state assembly. He had defeated a white Democrat in the primary and a white Republican incumbent on election day.

Some Black people had made enough money to settle on Staten Island, and one enclave of middle-class families lived in Merrick Park, Long Island. Most people of color, however, still preferred to live in New York's five boroughs.

For these African American New Yorkers, the postwar era brought promises, frustrations, and sometimes wrenching changes. Their struggles against segregation in housing, education, and jobs seemed to swing in a seesaw motion of progress one month and frustration the next. In 1945 New York became the first state to establish a State Commission Against Discrimination. This was only a symbolic beginning since, as

Black leaders pointed out, the agency lacked enforcement powers.

However, Black New Yorkers saw opportunity in the choice of their city as the first permanent home of the United Nations. They were thrilled to see African nations wrench free of colonial rule and their representatives serve on an equal basis in the UN General Assembly with former European rulers.

In New York, African Americans hoped their new neighbor perched on the East River might become a forum to air grievances before an international audience. In 1947 the NAACP's "An Appeal to the World," written by Dr. Du Bois and others, asked the UN to redress "the Denial of Human Rights to Minorities."

This was just the first salvo. A new global awareness among African Americans in New York began to mount. In 1951 civil rights attorney William L. Patterson's leftist Civil Rights Congress presented the UN with its "We Charge Genocide," a petition listing hundreds of acts of genocidal violence toward African Americans.[1] That year Paul Robeson's wife, Eslanda, and two others disrupted a UN conference on genocide. In February 1961 Black people in the UN visitors' gallery noisily protested the murder of the first president of the Congo, Patrice Lamumba. It later turned out that U.S. CIA agents had a role in Lamumba's assassination and in the dictatorship that replaced him.

Perhaps no one described Harlem during the postwar era better than resident James Baldwin. Born in 1924 to a working-class couple whose tenement on "dark and dirty" Park Avenue hovered over railroad tracks, Baldwin found his education not in school but in the six square miles of Harlem.

> Everything was falling down and going to pieces. And no one cared. And it spelled out to me with brutal clarity and in every possible way that I was a worthless human being. They [police] were brutal the night they stopped me and frisked me, and taunted me and said ugly things about me and my family. Then they knocked me down. And I wished I had a machine gun to kill them. And you begin to hate and you're changed into an enraged human being.

For years Louis Michaux's Harlem Home of Proper Propaganda sold books and attracted intellectuals.

In overcrowded schools, Baldwin felt "caged like an animal." In his community, the policeman was "an occupying soldier in a bitterly hostile country," and he had seen and suffered their injustice, incompetence, and brutality many times.[2]

But young Baldwin was a fighter, and by high school graduation, a talented poet and writer: "I knew I was black but I knew I was bright." Schools denied his heritage, so with "a feeling of no past, no present and no future" he spent afternoons reading about the heritage of his people at the Schomburg Library. To browse, he visited Michaux's Home of Proper Propaganda, a bookstore on Seventh Avenue near 125th Street.

In 1948 Baldwin, at twenty-four, was a young, eager writer who had been awarded two writing fellowships. But when he entered a restaurant and asked for a glass of water, a waitress said, "We don't serve Negroes here." He lost his temper, threw a glass of water from a nearby table at the waitress, missed her, and stormed out. He had discovered inside him a deep reservoir of hatred toward bigotry.

"Make It Plain" was Malcolm X's byword. Photo 1963.

Doubting that he could "survive the fury of the color problem," Baldwin left for France with little money, no knowledge of French, and no job. By 1951 he wrote his first book, *Go Tell It on the Mountain,* about growing up in Harlem, then two other novels; short stories; plays; and three books of essays. Writing, for Baldwin, was "an attempt to be loved," a "way to save myself and to save my family," and a way "to bear witness to the truth." Though he loved Harlem, Baldwin would spend most of his years living in Europe.

It was in Baldwin's Harlem that Malcolm X took his stand as a teacher and philosopher of his people. Born in 1925 in Omaha, Nebraska, Malcolm Little left the eighth grade to work in New York and took an apartment in the Braddock Hotel on 126th Street and a job as a waiter at Small's Paradise. Drawn into the exciting nightlife, he sought out the Apollo Theater, danced at the Savoy Ballroom, and slipped into Harlem's underworld. After a run-in with a crook, he had to leave town.

In 1946 and while living in Boston, Malcolm was arrested for a burglary and sentenced to ten years in jail. In prison he became an avid reader of history, and he corresponded with the Honorable Elijah Muhammad, founder of the Nation of Islam. Muhammad had started his society in Detroit in 1931. He enrolled elderly Black men in major cities who had rejected Christianity in favor of his version of the Islamic creed. Malcolm became his eager student and disciple.

Malcolm X addresses a Harlem rally in 1963.

In 1952 when Malcolm was released from Norfolk prison, Elijah Muhammad assigned him to mosques in Detroit, Philadelphia, and New York. J. Edgar Hoover's agents began to monitor the speeches and attend the meetings led by the dynamic young former convict.[3]

Muhammad appointed Malcolm his chief spokesperson and in June 1954 dispatched him to Temple #7 in Harlem on Lenox Avenue and 116th Street. It was the same year Reverend Martin Luther King Jr. became pastor of the Dexter Avenue church in Montgomery, Alabama. As a Muslim minister, Malcolm began a series of street lectures that brought new members to his storefront headquarters. His brother Wilfred Little recalled: "In those early days the main thing they were after was just gettin' rid of that inferiority complex that existed among our people and spreading this new idea. That's what Malcolm began to do."

Malcolm's sermons praised Allah and the Honorable Elijah

Muhammad, condemned white people as devils, and declared white racism irreversible. The media soon cast the preacher as a fanatic hater of whites, but everyone also found him charming and polite, with a finely honed sense of humor. Malcolm's angry response to white hatred was not personal but political. Soon he attracted his own loyal followers, a fact recorded by the Nation of Islam in Chicago and by the FBI in Washington.

In the late 1950s a number of young Black men were upset by the government's failure to enforce the Supreme Court's unanimous 1954 *Brown* decision that outlawed school segregation. Others were stirred by Africa's revolt against colonialism and attracted to Muhammad's mosques. The Nation of Islam provided a secure home, an iron discipline, and a formal dress code.

Novelist Claude Brown, born in 1937, was a young street thief when he noticed the changes Muslims brought to Harlem. Expelled from school four times by his ninth birthday, he had friends in jail, friends who had been murdered, and one whose goal was to be Harlem's best thief. From 1955 to 1959, Brown saw the Muslims take over 125th Street, Seventh Avenue, and reach deeper into Harlem. They offered males "an angry organization" and a sense of importance. He noticed that, except for hardened criminals, "just about everybody who came out of jail came out a Muslim." Their converts consisted of "men who were very uncertain about where they were, who they were or what they were going to do, the cats who had never been able to find their groove."

With Malcolm X heading its Harlem branch, the Nation of Islam, Brown found, gave people "food for thought, feeding them with a philosophy—if you could call it that—that provided some type of moral fortitude." Residents feared to contradict the Muslim speakers on Seventh Avenue. Some began to buy their newspapers "just to give some money to the cause." Brown believed "that even the people who weren't interested in or were indifferent to the Muslim movement sort of sympathized with them."

Broader than its religious base, the Nation of Islam beckoned to Harlem residents with its political and economic message of unity—"doing for ourselves, not depending on the white man." It attracted those who identified with Muslim anger toward whites and its prediction that "the days of the white man are numbered." For those society scorned, its scorching rhetoric was a fresh, illuminating alternative to leaders who counseled patience and integration with a hostile white society.

As the civil rights crusade gained momentum, Malcolm X challenged its basic assumptions and questioned its goals. He insisted that white men would never abandon their bigotry, never agree to racial desegregation and equality. Although the Nation of Islam remained aloof from public debate and protest, Malcolm X began to move in a more activist direction.

In 1957, when police arrested a member of his mosque, Johnson Hinton, for intervening with a police officer who had beaten a Black woman and man, Malcolm assembled history's first Muslim protest force in front of the Twenty-eighth Police precinct. Johnson, unattended by police, was bleeding profusely, and men and women from the Nation of Islam stood in formation as Malcolm negotiated Johnson's release to a hospital.

Muslims marched in formation behind the ambulance the fourteen blocks to a hospital and remained until doctors said Johnson was out of danger. "No man should have that much power," muttered a white police captain. The incident and Muslim self-discipline made Malcolm and his mosque a force in New York City. He continued to say Black people should be prepared to sacrifice their lives to defend their human rights.

Malcolm met and married Betty, a young Muslim nursing student, and they moved into a two-family house in Queens. By 1959 their first of six children was born. That year the couple also struggled with police, who stormed into their home without a warrant, fired shots, and arrested Betty for blocking their intrusion.[4]

In 1959 Malcolm X moved to a larger stage when, on behalf of Elijah Muhammad, he visited African and Middle Eastern countries. When a nationwide TV news special attacked the Nation of Islam and Malcolm for "black racism," it frightened whites but doubled the Muslim's national membership.

In 1960 Fidel Castro rented forty rooms at the Hotel Theresa for his UN delegation, and Malcolm was there to meet and speak with the Cuban leader. The president of Ghana, Kwame Nkrumah, arrived to talk with Malcolm in front of the hotel. That year Malcolm founded the Nation of Islam newspaper, *Muhammad Speaks.* Meanwhile, Hoover ordered his New York FBI and other offices to intensify surveillance of the Muslim minister. Even Malcolm's sister, Ella Collins, was now followed.

In 1961 Elijah Muhammad and Malcolm addressed ten thousand people at Harlem's 369th Armory. Temple #7 ran a restaurant and became a popular part of the Harlem local scene, which poet and writer Maya Angelou described in these words:

> The streets were clean in the sixties. The air would be crackling with excitement. The African Americans who call themselves Ethiopians would be out. The Black Jews would be out. The Nation of Islam, Baptists, Methodists, Holy Rollers, Seventh-Day Adventists, all the religious groups would be out. . . .

Malcolm appointed two of his brothers to manage mosques in Detroit and Lansing, and one of his new recruits, Louis X, later known as Louis Farrakhan, was sent to Boston. By then the Nation of Islam collected millions of dollars each year from its members, and Malcolm X was its best fund-raiser.

In the early 1960s Harlem was haunted by men who traded in heroin. "It seemed a kind of plague," wrote Claude Brown. "Every time I went uptown, somebody else was hooked, somebody else was strung out. People talked about them as if they were dead." Brown found that "a lot of cats were dying," and no one knew of anyone who had successfully kicked the heroin curse.

> Cats were starving for drugs; their habit was down on them, and they were getting sick. They were out of their minds, so money for drugs became the big thing. . . .
>
> People were more afraid than they'd ever been before. . . . They were afraid to go out of their houses with just one lock on the door. They had two three and four locks. People had guns

in their houses because of the junkies. The junkies were committing almost all the crimes in Harlem.

Meanwhile, Malcolm X continued to expand the scope of Temple #7. In January 1963 Nation of Islam pickets walked before the Criminal Court Building in lower Manhattan to protest the trial of two Muslims who clashed with police while selling *Muhammad Speaks.* In February he led a demonstration against police brutality in Times Square. Both were unheard of events for Muslims.

Soon Malcolm joined voter registration drives, spoke out against police brutality, and joined the Harlem Community Council. In a demonstration of international unity, he united with Harlem residents who offered greetings to UN delegates from new African nations. He invited the famous *Life* magazine photographer Gordon Parks inside Temple #7 to take pictures.

In 1963, although Elijah Muhammad spoke of leading his Nation of Islam into the political arena, nothing came of his words. Malcolm warned the country that "younger Black Muslims want to see some action."

Disturbing and divisive issues began to bubble to the surface for the Nation of Islam. In April 1963 Malcolm X confronted Elijah Muhammad about his relationships with nine Nation of Islam women who said they had given birth to his children. Muhammad did not offer a satisfactory explanation.

Malcolm's relationship with Elijah Muhammad began to deteriorate. After President Kennedy's murder, Malcolm said he was "glad." Pointing out that U.S. agents had carried out assassinations overseas, he called Kennedy's death an example of "chickens come home to roost." Muhammad, who had prohibited any Muslim public statements about Kennedy's death, suspended his disciple for ninety days. Malcolm X was never reinstated, and he began to hear talk of his death, which he believed came from his mentor's Chicago headquarters.

On March 8, 1964, Malcolm announced he was leaving the Nation of Islam. He said he would remain a Muslim and was "prepared to cooperate in local civil rights actions in the South and elsewhere . . . [to] heighten the political consciousness of Negroes and intensify their identification against white society." He said he would support better education, housing, and jobs as "imperatives" for his people, but he now favored a revolution. "I'm going to join in the fight wherever Negroes ask for my help."

Malcolm became increasingly blunt and defiant. Black people, he said, should only be nonviolent "when your enemies are nonviolent. Anything else would be stupid." He spoke more and more as a teacher as he urged people to arm for self-defense in three ways: first, respect themselves as people of African descent; second, increase their general knowledge and that of their children; and third, store arms in order to protect their families.

Casting himself as a revolutionary, Malcolm insisted that no people ever achieved freedom without a fight and asked his followers to prepare for action.

> I'm for the freedom of the 22 million Afro-Americans by any means necessary. *By any means necessary.* I'm for a society in which our people are recognized and respected as human beings, and I believe that we have the right to resort to any means necessary to bring that about.

The media emphasized the man's melodramatic rhetoric, but he saw his message reach a wide audience. Whites found his language terrifying, and people of color found it heartening. Both responses pleased him.

At a March 1964 press conference, five days after his break with Elijah Muhammad, Malcolm compared his people to a man trapped in a wolf's den and said, "I don't care who opens the door and lets me out." He offered a new plan for Black unity: "Whites can help us, but they can't join us. There can be no black-white unity until there is first some black unity. . . . We cannot think of unifying with others, until we have first united among ourselves." Then Malcolm announced he was going to organize a Muslim Mosque Inc. "as a religious base, and the spiritual force necessary." The "philosophy will be black nationalism."

We keep our religion in our Mosque. After our religious services are over, then as Muslims we become involved in political action, economic action and social and civic action.

On April 13 Malcolm left to spend five weeks in Mecca and Africa, this time representing himself in conferences with African revolutionaries of both races. On May 21, 1964, he returned from Africa sounding like a secular revolutionary and a socialist: "You can't have capitalism without racism."

Later that month in New York, Malcolm said, "In my recent travels into the Africa countries and others, it was impressed upon me the importance of having a working unity among all peoples, black as well as white." He urged a new approach: "We will work with anyone, with any group, no matter what their color is. . . ."

Were whites still devils, he was asked. He told a Harlem audience, "All of them don't oppress. All of them aren't in a position to. But most of them are, and most of them do." To many this was a glacial change in a man the media said represented overwhelming Black rage and violence.[5]

In a month Malcolm convened a new society, the Organization of Afro-American Unity (OAAU), headquartered at the Hotel Theresa, and threw himself into its work. His rhetoric and tone began to change. He made no reference to Black nationalism, and he began to denounce Elijah Muhammad as a "religious faker" and a racist. Malcolm remained warm, witty, and charming, and an unrelenting foe of racism and colonialism. By this time his media appearances had made him one of the most eagerly sought lecturers in America.

In July Malcolm left again for Africa and audiences with its leaders. Some assured him they would support his efforts for a Black united front, free of factionalism, in the United States. He urged Africa's rulers to help him bring charges of U.S. human-rights violations to the United Nations. After a chance meeting in Nairobi, Kenya, Malcolm also had long talks with Georgia activist John Lewis of the Student Nonviolent Coordinating Committee (SNCC) and other young civil rights volunteers. He appeared to be establishing links if not a bond between his

OAAU and the radical youths in the Southern movement.

By the time Malcolm returned from Africa that summer, a riot had erupted in Harlem. It represented the pent-up rage Malcolm and James Baldwin in his book *The Fire Next Time* had warned about. Rioting next erupted in sections of Brooklyn. Governor Rockefeller dispatched National Guard troops to restore order when rioting broke out in Rochester. The New York, Brooklyn, and Rochester upheavals represented the first salvo of six "long hot summers." From 1964 to 1969 urban riots struck major cities and many smaller ones from the Atlantic to the Pacific.

In November 1964, after he returned from another trip to Africa, Malcolm praised the three civil rights workers, including two white Jewish New Yorkers, slain by the Mississippi Klan. In January he offered his opinion that interracial marriage was a personal matter and could be part of an individual's "stride toward oneness." He no longer inveighed against whites as a class, but denounced white racists in the South and their less noisy friends in the North. At this time Louis X (Farrakhan) announced in *Muhammad Speaks* that Malcolm was "worthy of death." Malcolm's death threats increased.

That December 1964 Malcolm spoke before thirty-seven Mississippi SNCC youths visiting Harlem as a reward for their efforts on behalf of civil rights. "The most important thing we can learn to do today is think for ourselves," he told them.

> You get freedom by letting your enemy know that you'll do anything to get your freedom; then you'll get it. It's the only way you'll get it. When you get that kind of attitude . . . they'll call you an extremist or a subversive, or seditious, or a red or a radical. But when you stay radical long enough, and get enough people to be like you, you'll get your freedom.

By this time the Organization of Afro-American Unity, with a program written by historian Dr. John Henrik Clarke, faced FBI surveillance and was infiltrated by New York City's Police Bureau of Special Services (BOSS). Gene Robert, a BOSS agent, had managed to become Malcolm's security chief.[6]

Increasingly, Malcolm embraced broader social goals. On January 19, asked if he believed in a Black state, he answered, "No, I believe in a society in which people can live like human beings on the basis of equality."

Sensing that his family was in danger, he prowled his living room at night, rifle in hand. On February 14, at 2:30 A.M., Malcolm's home was firebombed, but he, his wife, and children escaped without injury. He had seven more days to live.

The next day Malcolm flew to Rochester and told an audience he had expected an attack on his family by the Nation of Islam. For the first time, he revealed that in December 1960, at Muhammad's request, he negotiated with Klan leaders in Atlanta. "From that day onward," he explained "the Klan never interfered with the Black Muslim movement in the South." Muhammad and George Lincoln Rockwell, head of the American Nazi movement, he added, "are regular correspondents with each other."[7]

On February 18, at Columbia University, Malcolm spoke of "living in an era of revolution." Victory, he insisted, required "unity of black and white revolutionaries." By this time his Sunday lectures at the Audubon Auditorium on 166th Street and Broadway drew many FBI agents, and city police ringed the hall. There was one exception: February 21, 1965, the day El-Hajj Malik El-Shabazz, as he now called himself, was shot to death. No police were to be seen. His chief bodyguard and undercover New York City police officer, Gene Robert, gave him mouth-to-mouth resuscitation. It was too late.

CHAPTER SIXTEEN

NEW YORK CITY DURING THE KING ERA

Some trace the beginning of the postwar civil rights crusade not to a picket line, freedom bus, or lunch counter, but a baseball diamond in Ebbets Field, Brooklyn, New York. Since the 1880s, major league baseball owners had effectively barred African Americans from the national pastime. Before and during World War II, petition drives by white and Black fans sought to end this sports barrier, but nothing happened. Then in 1947, an all-around college athlete, Jackie Robinson, signed a contract, put on a Brooklyn Dodger uniform, picked up a glove, and trotted out to a spot in the infield.

Jackie Robinson starts a double play at second base.

As a boy growing up in California, Robinson and his Black buddies were only allowed to swim in the YMCA pool on Tuesdays. At UCLA he excelled in football, track, and baseball, and as an officer in World War II, he challenged army discrimination, was court-martialed for it, and acquitted. His baseball career began with the Black Kansas City Monarchs of the Negro Leagues.[1]

In 1945 he was hired by the Dodger manager Branch Rickey, who saw Robinson as a player who might fill his small stadium with paying fans. Robinson and Rickey had long talks not about batting, grounders, or line drives, but on how to handle the hatred of fans, opposing players, and fellow teammates. Robinson was shipped off to the Dodgers Montreal farm team.

Robinson's first Dodgers season was marked by insults on and off the diamond, including anonymous death threats. As he walked to the plate one time, the other team let a black cat onto the field. In some segregated cities, the Dodgers stayed in one hotel and Robinson was sent to another. The hardest part for the young infielder was not striking back. However, as Robinson enjoyed a sparkling rookie year, the overheated fury of some whites began to fade. By the 1947 World Series, a color barrier had been breached: the Dodgers had hired Dan Bankhead, and the Cleveland Indians had hired Larry Doby.

By 1949, when Robinson was the National League's most valuable player, his daring base-stealing skills and his courage and unflagging tenacity had won the hearts of New Yorkers. He had become one of the most exciting players in major league baseball, and he led the lowly Dodgers to six pennants and a World Series victory.

Robinson also hit home runs off the field. He joined civil rights demonstrations and became a role model for young people. By the time he hung up his Dodger uniform in 1956, teams eagerly competed for the best players without regard to race. His skill and grace made it difficult for young fans to understand why there had ever been a color bar.

Reverend Adam Clayton Powell Jr. might be called the Jackie Robinson of New York political life. Beginning in 1945 he served twenty-six years in the U.S. Congress, changed the political landscape, and set an independent tone for Black officials. Only the fourth Black Congressman of the twentieth century, he was the first to represent New York and the first to enter Congress owing nothing to the white political machine.

Powell arrived in Washington as an activist legislator. In the

Capitol, he threw himself into the fight to desegregate federal buildings, city restaurants and theaters. His staff—an equal number of Black and white aides—was the most integrated in Congress.

Congressman Powell (left) embraced Malcolm X in 1964.

He confronted the worst racist in the House of Representatives, Mississippi's John Rankin. When Rankin announced he would not let "Powell sit by me," Powell answered that Rankin was "only fit to sit next to Hitler and Mussolini." Then Powell insisted on taking the nearest seat to Rankin at every opportunity. One day Rankin moved five times to escape a Powell in eager pursuit.

In 1956 Powell, displaying his independent streak, bolted the Democratic Party to support President Eisenhower's reelection bid. Four years later Powell returned to support Democrat John F. Kennedy, and in 1961 he became chairman of the powerful House Labor committee. By the next year, six Black New Yorkers had been elected to the state legislature.

Powell was the first to urge Congress to deny funds to any project that discriminated, the first in Congress to demand integration of the U.S. armed forces, and the first to see that Black journalists sat in the congressional press gallery. His "Powell Amendment" was an ongoing effort to attach antidiscrimination provisions to funding bills. He repeatedly argued for anti-lynching laws. Soon everyone knew he would shake things up.

Powell's Education and Labor committee rolled up an impressive legislative record: forty-eight of its recommended bills became laws—acts that benefited the poor, women, the elderly, and people of color. Powell worked closely with Senate leader Sam Rayburn and won the praise of President Lyndon Johnson.

Powell supported civil rights leaders and, responding to the rising militancy in urban America, was photographed with Malcolm X. Before the phrase "Black Power" became known,

Powell was its embodiment. In 1966, just days before Stokely Carmichael introduced this slogan during a march in rural Alabama, Powell used the words "black power" in a speech.

The NAACP building in New York City flew this flag from the 1920s to the 1940s. NAACP photo.

Powell repeatedly faced serious charges that he sometimes surrendered public interests for personal ones. He was often absent for House votes, and his government expenses were not carefully detailed. His personal life was filled with scandals that he handled with a public shrug. In January 1967 Congress stripped him of his seat and his chairmanship, but by April his constituents reelected him. Stripped again of his power by Congress, he won his case before the Supreme Court. The justices ruled that he had been treated in a way that was both unconstitutional and racist.[2]

From his post in Congress, Powell was more than one of Harlem's own—he was a dynamic, fearless watchdog who at times led the battle for equality in America. His actions also put to rest any notion that a Black public figure must act better than a white one. In 1972 Powell, by only 205 votes, was finally unseated in a primary election by another African American, Charles Rangel of Harlem.

In the years following World War II the NAACP, from its Manhattan offices, pursued its efforts to secure equal justice through the courts. Its interracial legal defense team was led by Thurgood Marshall, who arrived in the city in 1934 and lived with his wife in a small walk-up Harlem apartment. For decades he worked night and day on discrimination cases and traveled five thousand miles a year fighting them. In 1952 Marshall's legal team won cases that admitted qualified Black candidates to graduate schools, compelled unions to admit Blacks to membership, and desegregated a Kansas City swimming pool, a Louisville golf course, and Ford's Theater in Baltimore.[3]

Thurgood Marshall (center) and NAACP attorneys celebrate their Supreme Court victory in the 1954 *Brown* case ending legal school segregation.

But the goal of the NAACP was to overturn segregation in the nation's schools. Marshall asked the help of Dr. Kenneth Clark, an expert in social psychology who graduated from Columbia in 1940. Using dolls to study the impact of school segregation on young minds, Clark presented evidence that young Black children invariably chose a black doll as "the bad one" and a white doll as the nice one, their favorite, and even the one most like themselves. In 1954 his studies helped convince the Supreme Court to unanimously rule in the *Brown* case that schools must desegregate "with all deliberate speed."

New York—as the home of A. Philip Randolph, actors Harry Belafonte, Paul Robeson, Ossie Davis, and Ruby Dee, civil rights attorney Conrad Lynn, and Queen Mother Moore—was a natural meeting ground for civil rights activists. It was also a seedbed that produced many more who led the march to equality.

In 1929 Ella Baker, after graduating Shaw University, left Littleton, North Carolina, to settle in New York City. She had inherited her penchant for struggle from her former slave grandparents. In Depression Harlem she attended political meetings, helped start a consumer cooperative, and served as its first national director.

Baker taught literacy skills to neighborhood workers. She met activists such as A. Philip Randolph, Conrad Lynn, and men who became leaders in the new CIO unions. She worked with a

Harlem protesters in the early 1960s.

Black women's reform organization and also wrote for Black city papers. In 1935 in the *Crisis* she exposed the "Bronx slave market," where domestic workers were hired for pennies a day.

In 1940 the NAACP had Baker spend five months on the road, building grassroots clubs in the South, a network that fed into civil rights organizations. During the war she became director of branches for the NAACP, and in 1946 she became the first woman president of its New York branch in Harlem. By moving NAACP actions into the neighborhood, Baker turned her small club into one of the largest in the state.

In 1956 Baker joined with A. Philip Randolph, his assistant Bayard Rustin, and Stanley Levison to help raise funds for Dr. Martin Luther King Jr.'s plan to boycott the Montgomery bus lines until they desegregated. Then she was hired in Atlanta to work for King and coordinate King's Southern Christian Leadership Conference's (SCLC) voting-rights campaign and education projects. A civil rights fighter before the phrase was known, a woman in a world led by male ministers, Baker often had to battle to be heard.

In 1960 at Shaw University, Baker helped young students form the Student Nonviolent Coordinating Committee (SNCC). SNCC fulfilled her dream of a youthful group and a decentralized, democratic, group-leadership perspective. Baker also knew that the civil rights burdens of the 1950s and 1960s were "carried largely by women, since it came out of church groups. It was sort of second nature to women to play a supportive role."

In 1964 Baker helped SNCC launch the Mississippi Freedom Democratic Party, managed SNCC's Washington office, and directed its effort to win seats at the Democratic national convention. She sought to link struggles for civil liberties with those for civil rights and to unite activists of both races.

Baker's intellectual and political influence reached beyond the groups she led and the leaders she trained. Though she worked with Dr. King and Stokely Carmichael, she opposed the concept of individual leadership. A charismatic leader created by the media, she insisted, also could be one undone by the media. Also, a leader, she pointed out, might come to believe "his *is* the movement." She offered this advice: "You have to have a certain sense of your own value, and sense of security on your part, to be able to forgo the glamour of what the leadership role offers."[4]

Robert Moses, born in Harlem in 1934, was another key civil rights crusader. He graduated from Stuyvesant High School and then Hamilton College. But when his mother died, he left a Harvard doctoral program to care for his father and made a living as a high school math teacher.

In 1960 Moses left for Atlanta to work in Ella Baker's office. The next year he carried Baker's concept of group leadership to McComb, Mississippi. He ran the voter registration drive, conducted the town's first sit-in, and was jailed many times.

As Klan murders plagued Mississippi in 1963, Moses suggested that white students be recruited and trained to help fight the KKK reign of terror. Whites would be less exposed to violence, he noted, and if they were attacked, the world would learn the brutal truth about Mississippi. In 1964 college volunteers by the hundreds began to arrive for Mississippi's "Freedom Summer." As early arrivals unpacked, two young white New Yorkers, Michael Schwerner and Andrew Goodman, disappeared. Klansmen killed Schwerner and Goodman along with a young Black Mississippian, James Chaney.

Stokely Carmichael spoke for Black Power while leading a march against fear in Mississippi. Gordon Parks photo.

Another early New York activist was playwright Lorraine Hansberry, who lived with her white husband in Greenwich Village. In 1959 her *A Raisin in the Sun* opened on Broadway, and she became the youngest person to win a Critic's Circle Award. Her play ran for 538 performances, toured other cities, and became a theater classic. *A Raisin in the Sun* elevated Black drama in the city to a new high. The play is often revived and became a movie starring its original cast.

Hansberry spoke at street-corner rallies for the Greenwich Village–Chelsea NAACP chapter and its president, James Yates, who served from 1964 to 1968.[5]

Another important figure in the civil rights struggle was Stokely Carmichael. Born in Trinidad in 1942, he came to New York in 1953 and attended Bronx High School of Science. At nineteen, the tall young man was a freedom rider, and four years later he ran a voter registration drive in Lowndes County, Alabama, that raised the number of Blacks voting from zero to thirty-nine hundred. In June 1966 he introduced the Black Power slogan after he and Dr. King led a march against fear in Mississippi. Black Power, he explained, meant that African Americans had to have political control of their own communities and their legal systems, education, and economic resources.

New York played a key role in Dr. Martin Luther King Jr.'s leadership of the civil rights crusade. He first visited New York in 1956 after his famous Montgomery bus boycott had kept enough people of color from the buses for more than a year and bus company executives finally had agreed to desegregate the lines and hire Black drivers. In New York City, King's victory received, he reported, "the kind of welcome [the city] usually reserves for the Brooklyn Dodgers." When he spoke at the Concord Baptist Church, ten thousand people tried to push in, and four thousand dollars was collected.

Harry Belafonte (left) and Dr. Martin Luther King Jr. (right) in 1968 in New York City. Daily Challenge photo.

King met with Harry Belafonte, who was just about to release the first solo album to sell a million copies. Belafonte, born in 1927 in the West Indies, arrived in New York in the 1930s and served in the armed forces during World War II. King often stayed at the Belafontes' Manhattan apartment, where they talked into the night. The singer-actor hosted fund-raising concerts for King and introduced him to his potential supporters among entertainers and politicians. Belafonte concerts became an early and reliable source of funds for the civil rights movement.

In May 1960 Senator John F. Kennedy, seeking the presidency, visited Belafonte to ask for his aid with Black voters. Belafonte suggested that the senator ought to speak to Dr. King rather than to an entertainer.

Belafonte continued to raise bail money for King and other activists arrested in the South for challenging segregation laws. He also intervened repeatedly with Attorney General Robert Kennedy, seeking to protect the lives of jailed civil rights workers in the South.

Dr. King's New York visits did not go unnoticed by the FBI. When he was introduced to former councilman Benjamin J. Davis, J. Edgar Hoover ordered an investigation of King's friends. In Harlem, while signing copies of his *Stride Toward Freedom* in 1958, Dr. King was stabbed with a knife wielded by a deranged woman. For many hours he hovered between life and death.

By 1961 Dr. King found a staunch ally in New York governor

Nelson Rockefeller, a Republican seeking the presidential nomination. In June 1961 Rockefeller flew King on a private plane to Albany, New York, for a freedom rally, then to New York for a speech—and hired a film crew to document it.

On May 24, 1963, Robert Kennedy arranged a special meeting at his family's New York apartment near the Plaza Hotel. He invited James Baldwin to assemble a representative group of people of color so he could find out how they felt about President Kennedy and civil rights. Baldwin brought Lorraine Hansberry, Lena Horne, Dr. Kenneth Clark, Harry Belafonte, and Jerome Smith, a Freedom Rider who had been beaten and jailed in Mississippi. Smith, angry about failures by the federal government to protect people of color, said, "I'm close to the moment where I'm ready to take up a gun." Asked if he would fight for the United States, Smith said, "Never! Never!"

Kennedy tried to ignore Smith's views, but Hansberry said to Kennedy, "You've got a great many very, very accomplished people in this room, Mr. Attorney General, but the only man who should be listened to is that man over there." The attorney general believed that the president had edged the nation toward equality and could not understand such disloyalty. Kenneth Clark called the meeting "the most dramatic experience I ever had." Kennedy returned to Washington and asked Hoover about those present that evening, and Hoover was pleased to provide reams of data.

King continued to visit the city. In 1964, after marching in a New York picket line for Hospital Union Local 1199, he left for Oslo and his Nobel Peace Prize. Three weeks before his death in April 1968, he told the union's members: "You have provided concrete and visible proof that when black and white workers unite in a democratic organization like Local 1199 they can move mountains."

In April 1967 at the Riverside church, King delivered a historic speech against the war in Vietnam that broadened his focus from civil rights to a global crusade for justice and peace. He called the United States "the greatest purveyor of violence in the world today" and called on young men not to respond to draft calls.[6] He returned to the city for the last time in early 1968 and addressed a Carnegie Hall commemoration of the birth of W. E. B. Du Bois, where King paid tribute to his radical economic and political views.

Constance Baker Motley. Daily Challenge photo.

After the Montgomery bus boycott ushered in the modern drive for equality, Black New Yorkers struggled to lift their own burdens. Demographics were changing in New York and in the nation. By 1960 New York became the first Northern state with an African American population larger than any Southern state.

In New York and other cities, the Black unemployment rate was twice the white rate and sometimes triple, with far-reaching economic, medical, and social results. In 1961 at the AFL-CIO convention, A. Philip Randolph detailed how Black New Yorkers were denied economic opportunities. In the garment and publishing industries, they were confined to low-paid and unskilled classifications. Black men worked in hotels, not as bartenders but as busboys and scullery laborers, and only a token number were bellhops or waiters. Randolph said that in the city's construction industry, Black people were only 1 percent of apprentices. African Americans, he told the delegates, were "a permanently depressed segment of American society."

The New York City Youth Board found no Black apprentices working with plumbers, steamfitters, sheet metalworkers, plasterers, metal tradesmen, and other skilled craftsmen. Not until 1962 was the first Black elected to the executive board of the United Auto Workers (UAW).

Calls to end Northern school segregation were soon heard in New York. In 1961, in the New York suburb of New Rochelle, Black parents found their local NAACP was ineffective in arguing against segregated schools and housing. They hired Harlem attorney Paul Zuber, and within a year he won a case for open enrollment in their city.

In February 1964 the movement against school segregation in the city led to a massive demonstration as 464,000 pupils, mostly people of color but also including whites, boycotted city schools. The next month another demonstration had 267,000 pupils leaving their classrooms to protest.

New Yorkers also moved to increase their own political impact. Constance Baker Motley became the first Black woman elected to the New York State Senate. J. Raymond Jones, a longtime leader of Harlem Democrats, was the first of his race to lead the city's Democratic Party. Then, in 1965, Motley became the first Black woman to be elected borough president of Manhattan.

The summer of 1964 began the riots—soon dubbed the "long hot summers"—that swept urban America for the next four years. After the riots in Rochester and Harlem that summer, President Johnson announced, "Violence and lawlessness cannot, must not, and will not be tolerated." Langston Hughes wrote that he hoped the president included beatings and murders in Mississippi: "Some Harlemites interpret this to mean there will be no more head-bustings on the part of the police, or shooting of adolescents, black, white or Puerto Rican by men representing New York's Finest."

New York became a prime target for President Johnson's announced "war on poverty." Armies of federal civil servants were sent into Harlem and other urban centers. In the end only twenty-five dollars was spent for each Harlem resident in the government's war on poverty, too little to make major changes. When Johnson escalated the Vietnam War, his war on poverty, said Dr. King, was lost on the battlefields of Vietnam.

By 1967, except for Washington, D.C., which offered many government jobs, a greater proportion of African Americans, 5.7 percent, held white-collar jobs in New York than in any other major city, and another 5.8 percent held skilled crafts jobs. But African Americans in New York were 11.5 percent of the city's population and had an unemployment rate of 12 percent compared to a 4 percent jobless rate for whites.

The year was filled with important events. The Supreme Court outlawed more than a hundred years of state bans on interracial marriages. For the first time in history, President Johnson picked an African American, Thurgood Marshall of New York, for a seat on the Supreme Court. But problems continued to plague urban America. As summer rioting continued in ghetto areas, Dr. King announced a Poor People's March on Washington that would unite people across racial lines.

Malcolm X was assassinated in 1965, and Dr. King was assassinated in 1968. They had changed the way many people in the city felt and acted, but much had remained the same. In 1971 Professor Nathan Irvin Huggins wrote: "Harlem now connotes violence, crime, and poverty. For many, it represents a source of militancy, radical social change and black community culture."

Harlem had 336,364 people, 256 churches, and 125,000 church members. It also had 168 liquor stores that sold $34,368,000 in alcohol each year, with even more alcohol sold in bars. One-third of Harlem's people were divorced, widowed, or separated. Half lived in decaying dwellings, and the average annual family income stood at $3,723 ($6,000 was the poverty line). It had no high school of its own or unemployment office.

In 1964 writer Sylvester Leaks described Harlem as a "festering black scar on the alabaster underbelly of the white man's indifference." But it was also a place where people fought for their rights on picket lines, filled church choirs, came to fifty-four social agencies, and studied at the Schomburg Library. They attended dance palaces, fashion shows, and the Apollo Theater.[7]

Harlem schools remained a scandal. Educator Hope Stevens wrote:

> The system of public instruction has long been geared to depress the level of education of colored children. For many years the attitude of educational planners as well as teachers was that it didn't matter too much whether pupils in Harlem schools learned or did not learn. They were thought to be biologically inferior anyway and what was the point in expending energy to make them learn when the work that would be available to them would be in unskilled categories where minimum education would be adequate.

Despite electoral gains, some authorities believed Black city politics lacked substance. "We have a political frosting but no political cake," said attorney Paul Zuber. He believed prominent ministers surrendered to downtown bosses to gain civil service jobs for residents. In this arrangement a white elite used Black ministers to quash community dissent with token jobs.

Movie director Spike Lee was a child when Malcolm X lived in Harlem. Daily Challenge photo.

But King and Malcolm also had left Harlem and other Black communities an enduring legacy of self-assertion and racial pride. Malcolm X was the inspiration for the Black Panther Party. Founders Bobby Seale and Huey Newton first planned their community self-defense force in the wake of Malcolm's death. In New York Richard Moore (Dhoruba bin-Wahad) and Lumumba and Afeni Shakur, parents of Tupac Shakur, worked at the party's Harlem headquarters on Seventh Avenue.

Militant Puerto Rican Young Lords organized in New York and Chicago. Chicanos formed youthful defense units in Western cities. These radical clubs were subject to surveillance by local and federal government agents.

The year after Malcolm was assassinated, writer LeRoi Jones walked away from Greenwich Village and white people and moved to Harlem. As a cultural nationalist and leader of the Black Arts Theater, his "poems that kill" influenced a generation of artists. Like Malcolm, he rejected capitalism and said, "I see art as . . . a weapon of revolution."

In 1976 a Harlem school was named after Malcolm X, and in 1993 Spike Lee produced an epic Hollywood film on his life. He had become a hero to a generation of African Americans.

NEW YORK CITY POPULATION BY DECADES[8]

Year	Total City Population	Blacks
1940	7,454,995	458,444
1950	7,891,957	747,608
1960	7,781,984	1,087,931
1970	7,894,862	1,668,115

CHAPTER SEVENTEEN

THE DINKINS VICTORY

The 1980s brought a change to American urban politics. In the nine years that ended in 1983, the number of Black mayors rose from 108 to 240. They ruled from Los Angeles to Chicago to Birmingham. That year Jesse Jackson, a civil rights activist who had never held office before, entered the Democratic presidential primary and won 17 percent of the votes and 10 percent of the delegates to the Democratic presidential convention.

In 1988 Jackson finished a strong second behind Michael Dukakis. Jackson carried delegate majorities in Alabama, Georgia, Mississippi, Louisiana, and Virginia, and he placed second in Missouri, Massachusetts, North Carolina, and Texas—and in Vermont and Alaska, with populations almost as white as their winters. Jackson even won Michigan's vast white majority.

Then Jackson arrived for the pivotal New York primary. David Dinkins was borough president of Manhattan. Since the election of Hulan Jack in 1953, the Manhattan borough president's office had been the highest elected post for New York's African Americans. Other distinguished people of color followed Jack. One was Anna Hedgeman, born in 1899 in Iowa, a granddaughter of slaves. From 1954 to 1958, she served as part of Mayor Robert Wagner's cabinet. She had the distinction of being the only woman on the committee that planned Dr. King's 1963 March on Washington. Her contribution was to make sure it included a demand for jobs as well as freedom.[1]

Following Hedgeman, other African Americans rose to prominence in the city. In 1964 J. Raymond Jones became the leader of Tammany Hall and the first African American county political

Percy Sutton served as an attorney for Malcolm X. Daily Challenge photo.

boss in the nation. The following year Constance Baker Motley was elected Manhattan borough president. Then, in 1966 Motley was appointed as a federal judge. Percy Sutton, a captain in World War II, a Freedom Rider, and Malcolm X's attorney, became Manhattan borough president.

By 1972 African Americans were 19 percent of New York City's population and their power was still rising. Except for Staten Island, each borough had at least one Black district leader, and each had sent a man or woman of color to the state assembly. Every court except for the Court of Appeals had at least one African American judge. New York City sent two African Americans to Congress, two to the city council, and six to Albany as state senators from Manhattan, Brooklyn, and the Bronx.

In 1953 Shirley Chisholm had been a volunteer in Brooklyn's first successful effort to elect a Black judge. The daughter of a housecleaner from the West Indies, Chisholm, a teacher, worked hard for her Democratic club. In 1942 a college professor had told her to make politics her career and she had laughed, but not for long.

In 1964 Chisholm was elected to the New York Assembly, where she gained a reputation for voting her conscience. But this did not win her political friends. In 1968 Chisholm, able to speak Spanish, Bedford-Stuyvesant's second language, ran for Congress. She had little money, but her district was 70 percent Black, 80 percent Democratic, and had ten thousand more women registered voters than men. Campaigning as Fighting Shirley Chisholm—"Unbought and Unbossed"—she won in a landslide over the popular civil rights activist James Farmer. Brooklyn was finally represented by a person of color, and the U.S. Congress had its first Black congresswoman.

Chisholm rejected her assignment to the committee on forests as laughable and was appointed to the Veterans' Affairs committee. She opposed the Vietnam War as soon as she arrived and said she would "vote 'no' on every money bill that comes to the floor of this house that provides any funds for the Department of Defense." In 1970 she told Congress: "Racism and anti-feminism are two of the prime traditions of this country." She fought hard for aid for Native Americans, Chicanos, people of color, and working men and women.

Chisholm said to other women: "Your time is now, my sisters. . . . The law cannot do it for us. We must do it for ourselves. Women in this country must become revolutionaries. We must refuse to accept the old, the traditional roles and stereotypes." She also explained the value she placed on confrontational politics:

> Confronting people with their humanity and their own inhumanity—confronting them wherever we meet them: in the church, in the classroom, on the floor of the Congress and the state legislatures, in the bars, and on the streets. We must reject not only the stereotypes that others hold of us, but also the stereotypes that we hold of ourselves.

By 1970 Chisholm's borough of Brooklyn had more people of color than Manhattan. In 1972, as her district of Bedford-Stuyvesant was about to become the country's largest black ghetto, she announced her candidacy for the Democratic presidential nomination. She became the first woman of color in a major party to campaign for the highest office in the land. She garnered thousands of votes in primaries but dropped out for lack of campaign funds. Voters returned her to Congress five more terms. Chisholm once described her treatment as a woman and a person of color:

> The harshest discrimination that I have encountered in the political arena is antifeminism from males and brainwashed, Uncle Tom females. When I first announced that I was running for the United States Congress, both males and females advised me, as they had when I ran for the New York legislature, to go back to teaching—a woman's vocation—and leave politics to the men.

Congresswoman Shirley Chisholm campaigns for the Democratic presidential nomination in 1972. Courtesy Shirley Chisholm.

After retiring from Congress in 1983, Shirley Chisholm continued to battle for an America where all "meet on a basis of respect and equality." She added, "I hope I did a little to make it happen."[2]

When Jesse Jackson arrived in June 1988 for the New York primary, he faced its flamboyant mayor, Ed Koch, his self-appointed political spoiler. In the 1960s Koch was a volunteer in civil rights campaigns in Mississippi, but he had become more conservative in the twelve years he had been mayor.

During the Koch administration, ghetto residents reported mounting police abuse. In 1983 a congressional committee headed by John Conyers arrived in New York to record testimony about racist lawmen. Conyers was handed a list of black plainclothes officers who had been shot while in the line of duty by white cops. No Black officers shot any white undercover police officers. Some Black officers stated that white police fired at them even after they had identified themselves. After the Conyers hearings, Mayor Koch hired the city's first Black police commissioner, Benjamin Ward, a personal friend. But police abuse did not end.

Before Christmas 1986 Michael Griffith, twenty-three, and his two Black companions, were in a car that broke down in Howard Beach. When they went to search for a phone or tow truck, the three were surrounded by white youths with baseball bats. One man escaped, another was severely beaten, and Griffith was chased by the mob onto a highway, where he was run down and killed by an oncoming car. White policemen treated the bleeding victims as suspects. When residents of Howard Beach were unwilling to identify mob members, those arrested were granted bail. Black rage rose with each action by the justice system.

Reverend Al Sharpton, who had been inspired by Reverend Adam Clayton Powell Jr. and Martin Luther King Jr., led protest marches through Howard Beach, which needed a strong police presence to restrain local whites. Eventually some suspects were convicted not of murder but of lesser crimes and served short sentences. In the face of white crimes of hate, Mayor Koch said little. To him the many instances of police brutality stemmed from "a few bad apples."

But for the 1988 primary the mayor was ready for Jesse Jackson. Koch, reacting to the anti-Semitism espoused by a few Black activists, announced that any Jews who voted for Jackson were "crazy." Jackson lost the state and any chance for the nomination, but Jackson's campaign strategy of concentrating on voter registration had enrolled hundreds of thousands of young Black voters. And despite Koch, Jackson had carried New York City. This set the stage for a mayoral challenge by a black candidate.[3]

By the 1989 mayoral primaries, many African Americans lived in all five boroughs, particularly Manhattan, Brooklyn, and Queens. Black power had begun to grow. Some twenty people of color served in the state legislature, including four in the senate.

David Dinkins, Manhattan borough president, had read the

As a beaming Mayor Dinkins looks on, Nelson Mandela (left) is welcomed by Jesse Jackson (right). Daily Challenge photo.

recent primary statistics in New York after Jackson's campaign and decided to challenge Koch in the Democratic primary. A soft-spoken career politician, Dinkins was one of the first African Americans to serve in the U.S. Marines during World War II. He had a reputation for racial healing.

Though both candidates denounced the city's sporadic acts of racial violence, Dinkins's calm and gentle manner contrasted with Koch's ability to taunt his foes. Dinkins claimed he would reunite the city, and the mayor promised four more years of his popular oratorical style. Koch proved to be less a favorite among voters than he thought, and Dinkins decisively defeated him.

Dinkins then faced his Republican opponent, Rudolph Giuliani, a popular federal prosecutor. Though he had never held elective office before, he had served in Reagan's Justice Department. City politics soon became racially polarized.

Queens College professor Andrew Hacker said Giuliani's supporters knew he stood for "turning the city back to white New Yorkers. He doesn't even have to say it. When he talks about crime and the like, white people know what he means."

The 5 percent increase in African American voters handed Dinkins the fifty thousand votes needed to win City Hall. Compared to other first-time Black candidates for mayor, Dinkins polled 30 percent of the white vote. First-time Black mayoral candidates in other major cities had failed to capture more than a quarter of white voters. On the other hand, a Republican had captured the white vote by more than two to one in a city that is overwhelmingly Democratic.[4]

New York's 106th mayor said he was proud that "no matter how tough things got in this campaign, we refused to yield the moral high ground. We held to the high road, and we proved that it is the right road to victory." Dinkins promised "to be the mayor of all of the people—not just those who voted for me."

New York City's massive economic and social problems could not be solved quickly. Discrimination was still the rule. City Consumer Affairs commissioner Mark Green, a white man, filed suits against five agencies that coded job applications by race. Insurance companies, he found, assigned car owners higher rates based not on driving records but on their neighborhoods.

Since the 1960s, Green found, banks in ghetto areas had been closed down or required loan or account applicants to live or work within ten blocks of a branch, although they waived the policy for whites. This virtually denied people of color checking accounts and mortgages. Green also discovered that African Americans were rejected for mortgages twice as often as whites. In 1990 Green wrote:

> Until the day arrives when minorities can open a checking account at any bank, successfully hail a medallion cab, have mortgage applications fairly evaluated and get equitably priced insurance, there will be a steady and generous supply of grist for the mill of racial anger.

Mayor Dinkins and Lee Brown, his Black police commissioner, were unable to halt police abuses in ghetto neighborhoods. In the summer of 1992, Mrs. Annie B. Dodds, a community leader, summoned police to her Brooklyn home to end a fight between her sons. The police beat the sons and the mother. Mrs. Dodds took her complaint to the district attorney, and a grand jury indicted an officer. To African American congressman Ed Towns, the incident proved "that all of us are potential victims of police brutality."

During the Dinkins administration, the New York State justice system was investigated by former secretary of state Cyrus Vance and a judicial commission of seventeen legal experts. In 1991, after three years and half a million words, the commission found the system "invested with racism." It uncovered "two justice systems at work in the courts of New York state, one for whites and a very different one for minorities and the poor." Court officials in the city and state often allowed whites to use racial slurs against Black attorneys. Vance called the findings "a terrible condemnation of our society."

Perhaps the emotional high point in the Dinkins administration came in June 1990 with the arrival of Nelson Mandela, the South African freedom fighter just released after twenty-six years in prison. First Mandela spoke at Boys and Girls High School in Brooklyn, then a huge Manhattan ticker-tape parade brought him to City Hall and a welcome by Dinkins, Governor Mario Cuomo, Jesse Jackson, and others. The descendant of a slave who was now mayor of the city presented the former political prisoner with the key to New York.

In Harlem, Mandela received a tumultuous welcome on 125th Street. Winnie Mandela, learning that the woman who introduced her, Dr. Betty Shabazz, was the wife of Malcolm X, threw her arms around her. At Yankee Stadium, Dinkins and Mandela spoke to tens of thousands of cheering citizens. Mandela, waving a New York baseball cap, shouted, "You can see I'm a Yankee."

As mayor, Dinkins tried to renew friendships he had solidified as a politician. In a city with many Jewish voters, the mayor repudiated Reverend Louis Farrakhan of the Nation of Islam for his anti-Semitic diatribes. During the Gulf War, Dinkins visited an Israel under fire from Iraq's scud missiles. Some African Americans and other supporters complained he had more urgent work at home.

Dinkins stumbled badly during a violent outbreak in Crown Heights. The Lubavitchers, an ultra-Orthodox Jewish sect, had been granted many special privileges by city mayors, and the area's 89 percent Black population chafed at this unfairness. African Americans were underrepresented on local school boards. Hasidim Jews voted conservative Republican while Blacks voted liberal Democrat. Hasidim charged that poor Black youths menaced their safety, and they organized their own protection system, which included unarmed civilian patrol cars. Kosher signs in Hebrew and Kente cloth from Ghana, Rastafarian dread locks and black fedoras, shared the same streets but found little in common. Crown Heights was a fuse needing only a spark.

In August 1991 a car driven by Yosef Lifsh in the motorcade of the Lubavitchers' leader, Rabbi Schneerson, ran a red light, leaped a curb, and hit two black children. Gavin Cato was killed and his cousin Angela was severely injured. The driver was not charged with a crime, and he fled to Israel. Within hours of the accident, Yankel Rosenbaum, a rabbinical student from Australia, was surrounded on a Crown Heights street by Black youths who yelled anti-Semitic slogans and stabbed him. He died later at a local hospital. His wounds may have been misdiagnosed.

Three nights of Black random rioting followed. Reverend Herbert Daughtry and other local African American figures tried to end the rioting to no avail. Police commissioner Brown was slow to dispatch officers to halt the turmoil and even slower to tell Mayor Dinkins about the lawlessness. The mayor finally arrived and restored calm.

Knowing how white police treated people of color during previous riots, African Americans believed Dinkins was right to restrain them. The Lubavitchers condemned the mayor's actions as mob provocation and labeled the riot a "pogrom." (A pogrom is an anti-Semitic riot encouraged by legal authorities;

they grew out of the savage treatment of Jews in Europe before World War II.) The new, borrowed phrase further inflamed racial tensions in the city.

Reverend Al Sharpton (fourth from right) leads a march to protest New York police brutality. Daily Challenge photo.

Reverend Al Sharpton began to rise as a new African American political figure. He was an accomplished speaker even as a teenager. In the 1980s he came to prominence as a leader of protest marches against racial injustice. In January 1991 Reverend Sharpton prepared to lead a Brooklyn march honoring Dr. King's birthday. Suddenly, a white man plunged a knife into his chest. The minister recovered, the assailant was jailed, and racial tensions in the city remained high. The next year Sharpton entered the Democratic primary race for U.S. senator. The young minister had moderated his tone and become a respected community voice. Families victimized by racial violence often chose him to act as their official voice.

Sharpton held his own in debates with the other candidates and polled a 20 percent share of the vote. He placed third and made a respectable showing for a man the media had pictured as a clown with dangerous ideas.

In the summer of 1992, Mayor Dinkins tried to restore his image when he spoke at the Democratic National Convention taking place in New York. But the Crown Heights riots had tarnished his reputation as an administrator and a peacemaker.

In the 1993 election, Dinkins and Giuliani faced each other again, and race was a major if often silent issue. Giuliani harped on "crime," "Crown Heights," and "pogrom," and Dinkins tried to vindicate his record.

At Hostos Community College in the Bronx, the mayor

addressed a largely minority student body. He hardly sounded like a man fighting for his political life. He spoke of his parents separating when he was six, and how his mother and grandmother "cooked and cleaned and worked for other people as domestics for a dollar a day. I was poor but I didn't know it. They put their arms around me and they loved me." The mayor spoke of childhood friends in prison or on drugs and left his audience with a note of encouragement: "And I tell young people you can be anybody you want to be if you can learn to reason. And you can. You can be mayor, no doubt about that."[5]

Two million New Yorkers went to vote, and Democrats again outnumbered Republicans by five to one. The mayor lost by forty-four thousand votes. Only ninety-two thousand votes had shifted between his victory in 1989 and this defeat. He was as gracious in defeat as he had been as mayor. He was offered a teaching job at Columbia University and seemed pleased to be leaving City Hall for less hazardous work.

During the Dinkins administration, more people of color lived in New York than any other city. New York stood as the symbol and mecca of the African diaspora. According to the 1990 U.S. census, New York City's 7,322,564 people included 3,432,978 African Americans living in all five boroughs: Manhattan had 1,847,040; the Bronx, 369,113; Brooklyn, 797,802; Queens, 390,842; and Richmond, 28,172.

In 1990 New York State's African American elected officials numbered 263, with 138 of these serving on local school boards. This total also included four in Congress, five in the state senate, sixteen in the state assembly, four mayors of cities, twenty-nine who sat on municipal governing councils, forty-five judges, and two magistrates. Black women comprised 102 of the elected officials (including six judges), and seventy-seven more served on local school boards.[6]

CHAPTER EIGHTEEN

A CITY OF BLACK HEROES AND LANDMARKS

Between their arrival around 1626 and the election of David Dinkins in 1989, people of African descent have been an integral part of New York City's heritage and have made special contributions to its history.

New York gave birth to the first Black newspaper, the earliest Black church, the NAACP, the Urban League, the United Negro Improvement Association, and the National Council of Negro Women. Before the Revolution, Black citizens fought against slavery; before the Civil War, they carried out nonviolent civil rights demonstrations and sit-ins; and in each war the United States fought in, they fought for their freedom and their country.

The city has welcomed leading Black shakers and makers of U.S. history from Frederick Douglass, Harriet Tubman, and Sojourner Truth to Marcus Garvey, Paul Robeson, W. E. B. Du Bois, Langston Hughes, and Malcolm X. The world's greatest jazz innovator, Louis Armstrong, made recording history in the city and lived out the last decades of his life in Queens.

Before he sat as an associate justice on the U.S. Supreme Court, for two decades Thurgood Marshall served as the NAACP general legal counsel in New York. Ronald McNair rose from poverty in Harlem to become an astronaut. Ronald Brown, also born to a poor Harlem family, became the first Black chairman of the Democratic National committee and served in President

Clinton's cabinet. Spike Lee graduated from New York University to become a filmmaker and a household name.

In New York, TV networks attracted figures such as Gil Noble, whose pioneering "Like It Is" opened opportunities for other talented people of color. Max Robinson, Charlayne Hunter-Gault, Bob Teague, Carol Jenkins, Norma Quarles, John Johnson, and Tony Brown followed in his pioneering footsteps.

From *Freedom's Journal* in 1827 forward, New York has been home to Black publications such as *Crisis, Opportunity,* and *Freedomways.* Currently *Enterprise* boasts more than a quarter of a million monthly circulation; *Essence,* a magazine for Black women, has a monthly circulation of 650,000; and *Encore* has a 170,000 circulation.

Louis Armstrong in 1969, when he lived in Queens.

New York intellectuals included Roscoe Brown, who served as president of Bronx Community College and consultant to Mayor Dinkins. Dr. Mary Schmidt Campbell, a former executive director of the Studio Museum in Harlem, became the city's Commissioner of Cultural Affairs. Dr. Kenneth B. Clark, an internationally known scholar, served as a New York Regent, a director of the state educational system. Professor Manning Marable, chair of the Black Studies Department at Columbia University, is the author of many important works. James Baldwin and Claude Brown wrote poignant novels describing a Harlem whose dangers and wonders they knew as children.

Professor John Henrik Clarke, a philosopher and world-renowned scholar on Africa, taught at Hunter College, edited many books and publications, such as *Harlem Quarterly* and *Freedomways,* and lived for decades on a quiet Harlem street.

Playwright Lorraine Hansberry in New York. Daily Challenge photo.

Ralph Ellison, author of *Invisible Man,* an acclaimed 1952 novel, was the first of his race to win a National Book Award. He won a presidential medal of freedom and for decades taught at New York University.

Lorraine Hansberry lived in Greenwich Village, where in 1959 she wrote the award-winning play *A Raisin in the Sun.* Historian and theologian Vincent Harding, who grew up in the city and attended Columbia University, joined the civil rights crusade in the South and became director of the Martin Luther King Jr. Center in Atlanta. June Jordan, born in New York City, attended Barnard College and became a professor of English and a writer of children's books, poetry, and essays.

New York–born Audre Lorde graduated from Hunter College, wrote many books of poetry and essays, and was poet laureate of New York State at the time of her death. Professor Gloria Naylor, born in the city and graduated from Brooklyn College, wrote *The Women of Brewster Place,* which won an American Book Award.

Toni Morrison served as an editor for Random House in New York before she earned the Pulitzer Prize in 1988 and the Nobel Prize in 1994. Alice Walker, educated at Sarah Lawrence College in Bronxville, New York, writes novels, books of poetry, and essays and has also won the Pulitzer Prize.

Angela Davis moved to New York City in 1959 from Birmingham and attended the Elizabeth Irwin High School on Charlton Street on a scholarship. She graduated from Brandeis University and studied at the Sorbonne in Paris. She became one of the world's most well-known political activists.

General Colin Powell, born in 1937 to Jamaican immigrant parents in Harlem, grew up on Kelly Street in Hunts Point, the Bronx. He was educated at City College, and after two tours of active duty in Vietnam in which he was seriously wounded, he returned a decorated veteran. General Powell served as Chairman of the Joint Chiefs of Staff during the Persian Gulf War; then he retired, wrote a highly popular autobiography, and was chosen by most voters polled as their favorite choice in 1995 to serve as president of the United States.

In 1991 Mayor Dinkins welcomed General Colin Powell to Yankee Stadium. Daily Challenge photo.

The rebirth of interest in the African American heritage in the United States has led to cultural gains for the entire city and the preservation of important landmarks.[1] Some trace this rebirth to 1953, when Seventh Avenue from 110th Street to 155th Street was renamed George Washington Carver Boulevard in honor of the noted scientist.

The Studio Museum in Harlem, founded in 1967 in a loft above a liquor store on Fifth Avenue, has expanded to a bigger location on West 125th Street. It is dedicated to collecting, exhibiting, and documenting African American culture—paintings, sculpture, photography—and has exhibited the work of Elizabeth Catlett, Jacob Lawrence, and Romare Bearden.

By the 1970s the Studio mounted exhibitions that toured Black colleges and galleries across the country. The museum acquired the vast film archives of photographer James VanDerZee. In 1987 it mounted a triumphal three-year national tour for its exhibit on the Harlem Renaissance. It attracts a hundred thousand visitors a year.

Beginning in the 1970s, Black neighborhoods in all five boroughs have remembered their citizens of distinction. In 1973 Mount Morris Park on Fifth Avenue between 123rd and 124th streets was renamed Marcus Garvey Park. In 1974 "Harlem Week" was founded by businessman Lloyd Williams and in 1994 it celebrated its twentieth year under the slogan "It's up to us."

Harlem Magazine in 1994 reported, "Tour buses stop and deliver hundreds of thousands of visitors from throughout the region, country, and the world to Harlem's churches, restaurants, historic sites, museums, major events and stores." That year saw the birth of efforts to preserve Harlem's heritage: an Apollo Theater Foundation and Striver's Center Development Project.

Harlem Week was launched in earnest in 1975 with borough president Percy Sutton renaming all of Seventh Avenue in Harlem after Adam Clayton Powell Jr. In 1977 the name of Eighth Avenue was changed to honor Frederick Douglass.

Other Harlem landmarks formed a walk through history: Duke Ellington Drive, Langston Hughes Place, Nat King Cole Walk, African Square, Mary McLeod Bethune Place.

In 1974 the Adam Clayton Powell Jr. Office Building, costing thirty-six million dollars, was dedicated. Standing twenty stories tall on 125th Street and Lenox Avenue, it took eight years of planning and was the work of Black architects, construction companies, electrical companies, and superintendents. Under a special program run by Dorothy Gordon, the project also trained community people without skills.

The Powell office building's first tenant was the State Division of Human Rights, and twenty other state agencies followed. It employs about eighteen hundred people, including civil court workers.

Brooklyn has acknowledged its African American past. In 1975 the Bedford-Stuyvesant Restoration Commercial Center, at a cost of six million dollars, was opened between Fulton and Herkimer streets. Initiated by Robert Kennedy eight years before, it had been financed by banks, foundations, and the federal Office of Economic Opportunity. Franklin Thomas, a former ambassador, served as its first president.

The center offered office space, commercial space, and room for thirty-two stores, as well as a skating rink. James L. Hicks, in the *Amsterdam News*, called it a "Cinderella story." It used local people, including many women who worked as carpenters and laborers. Hicks found children who proudly said, "I helped build that."

Under its director, Joan Maynard, the Society for the Preservation of Weeksville and Bedford-Stuyvesant History since 1968 has preserved an elusive portion of New York's Black past. The society not only has renovated the Hunterfly Road houses, the oldest-known existing buildings in Bedford-Stuyvesant, but by 1985 it opened them to schools and the public as a museum.[2] An estimated three thousand children, from schools in all five boroughs, visit the restoration site each year. Ms. Maynard summarized her society's approach:

> The Weeksville Society understands that its principal product, knowledge of and pride in self and heritage, is an essential element in positive community development, since it taps the positive, creative energy within the community, which allows it to play a central role in its own salvation as well as the larger community of the city.

On Staten Island in 1975, a ten-acre park at Broadway and Richmond Terrace was dedicated to Laurence C. Thompson, the first Black serviceman killed in Vietnam. His mother attended the ceremonies along with borough president Robert T. Connor and other dignitaries.

The Schomburg collection of African American history and culture, materials purchased in 1926 from Arthur Schomburg through a grant from the Carnegie Corporation, has been opened to the public since January 1927. In 1973 the site in Manhattan was designated a research library and renamed the Schomburg Center for Research in Black Culture.[3]

In 1980 city dignitaries were present at the dedication ceremonies for the new building of the Schomburg Center, designed by famous architect J. Max Bond Jr. It offers researchers over

New York's West Indian Day Parade draws millions to Brooklyn each Labor Day. Daily Challenge photo.

125,000 volumes in English and other languages, 400 Black newspapers on microfilm, 2,800 rare books and pamphlets, 210 manuscript collections, 150,000 photographs, over 600 movies and videos, African artifacts and works of art, and a collection of children's literature. Every year an estimated thirty thousand people visit the Schomburg, which the *New York Times* calls "one of the city's most astonishing treasures."

In May 1987 Lenox Avenue in Harlem became Malcolm X Boulevard in a rainy one-hour ceremony attended by his wife, Dr. Betty Shabazz. Poets recited, percussionists performed, and politicians spoke. State senator David Patterson said, "We, the living, must carry Malcolm's dream on. We must not only change the street signs . . . we must also change our environment to the conditions that people such as Malcolm struggled for."

In May 1995 Harlem honored a local hero when it designated

the corner of Fifth Avenue and Central Park North "Duke Ellington Circle." Former mayor Dinkins was present and a band played "Take the A Train." The circle will feature a fifty-foot bronze statue of America's greatest composer and the man who helped show the way to Harlem.[4]

By the time Mayor Dinkins left office, dozens of historic African American sites in the city and state had been designated national landmarks by the federal government.[5] Those listed in editor Beth L. Savage's *African American Historical Places* (Washington, D.C.: Preservation Press, 1994) include:

· The Louis Armstrong Home at 3456 107th Street, Queens, New York, where the seminal jazz figure lived from 1940 until his death in 1971.

· The Ralph Bunche Home at 115-125 Grosvner Road, Queens, where the Nobel Prize-recipient lived from 1952 to 1971.

· The Jackie Robinson Home at 1224 Tilden Street, Manhattan.

· The Apollo Theater, which opened in 1914, at 253 W. 125th Street.[6]

· The Dunbar Apartments at 149th to 150th Streets between Seventh and Eighth avenues, which in 1926 was the first Black cooperative apartment building; was home to Dr. W. E. B. Du Bois, Paul Robeson, and Countee Cullen, among many others; and contained a garden, a school, nursery classes, the first Black-owned bank in Harlem, and stores.

· The Duke Ellington apartment 4D at 935 St. Nicholas Avenue, where the great composer lived from 1931 to 1961.

· The Harlem River Houses, built in 1937 with federal funds, city government aid, and community involvement, which was the country's first federal housing project

· The Matthew Henson apartment 3F at 241 West 150th Street, where the noted explorer with the Peary expedition to the North Pole in 1909 lived out the last decades of his life.

· The Langston Hughes Home at 20 East 127th Street, where the prolific poet lived longer than any other location in the city.

· The James Weldon Johnson Home at 187 W. 135th Street, the

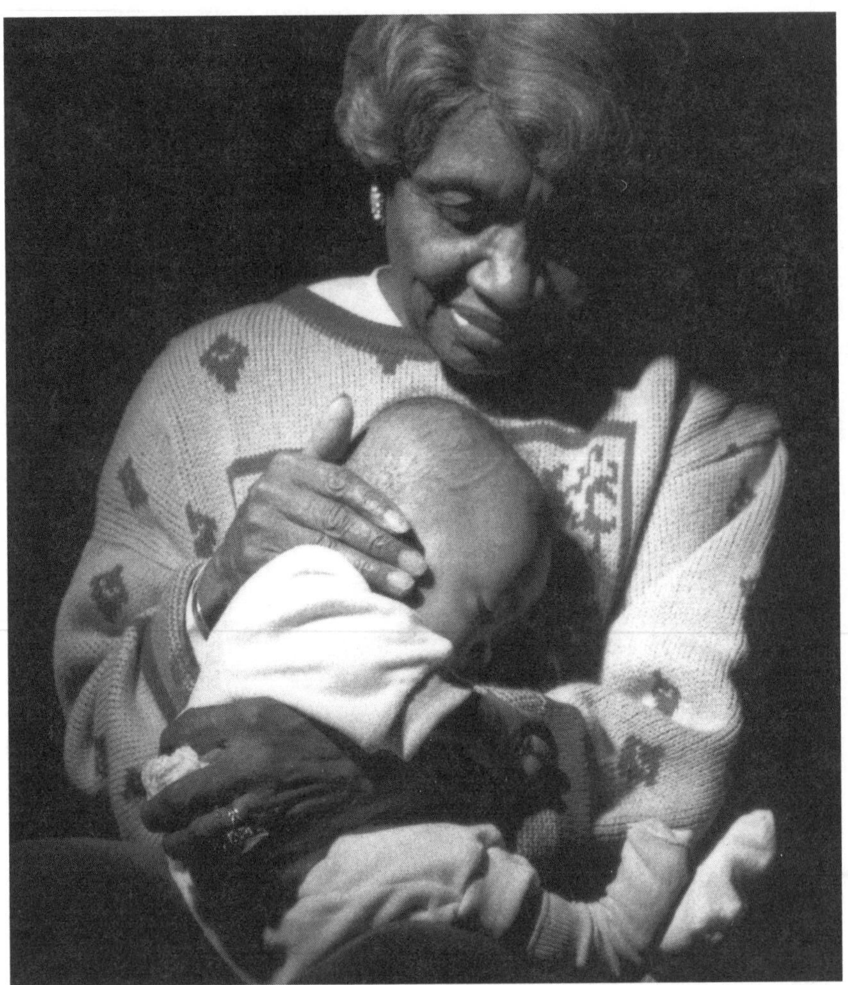

Mother Hale and an infant in her care. Courtesy of Hale House.

residence of the multitalented civil rights advocate and poet.

• The Claude McKay Home at 180 West 135th Street, where the radical novelist and poet lived between 1942 and 1946.

• The Paul Robeson Home at 555 Edgecomb Avenue, where the world-famous baritone and activist lived between 1939 and 1941.

• *The New York Amsterdam News* building at 2293 Seventh Avenue, where the Harlem newspaper ran its operations from its founding in 1909 to 1916.

• The 369th Regiment Armory at 2366 First Avenue, the home of the immortal Harlem Hellfighters of World War I.

• In 1970 Clara Hale opened Hale House to care for babies stricken with disease or abandoned by their mothers. Today Hale

House at 154 W. 122nd Street is a beacon of hope to an entire community.

Perhaps no federal landmark has offered such profound implications for New Yorkers and the entire country as the African Burial Ground. In June 1991, during excavations for a new federal office building in Manhattan's downtown business district, workers stumbled on a burial site of nearly six acres. Bulldozers had uncovered the final resting place from 1712 to 1795 for twenty thousand or more New Yorkers of African descent. The site is located in the City Hall area and is bounded by Broadway, Elk, Duane, and Reade Streets. During its four active generations, it had been just beyond the city wall.

The cemetery quickly became a major American anthropological find.[7] To prevent further excavation that would destroy the burial ground, state senator David Patterson and Howard Dodson, Chief of the Schomburg Center, led picket lines, and for eighteen months New Yorkers of every race joined in chants, marches, and vigils. The goal of the protesters was to see that the dead were preserved, that no building was erected over them, that the graves' artifacts and bodies were subject to thorough study, and that bodies were properly reburied.

In July 1992 Mayor Dinkins, who supported the restoration, was told the federal government had agreed to halt further construction at the site and to finance a scholarly study of its contents. In February 1993 the New York City Landmarks Preservation Commission considered what to do. The current rector of St. Trinity George's Episcopal Church, Reverend Thomas F. Pike, sat on the landmark panel. While the burial ground was being used in the 1700s, Trinity Church had a chapel, St. George's, that conducted a school for slave children. Before the vote, Reverend Pike addressed his fellow commissioners:

> The designation cannot undo the fruits of slavery, prejudice and exploitation that brought the burial ground into existence and later contributed to its convenient disappearance from the city's active memory. Today we are recognizing the lives of thousands

> of men, women and children who were African Americans. Their struggles against incredible odds, their capacity to experience joy, hope and love in a hostile environment has consecrated the soil in which they were buried.[8]

The commission voted unanimously to create the African Burial Ground and the Commons Historical District.

Later that year Howard University was designated custodian of the remains, and forty of its researchers began to examine every aspect of the site, artifacts, and the remains. State senator Patterson was pleased to announce that the General Services Administration agreed that "a world-class museum be erected to commemorate the history of what the archaeological dig uncovered; that landmark status be granted by the national and city agencies, and that the remains be reinterred on the site." The federal government next designated the burial ground a United States landmark and allocated three million dollars for a museum. Some scholars believe the site is the single most important anthropological find in recent United States history.

The remains were taken to Howard University for four years of study by twenty-eight students and professional anthropologists. Soon Dr. Michael Blakey, the project's director, reported finding a high child mortality rate compared to New York's Europeans, and many bodies that showed childhood nutritional problems including anemia. Adults showed heavy workloads—including carrying heavy loads on the head—and a high rate of infectious diseases. Burials in resting positions or squatting or sitting on a small stool, typical of Ghana, have been found at the site. Early examination showed that some had followed the West African custom of filing their teeth. One grave included a Ghanaian *adinkra* symbol called *Sankofa,* which means "look to the past to inform the future; you can always correct your mistakes."

The exploration of the African Burial Ground may reveal other important secrets about the early African residents of New York City.

ENDNOTES

CHAPTER 1: THE AFRICANS OF NEW AMSTERDAM

1. Peter Bakker, "First African in New Netherlands, 1613–1616," *Halve Maen* LXVIII, no. 3 (Fall 1995): 50–52. This article cites documents from international scholarly linguistic journals and French, Portuguese, and U.S. anthropological and historical publications. The *Halve Maen* (or *Half Moon*) has been issued since 1885 by the Holland Society.

2. Ibid. For other Africans as New World language experts also see Rayford Logan, "Estevanico, Negro Discoverer of the Southwest," *Phylon* (1941): 325–333; *Journals of the Commissioners of the Indian Trade, 1710–1718,* in Peter H. Wood, *Black Majority: Negroes in Colonial South Carolina* (New York: Knopf, 1975), 115, which states, "Timboe's role as a highly valued interpreter is emblematic of the intriguing intermediary position occupied by all Negro slaves during these [colonial] years."

3. I. N. Phelps Stokes, *The Iconography of Manhattan Island 1498–1909* (New York: Robert H. Dodd, 1916), II, 105, which states that the Dutch colony "came several times to a complete standstill."

4. The 1626 arrival of Africans is confirmed in Elizabeth Donnan, *Documents Illustrative of the History of the Slave Trade* (Washington, D.C.: Carnegie Institution, 1932), III, 405; E. B. Callaghan, ed., *Documents Relative to the Colonial History of the State of New York* (New York: 1856), I, 162, which states "1625 or 1626"; James Franklin Jameson, ed., *Narratives of New Netherland* (New York: Johns Hopkins University Press, 1909), 129 footnote; and Stokes, I, 13, which states "about 1626."

5. After 1628 there are no African population figures for New Netherlands. Population estimates in this chapter are from Michael Kammen, *Colonial New York: A History* (New York: Scribners, 1975). Stokes, I, 11, mentions thirty homes made of "bark of trees" and cites the earliest historian of New Netherlands on the scene, Dr. Nicolaes van Wassenear, on "Manhates" (one European spelling for an Indian word meaning "island").

6. Joyce D. Goodfriend, "Burghers and Blacks: The Evolution of a Slave Society in New Amsterdam," *New York History* (April 1978): 125–130.

7. Donnan, 129–130, quoting a New Netherlands' overseer's testimony in 1639 about slave jobs.

8. Kammen, 37; William Loren Katz, *A History of Multicultural America* (Austin: Stech-Vaughn, 1993), 39–40.

9. The Primero murder story and its aftermath are taken from "Dutch Council Minutes" in Stokes, IV, 93, which states "Manuel and those who were implicated with him were the same slaves who received emancipation by the ordinance of February 25, 1644"; Stokes, VI, 75–76; Mrs. Schuyler Van Rensslear, *History of the City of New York in the Seventeenth Century* (New York: Macmillan, 1909), 230. For the most thorough chronicle of New York slavery, see Edgar J. McManus, *A History of Negro Slavery in New York* (Syracuse: Syracuse University Press, 1966).

10. E. B. O'Callaghan, *History of New Netherlands; or New York under the Dutch* (New York: Weed Parsons Co, 1845), 224–225, 227, 268; Christopher Moore, "Land of the Blacks," *Seaport* XXIX, no. 3, 10.

11. Stokes, I, 21, 23; IV, 98, 100.

12. Moore, 10; Kammen, 46, notes that the protest of the "Eight Men" persuaded the Dutch West India Company to recall Kieft. Peter Stuyvesant replaced him in 1645 but did not arrive in New Amsterdam for two years.

13. O'Callaghan, ed., I, 36–37; see also endnote nine.

14. Stokes, VI, 76.

15. Some sources claim at this time Africans did serve in the Dutch militia, but evidence is only in secondary sources. This writer's view of the Black land grants as a buffer zone, based on chronology and interpretation of events, was reinforced in March 1996 after talks with historians Dr. Sherill D. Wilson and Emilyn Brown of the African Burial Ground Project.

16. Stokes, VI, 73, 75.; a fine and useful secondary source on Black New Amsterdam is James Weldon Johnson, *Black Manhattan* (New York: Knopf, 1930). Reprint (Atheneum, 1968), 4–7.

17. A. Leon Higgenbotham Jr., *In the Matter of*

Color (New York: Oxford University Press, 1978), 100–109, documents various aspects of New Amsterdam's "half-slavery."
18. Stokes, VI, 100; Johnson, *Black Manhattan,* 5–7.
19. Stokes, VI, 76, citing "Year Book of the Holland Society," 1900, 131; Herbert Aptheker, ed., *And Why Not Every Man?* (Berlin: Seven Seas, 1961), 27–28, includes the petitioner's dramatic plea.
20. Stokes, IV, 96; VI, 73.
21. John Fanning Watson, *Annals and Occurrences of New York City and State in the Older Times* (Philadelphia: 1846), 171, in Johnson, *Black Manhattan,* 10.
22. Stokes, VI, 74–76, 104.
23. Roi Ottley and William J. Weatherby, eds., *The Negro in New York* (New York: Praeger, 1967), 8–12.
24. Goodfriend, "Burghers and Blacks," 132–143.
25. Stuyvesant's excuse can be found in Donnan, III, 434, which cites New York Collection Documents, II, 430; confirmation that three hundred Africans arrived on the *Gideon* only two weeks before the British appears in the records of the Council of New Netherlands to Directors, August, 17, 1664, cited in Goodfriend, "Burghers and Blacks," 138.
26. Higgenbotham, 116–123, documents British harsh slave laws.

CHAPTER 2: IN BRITISH NEW YORK

1. Kenneth T. Jackson, ed., *The Encyclopedia of New York City* (New York: Yale University Press, 1995), 112.
2. On relations between Africans and Native Americans see Ottley and Weatherby, chapter 2; also William Loren Katz, *Black Indians: A Hidden Heritage* (New York: Atheneum, 1986), chapters 8, 10.
3. Johnson, *Black Manhattan,* 7–10.
4. For conflicting versions of this revolt in a single volume see Jackson, ed., 112, 804, 1077.
5. Sidney Kaplan and Emma N. Kaplan, *The Black Presence in the Era of the American Revolution,* rev. ed. (Amherst: University of Massachusetts Press, 1989), 191–200.
6. E. B. Greene and V. D. Harrington, *American Population Before the Federal Census of 1790* (New York: 1932), cited in Rosenwaike, 8.

CHAPTER 3: SLAVERY OR FREEDOM IN A REVOLUTIONARY ERA

1. For an early discussion, see William C. Nell, The Colored Patriots of the American Revolution (Boston: 1855). Reprint (New York: Anno Press, 1968).
2. Benjamin Quarles. "Lord Dunmore as Liberator," The William and Mary Quarterly XV, 494–505.
3. Benjamin Quarles, The Negro in the American Revolution (Chapel Hill: University of North Carolina Press, 1961), surveys the Black experience of fighting for freedom in the armed forces of the Americans and the British.
4. Shane White, Somewhat More Independent: The End of Slavery in New York City (Athens, GA: University of Georgia Press, 1991), chapters 1–3.
5. For data on Africans who joined the Ramapos Indians during the Revolution, see Ralph Sessions, Woodsmen, Mountaineers and Bockies: The People of the Ramapos (New City, NY: Historical Society of Rockland County, 1985), 3–13.
6. William Loren Katz, Eyewitness (New York: Simon & Schuster, 1995), 41–42.
7. Ottley and Weatherby, eds., 53–56.
8. E. B. Greene and V. D. Harrington, American Population Before the Federal Census of 1790 (New York, 1932), for 1771, and citing New York Secretary of State and Census of State of New York for 1865 (Albany, 1867) for 1786 and 1790; all cited in Ira Rosenwaike, Population History of New York City (Syracuse: Syracuse University Press, 1972), 8, 18.

CHAPTER 4: EDUCATION IN OLD NEW YORK

1. Dorothy Porter, "The Organized Educational Activities of Negro Literary Societies: 1828–1846," Journal of Negro Education V, 556–576.
2. Luc Sante, Low Life of Old New York (New York: Farrar, Straus, Giroux, 1991), presents information on Five Points; see also Jackson, ed., 414–415.
3. Dixon Ryan Fox, "The Negro Voter in Old New York," Political Science Quarterly XXXII, 252–275.
4. Charles C. Andrews, The History of the African Free Schools (New York: Mahalon Day, 1830), describes the staff, students, buildings, and progress

of the city's first public schools.

5. Ibid., 133–134.

6. Alexander Crummell, The Eulogy on Henry Highland Garnet (Washington, D.C.: 1882), in Katz, Eyewitness, 153–154.

7. See Rayford W. Logan and Michael Winston, eds., Dictionary of American Negro Biography (New York: W. W. Norton Co., 1982), entries on Garnet, Crummell, and Ward; also see Samuel R. Ward, Autobiography of a Fugitive Negro (London: John Snow, 1855).

8. See Logan and Winston, eds., for entries on Aldridge and Molineaux.

9. Census of the State of New York for 1865, cited in Rosenwaike, 18.

CHAPTER 5: EMANCIPATION COMES TO NEW YORK

1. See George Livermore, An Historical Research Respecting the Opinions of the Founders of the Republic on Negroes as Slaves, as Citizens and as Soldiers (Boston: 1862). Reprint (New York: Anno Press, 1969).

2. Arthur Zilversmit, The First Emancipation (Chicago: University of Chicago Press, 1967), 139–200, focuses on emancipation in New York and New Jersey.

3. Robert Wilson Schufeldt, "Secret History of the Slave Trade to Cuba," Journal of Negro History LV, no. 3 (July 1970): 218–235. He reported in 1859 seventy vessels left New York on slave-trading missions.

4. See also Nathaniel Paul, An Address, Delivered on the Celebration of the Abolition of Slavery in the State of New York, July 5, 1827 (Albany: John B. Van Steenbergh, 1827).

5. Freedom's Journal I (March 16, 1827): 1; copy at the Schomburg Center for Research in Black Culture.

6. "Matilda," Freedom's Journal I (August 10, 1827), cited in Herbert Aptheker, ed., A Documentary History of the Negro People in the United States (New York: Citadel, 1951), I, 89.

7. Joan Maynard and Gwen Cottman, Weeksville Then and Now (Brooklyn: Weeksville Society, 1983), 5, and see also 9–21 for additional information.

CHAPTER 6: ABOLITION'S BLACK VANGUARD

1. Daniel K. Meaders, Isaac Hopper's Tales of Oppression, 1780–1843 (New York: Garland, 1994), 1–31, details Hopper's daring career.

2. Benjamin Quarles, Black Abolitionists (New York: Oxford University Press, 1969), surveys abolitionists in New York and elsewhere; see also Ottley and Weatherby, 93–108.

3. Douglass's story has been told in three autobiographies; for his role at Seneca Falls in 1848 see Laura Curtis Bullard, Our Famous Women (Hartford, CT: 1884), 613–614, cited in Katz, Eyewitness, 180.

4. Narrative of Sojourner Truth (New York: 1878). Reprint (Anno Press, 1968). See also Patricia C. McKissack and Frederick McKissack, Sojourner Truth (New York: Scholastic, 1992).

5. Samuel J. May, Some Recollections of Our Antislavery Conflict (Boston: 1869), 127–128; cited in Katz, Eyewitness, 172.

6. Herbert Aptheker, Abolitionism: A Revolutionary Movement (Boston: Twayne, 1989), 47–48, details attacks in New York City.

7. Katz, Eyewitness, 145, 159–160.

8. David Walker, Walker's Appeal, and Henry Highland Garnet, An Address to the Slaves of the United States (New York: John Brown, 1848). Reprint (New York: Anno Press, 1968).

9. Census statistics cited in Rosenwaike, 44–45.

CHAPTER 7: THE CIVIL WAR ERA

1. Leon F. Litwack, North of Slavery (Chicago: University of Chicago Press, 1961), 247–277; see also Katz, Eyewitness, 184–190, 195–196.

2. New York Tribune, July 19, 1854, cited in C. Peter Ripley et al., eds., Witness for Freedom (Chapel Hill: University of North Carolina Press, 1993), 60–61.

3. Douglas Martin, "Before Park, Black Village," New York Times, April 7, 1995, B-1–2.

4. Aptheker, ed., Documentary History, I, 398–402.

5. Robert Ernst, "The Economic Status of New York City Negroes," Negro History Bulletin (March 1949): 131–139.

6. See Jerome Mushkat, Fernando Wood: A Political Biography (Kent, OH: Kent State University Press, 1990).

7. Clinton Cox, Undying Glory (New York: Scholastic, 1991), 26, 59, 69, 71, 100, 119, 140, for the role of New York volunteers in the 54th Massachusetts Regiment.

CHAPTER 8: FROM THE ASHES OF THE DRAFT RIOTS

1. A Draft Riot chronology is detailed in Iver Bernstein, The New York City Draft Riots (New York: Oxford University Press, 1990), chapter 1.
2. Ibid., 10, 11, 13, 35, 45, 46, 50–60, 63.
3. Cox, 70–71.
4. Albert P. Blaustein and Robert L. Zangrando, eds., Civil Rights and the American Negro (New York: Washington Square Press, 1968), 268–281.
5. For McCabe's career in Kansas and Oklahoma see William Loren Katz, Black Indians: A Hidden Heritage (New York: Atheneum, 1986), 149–153; also see entry for McCabe in Dictionary of American Negro Biography (New York: W. W. Norton, 1982), 410–412.
6. Ottley and Weatherby, 145–152, 156–164.
7. Johnson, Black Manhattan, 8–11, 14–17, details early Black theater participation in the city.
8. For the career of Mary Church Terrell, see Darlene Clark Hine et al., eds., Black Women in America (New York: Carlson, 1994), 1157–1159.

CHAPTER 9: TURNING INTO A NEW CENTURY

1. Johnson, Black Manhattan, 126–127; see also Ottley and Weatherby, 166–168.
2. W. E. B. Du Bois, The Black North in 1901 (New York: Anno Press, 1969). A reprint of the original Times articles.
3. Hine et al., eds., 1109–1112.
4. C. R. Gibbs, Black Inventors (Silver Spring, MD: Three Dimensional Publishing, 1995), details the contributions of Woods, 196–199, and Latimer, pp. 163–165 .
5. George E. Haynes, The Negro At Work in New York City (New York: Columbia University, 1912), is an early Black survey of the city.
6. David Levering Lewis, W. E. B. Du Bois: Biography of a Race (New York: Henry Holt, 1993), 255–264, 429–431.

CHAPTER 10: MOVING TO HARLEM

1. Gilbert Osofsky, Harlem: The Making of A Ghetto (New York: Harper & Row, 1965), 94–99.
2. Ibid., 113–117.
3. David Levering Lewis, When Harlem Was In Vogue (New York: Oxford University Press, 1989), 110–111. Lewis's is clearly the definitive study of this era in Harlem.
4. Ibid., 3–10.
5. Cited in Katz, Eyewitness, 381–382.

CHAPTER 11: MARCUS GARVEY CAPTURES HARLEM

1. See Theodore Vincent, Black Power and the Garvey Movement (Berkeley: Ramparts Press, 1971), for a discussion of various Harlem radicals.
2. Hugh Mulzac, A Star to Steer By (New York: International Publishers, 1963), 74–79.
3. Lewis, When Harlem Was in Vogue, 34–43, has an excellent summary of Garvey's movement.
4. Ibid., 44.
5. Kenneth O'Reilly, Black Americans: The FBI Files (New York: Carroll and Graf, 1994), 139–167, profiles Garvey as the first Black FBI target.
6. Lewis, When Harlem Was in Vogue, 214.

CHAPTER 12: A CULTURAL RENAISSANCE

1. Lewis, *When Harlem Was In Vogue,* is a careful, reliable evaluation of the Harlem Renaissance.
2. Harry H. Pace, November, 17, 1939, quoted in Ottley and Weatherby, 232–235.
3. Oscar Micheaux, *The Conquest* (Lincoln, NB: Western Book Co., 1913). Reprint (from new Learthern Dorsey introduction, 1994), xi–xxi.
4. See Blanche E. Ferguson, *Countee Cullen and the Negro Renaissance* (New York: Dodd Mead, 1966).
5. Langston Hughes, *The Big Sea* (New York: Hill Wang, 1940), 81–85; see also Langston Hughes, "My Early Days in Harlem," in John Henrik Clarke, ed., *Harlem: A Community in Transition* (New York: Citadel, 1964), 62–64.
6. James Weldon Johnson, *Along This Way* (New York: Viking, 1933), 374–414, is his personal odyssey during the Harlem Renaissance.
7. See Hine et al., eds., I, 598–602, for a sketch of

Hurston; also see biographies of other women figures in the Harlem Renaissance.

8. See Lewis, *When Harlem Was In Vogue,* for the best clear-eyed look at white and Black responses to Harlem at this time.

9. Chris Albertson, *Bessie* (New York: Stein & Day, 1974), 196–197; see also Jack Schiffman, *Uptown: The Story of Harlem's Apollo Theater* (New York: Cowles, 1971), for a white businessman's view of the period.

10. Logan and Winston, eds., *Dictionary of American Negro Biography,* 546-548 (on Schomburg), and elsewhere in the volume for biographies of Du Bois, Woodson, James Weldon Johnson, and Charles Johnson.

CHAPTER 13: HARD TIMES HIT NEW YORK

1. Alain Locke, ed., *The New Negro* (New York: A & C Boni, 1925), 127–150, provides examples of early Harlem Renaissance poetry, and sections focus on fiction, drama, music, and essays.

2. Lewis, *When Harlem Was In Vogue,* 282–307, deftly traces how the Great Depression terminated the Harlem Renaissance.

3. Ottley and Weatherby, 265–275, details the impact of the hard times on Harlem.

4. Loften Mitchell, "Harlem Reconsidered," *Freedomways* (1964): 469–470.

5. James Yates, *Mississippi to Madrid* (Seattle: Open Hand Publishers, 1989), 80.

6. Roi Ottley, *New World A-Coming* (New York: 1943). Reprint (New York: Anno Press, 1968), 82–83, 88–89.

7. Data on Salaria Kee provided by Dr. Francis Petai, the New York office of the Veterans of the Abraham Lincoln Brigade, and in Salaria Kee, *A Negro Nurse in Republican Spain* (New York: North American Committee to Aid Spanish Democracy, 1938).

8. Mayor's Commission Report cited in Ottley and Weatherby, 275–280.

9. Robin D. G. Kelley, in Abraham Lincoln Brigade Archives, *African Americans in the Spanish Civil War* (New York: G. K. Hall, 1992), 5–20, traces Black Communists in New York City in the 1930s.

10. For the long advocacy career of A. Philip Randolph, see Daniel S. Davis, *Mr Black Labor* (New York: Dutton, 1972), 41–80.

11. U.S. Bureau of the Census, in Rosenwaike, 141.

CHAPTER 14: FIGHTING FOR THE DOUBLE V

1. Robin D. G. Kelley in Abraham Lincoln Brigade Archives, *African Americans in the Spanish Civil War* (New York: 1992), 16–18.

2. William Loren Katz and Marc Crawford, *The Lincoln Brigade* (New York: Atheneum, 1989), chapters 11, 12.

3. Herbert Garfinkel, *When Negroes March* (New York: Atheneum, 1969), chapters II, III, and pp. 186–193.

4. Mulzac, chapters 11–13.

5. Hine et al., eds., II, 1106–1108.

6. Quoted in Dorothy and Thomas Hoobler, *The African American Family Album* (New York: Oxford University Press, 1995), 76–77.

7. Langston Hughes, "Harlem III," *New York Post* (July 23, 1964), in Katz, *Eyewitness,* 464–465.

8. See Benjamin J. Davis, *Communist Councilman from Harlem* (New York: New World, 1969).

9. Paul Robeson, *Here I Stand* (Boston: Beacon Press, 1958), 63–74.

10. Mulzac, 242–243.

CHAPTER 15: MALCOLM X IN NEW YORK

1. William L. Patterson, *We Charge Genocide* (New York: Civil Rights Congress, 1951), cited in William L. Patterson, *The Man Who Cried Genocide* (New York: International Publishers, 1991), is the first full-length study of white violence.

2. Interview with Dr. Kenneth B. Clark, "A Conversation with James Baldwin," May 24, 1963, WGBH-TV, Boston, cited in Clarke, ed., 123–130.

3. Malcolm X and Alex Haley, *The Autobiography of Malcolm X* (New York: Grove Press, 1965), is still an authoritative account.

4. Ibid.

5. Bruce Perry, ed., *Malcolm X: The Last Speeches* (New York: Pathfinder, 1989); see also O'Reilly, ed., 442–511.

6. Clayborne Carson, ed., *Malcolm X: The FBI File* (New York: Ballantine, 1991); the lengthy introduction is very valuable.

7. See film by Spike Lee, *Malcolm X*; see also

Clayborne Carson, "Malcolm X," in Mark C. Carnes, ed., *Past Imperfect: History According to the Movies* (New York: 1995), 278–283.

CHAPTER 16: NEW YORK CITY DURING THE KING ERA

1. See Jackie Robinson, *I Never Had It Made* (New York: Putnam, 1972), and recent biographies of the Dodgers superstar.
2. See chapter on Powell in John Hope Franklin and August Meier, eds., *Black Leaders of the Twentieth Century* (Chicago: University of Illinois Press, 1982).
3. Michael D. Davis and Hunter R. Clark, *Thurgood Marshall* (Seacaucus, NJ: Carol Publishing Group, 1992), traces his work for the NAACP in New York City.
4. Shyrlee Dallard, *Ella Baker* (New York: Silver Burdett, 1990), 26–122.
5. Yates, 112.
6. Quoted in Clayborne Carson et al., eds., *Eyes on the Prize Civil Rights Reader* (New York: Penguin, 1991), 387–393.
7. Sylvester Leaks, "Talking about Harlem," in Clarke, ed., 13–15, and including statistics from Protestant Council of New York City.
8. U.S. Bureau of the Census, in Rosenwaike, 141.

CHAPTER 17: THE DINKINS VICTORY

1. Edwin R. Lewinson, *Black Politicians in New York City* (New York: Twayne, 1974), is a careful study of this century's racial city politics.
2. For information on Black women politicians see Hine et al., eds., vols. I, II.
3. See*New York Daily Challenge* articles in Katz, *Eyewitness,* chapters 23, 25.
4. Andrew Hacker, *Two Nations, Black and White, Separate, Hostile and Unequal* (New York: Scribners, 1992), 204–206, 209.
5. Mayor David Dinkins speech of October 30, 1993, quoted in Katz, *Eyewitness,* 606.
6. U.S. Census figures for New York State cited in Alfred N. Garwood, ed., *Black Americans: A Statistical Sourcebook* (Boulder, CO: Numbers and Concepts, 1993), 9, 11, 12.

CHAPTER 18: A CITY OF BLACK HEROES AND LANDMARKS

1. Sherill D. Wilson, ed., *Through Black Eyes: Revisioning New York History* I (November-December 1991; premier issue); see also Joan Maynard, "When Children's Dreams Become Reality: The Society for the Preservation of Weeksville and Bedford-Stuyvesant History," in Beth L. Savage, ed. *African American Historic Places* (Washington, D.C.: National Park Service, 1995), 77–82.
2. Weeksville Society, P.O. Box 130120, St. John Station, Brooklyn, NY, 11213.
3. "The Schomburg Library Opened to Students," *Opportunity* (June 1926): 187.
4. A 1994 view of Harlem appears in "Make Me Dream Tall!: Harlem Recalled," *New York Sunday Times,* February 6, 1994, Neighborhood Report, 1, including statistics on population, housing, high school graduates, unemployment, and income.
5. The Eastman Kodak Company, *Garvey Historic Sites* (New York: Eastman Kodak, 1987).
6. A 1993 view of 125th Street is in Ian Fisher, "Street of Dreams," *New York Times,* April 11, 1993, Styles, 1, 9. On Harlem becoming a tourist attraction see Pamela Newkirk, "A Must See for Foreigners: Harlem," *New York Sunday Times* August 8, 1996, Styles, 53, which reported: "Not since the 1920's, when Harlem lured legions of pleasure-seekers from downtown and around the world, has the neighborhood been so in vogue."
7. Bruce Frankel, "Black Cemetery in NYC New Key to Colonial Times," *USA Today,* September 15, 1992, 10-A; and see Spencer P. M. Harrington, "New York's Great Cemetery Imbroglio," *Archaeology* (March–April 1993): 29–38.
8. David W. Dunlap, "A Black Cemetery Takes Its Place in History," *New York Times,* February 28, 1993, E-5.; see also Joel Siegel, "City Goofed in Cemetery Dig," *New York Daily News,* February 17, 1993, 7, 20.

BIBLIOGRAPHY

Abraham Lincoln Brigade Archives. *African Americans in the Spanish Civil War.* New York: G. K. Hall & Co., 1992.

Albertson, Chris. *Bessie.* New York: Stein & Day, 1974.

Allen, William G. *The American Prejudice Against Color.* London, 1853. Reprint. New York: Anno Press, 1968.

Andrews, Charles C. *The History of the African Free Schools.* New York: Mahlon Day, 1830.

Aptheker, Herbert. *Abolitionism: A Revolutionary Movement.* Boston: Twayne, 1989.

Aptheker, Herbert, ed. *A Documentary History of the Negro People in the United States, 1661- 1968.* New York: Citadel Press, 1951–1991, 7 volumes.

Bernstein, Iver. *The New York City Draft Riots.* New York: Oxford University Press, 1990.

Blaustein, Albert P., and Robert L. Zangrando, eds. *Civil Rights and the American Negro.* New York: Washington Square Press, 1968.

Boyd, Herb, and Robert L. Allen, eds. *Brotherman: The Odyssey of Black Men in America.* New York: Ballantine, 1995.

Carleton, George Washington. *The Suppressed Book about Slavery.* 1864. Reprint. New York: Anno Press, 1968.

Carnes, Mark C., ed. *Past Imperfect: History According to the Movies.* New York: Carnes, 1995.

Carson, Clayborne. *Malcolm X: The FBI File.* New York: Ballantine, 1991.

Carson, Clayborne, et al., eds. *Eyes on the Prize Civil Rights Reader.* New York: Penguin, 1991.

Charters, Samuel B., and Leonard Kunstadt. *Jazz: A History of the New York Scene.* New York: Doubleday, 1962.

Clark, Kenneth. *Dark Ghetto.* Middleton, CT: Wesleyan University Press, 1955.

Clarke, John Henrik, ed. *Harlem: A Community in Transition.* New York: Citadel, 1964.

Cox, Clinton. *Undying Glory.* New York: Scholastic, 1991.

Cullen, Countee. *Color.* New York: Harper & Brothers, 1925.

Dallard, Shyrlee. *Ella Baker.* New York: Silver Burdett, 1990.

Davis, Benjamin J. *Communist Councilman from Harlem.* New York: International Publishers, 1969.

Davis, Daniel S. *Mr. Black Labor.* New York: Dutton, 1972.

Davis, Michael, and Hunter R. Clark. *Thurgood Marshall.* Seacaucus, NJ: Carol Publishing, 1992.

Donnan, Elizabeth. *Documents Illustrative of the History of the Slave Trade.* Washington, D.C.: Carnegie Institution, 1932.

Douglas, Ann. *Terrible Honesty.* New York: Farrar, Straus & Giroux, 1995.

Douglass, Frederick. *The Life and Times of Frederick Douglass.* Reprint. New York: Collier Books, 1962.

Du Bois, W. E. B. *The Black North in 1901.* Reprint. New York: Anno Press, 1969.

Dunbar, Paul Laurence. *The Sport of the Gods.* New York: Dodd Mead, 1902.

Ellis, Edward Robb. *The Epic of New York City.* New York: Coward McCann, 1966.

Ferguson, Blanche E. *Countee Cullen and the Negro Renaissance.* New York: Dodd Mead, 1966.

Fisher, Rudolph. *The Walls of Jericho.* 1928. Reprint. Ann Arbor: University of Michigan Press, 1994.

Franklin, John Hope, and August Meier, eds. *Black Leaders of the Twentieth Century.* Chicago: University of Illinois Press,1982.

Garfinkel, Herbert. *When Negroes March.* New York: Atheneum, 1969.

Garvey, Amy Jacques, ed. *Philosophy and Opinions of Marcus Garvey.* 1923. Reprint. New York: Anno Press, 1968.

Garwood, Alfred N., ed. *Black Americans: A Statistical Sourcebook.* Boulder, CO: Numbers and Concepts, 1993.

Gibbs, C. R. *Black Inventors.* Silver Spring, MD: Three Dimensional Publishing, 1995.

Gibson, Althea. *I Always Wanted to Be Somebody.* New York: Harper, 1958.

Hacker, Andrew. *Two Nations, Black and White, Separate, Hostile and Unequal.* New York: Scribners, 1992.

Haynes, George E. *The Negro at Work in New York City.* New York: Columbia University Press, 1912.

Higgenbotham, A. Leon. *In the Matter of Color.* New York: Oxford University Press, 1978.

Hine, Darlene Clark, et al., eds. *Black Women in America.* New York: Carlson, 1994.

Horne, Gerald. *Black Liberation—Red Scare: Ben Davis and the Communist Party.* Canbury, NJ: Associated University Presses, 1994.

Howard University Graduate School, eds. *The New Negro: Thirty Years Afterward.* Washington, D.C.: Howard University Press, 1954.

Hughes, Langston. *The Big Sea.* New York: Knopf, 1940.

———. *Simple Speaks His Mind.* New York: Simon & Schuster, 1950.

Hurston, Zora Neale. *Their Eyes Were Watching God.* Philadelphia: Lippincott, 1937.

Jackson, Kenneth T., ed. *The Encyclopedia of New York City.* New York: Yale University Press, 1995.

Jameson, J. Franklin. *Narratives of New Netherlands 1609–1664.* New York: Johns Hopkins University Press, 1909.

Johnson, James Weldon. *Along This Way.* New York: Viking, 1930.

———. *Black Manhattan.* New York: Knopf, 1930. Reprint. New York: Anno Press, 1968.

Kammen, Michael. *Colonial New York: A History.* New York: Scribners, 1975.

Kaplan, Sidney, and Emma N. Kaplan. *The Black Presence in the Era of the American Revolution.* Revised edition. Amherst: University of Massachusetts Press, 1989.

Katz, William Loren. *Black Indians: A Hidden Heritage.* New York: Atheneum, 1986.

———. *Eyewitness: A Living Documentary of the African American Contribution to American History.* New York: Simon & Schuster, 1995.

Katz, William Loren, and Marc Crawford. *The Lincoln Brigade: A Picture History.* New York: Atheneum, 1989.

Kiser, Clyde V. *Sea Island to City.* New York: Atheneum, 1932.

Klein, Milton M., ed. *New York: The Centennial Years 1676–1976.* Port Washington, NY: Kennikat Press, 1976.

Larsen, Nella. *Passing.* 1929. Reprint. New York: Anno Press, 1969.

Lewinson, Edwin R. *Black Politics in New York City.* New York: Twayne, 1974.

Lewis, David Levering. *W. E. B. Du Bois: Biography of a Race.* New York: Henry Holt, 1993.

———. *When Harlem Was in Vogue.* New York: Knopf, 1981.

Litwack, Leon. *North of Slavery.* Chicago: University of Chicago Press, 1961.

Livermore, George. *An Historical Research Respecting the Opinions of the Founders of the Republic on Negroes As Slaves, As Citizens and As Soldiers.* 1862. Reprint. New York: Ann Press, 1969.

Locke, Alain, ed. *The New Negro.* New York: A. and C. Boni Publishers, 1925.

Logan, Rayford, and Michael R. Winston, eds. *Dictionary of American Negro Biography.* New York: W. W. Norton, 1982.

Malcolm X and Alex Haley, *The Autobiography of Malcolm X.* New York: Grove Press, 1966.

McKay, Claude. *Home to Harlem.* New York, 1928.

McKissack, Patricia C., and Frederick McKissack. *Sojourner Truth.* New York: Scholastic, 1992.

McManus, Edgar J. *A History of Negro Slavery in New York.* Syracuse: Syracuse University Press, 1966.

Meaders, Daniel K., ed. *Isaac Hopper's Tales of Oppression, 1780–1843.* New York: Garland, 1994.

Mulzac, Hugh. *A Star to Steer By.* New York: International Publishers, 1963.

Nell, William C. *The Colored Patriots of the American Revolution.* 1855. Reprint. New York: Anno Press, 1969.

O'Callaghan, E. B., ed. *Documents Relating to the Colonial History of the State of New York.* Albany: Weed Parsons & Co., 1851.

O'Reilly, Kenneth. *Black Americans: The FBI Files.* New York: Carroll & Graf, 1994.

Osofsky, Gilbert. *Harlem: The Making of a Ghetto, 1890–1930.* New York: Harper & Row, 1966.

Ottley, Roi. *New World A-Coming: Inside Black America.* 1943. Reprint. New York: Ann Press, 1969.

Ottley, Roi, and William J. Weatherby, eds. *The Negro in New York: An Informal Social History, 1626–1940.* New York: Praeger, 1969.

Ovington, Mary White. *The Walls Came Tumbling Down.* New York: Harcourt, Brace, 1947.

Patterson, William L. *"We Charge Genocide."* New York: Civil Rights Congress, 1951.

Paul, Nathaniel. *An Address, Delivered on the Celebration of the Abolition of Slavery in the State of New York.* 1827. Reprint. New York: Anno Press, 1968.

Perry, Bruce, ed. *Malcolm X: The Last Speeches.* New York: Pathfinder, 1989.

Petry, Ann. *The Street.* Boston: Beacon Press, 1946.

Quarles, Benjamin. *Black Abolitionists.* New York: Oxford University Press, 1969.

———. *The Negro in the American Revolution.* Chapel Hill: University of North Carolina Press, 1961.

Rampersad, Arnold. *The Life of Langston Hughes.* New York: Oxford University Press, 1986.

Riker, James. *Revised History of Harlem: Its Origin and Early Annals.* New York: New Harlem Publishing Co., 1904

Ripley, C. Peter, et al., eds. *Witness for Freedom.* Chapel Hill: University of North Carolina Press, 1993.

Robeson, Paul. *Here I Stand.* New York: Othello Associates, 1958.

Robinson, Jackie. *I Never Had It Made.* New York: Putnam, 1972.

Rosenwaike, Ira. *Population History of New York City.* Syracuse: Syracuse University Press, 1972.

Sante, Luc. *Low Life of Old New York.* New York: Farrar, Straus, Giroux, 1991.

Savage, Beth L., ed. *African American Historic Places.* Washington, D.C.: 1993.

Scheiner, Seth M. *Negro Mecca: A History of the Negro in New York City, 1865–1920.* New York: New York University Press, 1965.

Schiffman, Jack. *Uptown: The Story of Harlem's Apollo Theater.* New York: Cowles, 1971.

Sessions, Ralph. *Woodsmen, Mountaineers and Bockies: The Peoples of the Ramapos.* New City, NY: Historical Society of Rockland County, 1985.

Stokes, I. N. Phelps. *The Iconography of Manhattan Island 1498–1909.* New York: Robert H. Dodd, 1916.

Strickland, William. *Malcolm X: Make It Plain.* New York: 1994.

Truth, Sojourner. *Narrative of Sojourner Truth.* 1878. Reprint. New York: Anno Press, 1968.

Van Rensselear, Mrs. Schuyler. *History of the City of New York in the Seventeenth Century.* Vols. I, II. New York: Macmillan Co., 1909.

Vincent, Theodore. *Black Power and the Garvey Movement.* Berkeley: Ramparts Press, 1971.

Walling, William English. *Proceedings of the National Negro Conference, 1909.* 1909. Reprint. New York: Anno Press, 1968.

Ward, Samuel Ringgold. *Autobiography of a Fugitive Negro.* London: John Ward, 1855.

White, Shane. *Somewhat More Independent: The End of Slavery in New York City, 1770–1810.* Athens: University of Georgia Press, 1991.

White, Walter. *A Man Called White.* New York: Viking Press, 1948.

Wood, Peter H. *Black Majority: Negroes in Colonial South Carolina.* New York: Knopf, 1975.

Yates, James. *Mississippi to Madrid.* Seattle, WA: Open Hand, 1989.

Zilversmit, Arthur. *The First Emancipation.* Chicago: 1967.

INDEX

ACKNOWLEDGEMENTS

Ernest Kaiser, friend for more than three decades, poured his more than half-century of knowledge into a line-by-line examination of this manuscript. Dr. Joan Maynard supplied valuable photographs of Weeksville, Dr. Daniel Meaders volunteered runaway notices, and Bruce Kayton, knowledgeable walking-tour guide, identified ancient street maps. Dr. Sherill Wilson and her African Burial Ground staff proffered original documents and sage advice. My father's great collaborators, with experiences that spanned decades—Walter Christmas, Ernest Critchlow, Ruth Jett, and Viola Scott—again proved invaluable in so many ways.

Over the years I also have been enlightened and inspired by probing conversations with educators Dr. Beryle Banfield, Dr. William Serialle, Nancy Brown, artist David Brown, Imotep Gary Bird, Gerard Lewison, Dr. Harvey Robins, Dr. Leonard Jeffries, sociologist Al Pinkney, documentarian St. Clair Bourne, talk show hosts Smorie Marksman, Pat Prescott, Bob Law, Utrice Leid, Dred Scott Keyes, Amy Goodman, Bernard White, Sandy Jackson, Mark Riley, Ann Tripp, Dr. Betty Shabazz, editors Dawad Philip, Marcia Marshall, and Esther Jackson, scholars Dr. John Henrik Clarke, Wesley Brown, Vivian Anderson, Charlayne Haynes, Herb Boyd, Dr. Gloria Joseph, Max and Jean Carey Bond, Paula Giddings, activists Chief Oceola Townsend, Sundancer, Ken Little Hawk, and Day Star, composer Charles Jones, writers Playthell Benjamin and Warren Halliburton, archivists Mrs. George E. Haynes and Dr. Sara Dunlap Jackson, and jazz immortals Bunk Johnson, Louis Armstrong, Art Hodes, Sandy Williams, Sidney Bechet, and James P. Johnson.

This book pursues courageous paths blazed by the awesome scholarship of Dr. James W. Pennington, Langston Hughes, James Weldon Johnson, Mr. Kaiser, Dr. Clarke, and more recently by Dr. David Levering Lewis and Dr. Ann Douglas.